Ohnalee

Ohnalee

Mermaid of Heceta Head

August 28, 2013

Best Regards

Judith Gilman

Judith Gilman

Cover Design—Mouse Grafix
Author Photo—Amanda Lee Forbes Hill
Interior Drawings by Judith Gilman, computer enhanced by Mouse Grafix

Library of Congress Control Number: 2007904887
ISBN: Hardcover   978-1-4257-8674-8
                 Softcover   978-1-4257-8666-3

This book was printed in the United States of America.

To order additional copies of this book, contact:
Xlibris Corporation
1-888-795-4274
www.Xlibris.com
Orders@Xlibris.com
37258

Dedication

I dedicate this book to the loving sprites and spirits who share my continuing voyage of exploration and adventure. They are as brave and beautiful as Ohnalee, as charismatic as Mokeema, and as strong and opinionated as Aquinae Magena. There is more than a little of my daughters Barbara, Lauri, and Mary Katherine in my story, as memories of our life on and under the warm waters of the Bahamas and Caribbean flow into the characters in my book. Captain Dan looks on with a mischievous grin of approval as I walk new paths and open new doors, always remembering the sound of his strong voice and the magnetic force of his personality.

I give special thanks to my oldest child, Barbara Colborn who has been a great collaborator and seems to know Ohnalee as well as I do. Her ideas have infused my characters with extra power and vitality, but praise cannot be given to Barbara without mentioning her little sister Lauri Hathaway, as these two are like separate sides of the same rare gold coin. You can't lose on a flip of this coin; heads you win, tales you win again. Thanks Lauri, for always supporting and understanding your Mother, and for being a perceptive and thorough editor.

And to all the children far away, I send my love.

CAPTAIN'S LADY STORE – 2006

Built by O. W. Hurd, Circa 1905. This structure was Florence's first telephone company. Switchboards were downstairs, with operator quarters on the second floor. The design is a good example of early commercial architecture with scrolled cornice brackets along the false front.

Chapter 1

THE DISCOVERY

It was the second of May when I reached the border between Idaho and Oregon, returning home after my annual winter job in Colorado. The fuel gauge was flirting with the empty mark, so I stopped at the first gas station I saw in Ontario, on the Oregon side of the border, thrilled there was no reason to jump from my comfortable seat to fill the gas tank. In Oregon, filling one's own gas tank is not legal, so after a long winter living and working at 10,200 feet in the historic mining town of Leadville, Colorado, this was a definite treat. Pumping gas into your vehicle, while standing in blowing snow in below zero temperatures is not my idea of fun.

My daughter Barbara and I passed quickly through Bend and Sisters, then climbed up over Santiam Pass before descending toward Eugene, traveling along the scenic McKenzie River. Massive ancient trees thickly lined both sides of the road and we could still see a few patches of dirty black snow left over from the last storm.

Green was never my favorite color before I moved to Oregon, but now my heart danced with delight to be almost home. Colorado is a beautiful state, with scenery that takes your breath away, but when I return to my job each November, the blossoms of the high country have already disappeared beneath the first dusting of snow.

The world outside my office and the cabin where I live is awesome and spectacular, with craggy peaks reaching to the heavens, but the dominant shades of the world in the west are beige and brown, white and gray, with cliffs of red and rust that change to shades of misty silvery pink and feathery gray as the sun slips beneath the horizon. In winter, the earthy colors of the land are blanketed with fine sparkling white powder that fades to gray then dirties to brown as it melts and is plowed off the roads, temporarily spoiling the unsullied purity of the surrounding hillsides. The bright yellow sun bounces down from the clear blue skies and fluffy white clouds of winter, reflecting on the shimmering landscape, melting the snow during the day, then leaving it to refreeze in the cold dark of the evening. Snow, melt, freeze, snow again, more fresh powder—it's a winter wonderland of constantly changing visions and vistas.

Homes are often made of logs, or are painted brown and beige, with interior mountain décor that tends to be heavy and conservative in color and design. Leather furniture and banisters made from deer antlers reflect the exterior colors of the countryside, with the golden colors of the sun beaming from a hot crackling fire in a stone fireplace. My cabin is cozy and warm, with interior wooden walls and neutral colors, a total contrast to the historic building where I live on the Oregon Coast.

The heavy rains that drench Oregon in the late fall and winter nourish the plants and flowers, bringing them to full arousal in the spring when they explode with passion and color, frosting the earth with every imaginable shade and hue of green from the palest icy mint green, to brilliant dark emerald green, and everything in between. Often when I return home at the end of April, the tree branches still droop heavily with a blanket of fresh, wet spring snow, but at their feet, colorful flowers and ferns struggle to break through the crusty ceiling, poking their heads up toward the sun.

Wild rhododendrons bloom profusely in an exuberant pink and white rhapsody, decorating the lush green lawns and gardens of the homes and cottages along the river, awaking my senses with their exotic beauty. The early pioneers thought the flower signified the ever-constant cycle of death and rebirth, and anxiously watched for the first multihued bloom on the hills and fields. Modern-day residents of the state look forward to the appearance of this flower as a sign winter is on the way out, with summer just around the corner.

My winter gig provided the cash to paint my building during my absence, so when I arrived back in Florence, I thought it looked resplendent in a pale shade of green, with garnet red for the doors and trim.

Unfortunately, plans to put on a new roof would have to wait for next winter, and I hoped the missing shingles would not result in damage from water leaking into the crawl space under the steep roof. Despite fleeting flashes of curiosity about the area, in the nine years since my husband and I purchased this building, neither of us had ever looked into the attic which was only accessible through a small hatch in the ceiling of the living room.

"Barb," I said to my daughter, "we really need to take a peek into my attic sometime soon."

"Let's do it," she agreed with enthusiasm, "I'll hold the ladder so you can stick your head through the opening to have a look."

"This week for sure," I promised, "but I am worried there could be spiders up there, so it doesn't sound like fun."

Remember to get some bug spray first, I thought, wondering if the Mother of All Spiders was waiting in the darkness.

It was actually late July when Barbara and Lauri arrived at my building with a sturdy paint-spattered stepladder. My daughters were excited, speculating we might find something valuable as the building was constructed about 1904.

"Hold on a minute," I said, deciding to change my clothes before the expedition into the unexplored mysteries of the garret. Stepping out of the embroidered jeans and the gauzy shirt purchased that day from my favorite shop in Florence, I removed the pendant that had been passed down from my grandmother to my mother and then to me. The piece was a scallop shell imbedded in silver with a magnificent turquoise stone at the top, framed with an intricate filigree.

Mother said she didn't know much about the history of the pendant, but it was my favorite piece of jewelry, and I wore it often.

With the pendant safely back in its box on the marble top of my antique dresser, I slipped into a favorite pair of old jeans, then pulled one of Danny's Tortola tee shirts over my head. Barefooted as usual, I returned to the living room to begin the treasure hunt.

The only way to reach the ceiling in the living room was to stand the ladder on top of the dining room table, but that was easier said than done as the table was no longer used for fancy dining. Instead of fancy Lenox dishes and a romantic candlelit dinner for two, the table now hosted an artistic arrangement of my favorite things.

The copper ship's horn came off *Capricorn Lady*, the '71 Trumpy motor yacht my husband Danny and I owned from 1980 to 1999. We took guests from around the world for one-week vacations on that boat, and Danny always blew the horn on New Year's Eve to compete with the loud electric horns in the wheelhouses of the luxury yachts anchored in Gorda Sound. *He had a great pair of lungs,* I thought, as no one else could blast that horn like Danny, but unfortunately those lungs were invaded by a cancerous tumor that finally killed him. Danny was the last person to blow that horn, and I liked to hold it to my lips, hoping to catch just a bit of the breath he left behind.

When I saw the elegant painted Chinese statue in an antique shop in St. Thomas in the Virgin Islands in about 1981, I knew it was the perfect thing to place on the mahogany table in the salon of the *Lady*. We were still struggling at the time, and money was short, so it took three months to get it out of layaway. I'm not certain if this statue represents Confucius, the Grand Master of All Ages, or a Chinese emperor, but Dan called him "Mr. Foo," and I was always careful to place him in my bed in the crew area while we were at sea so he wouldn't fall over and get damaged. When we were safely at anchor or at the dock, he was returned to his duty station, overseeing the action. The statue has a funny grin and mischievous, twinkling eyes, and Dan often made up naughty stories about what Mr. Foo was muttering under his breath as he watched the charter guests at play. These days, Mr. Foo smiles at me as I write. We have both come a long way from our life cruising the sunny islands of the British Virgins. I cradled him carefully in my arms, then laid him comfortably on the sofa in preparation for our attic expedition.

The Baccarat "vazzzz" was a gift from one of our first charter groups on *Capricorn Lady*. After a particularly crazy night of drinking and partying, the Texas oil folk traveled to St. Thomas on the ferry for a day, returning to Tortola with a gift for "Cookie," meaning me, the ship's Chef as well as a licensed USCG Captain. I placed a bouquet of island flowers in the heavy crystal container, positioning it on the table on the aft deck. It traveled the islands all that week, so heavy it never fell, despite some pretty rough seas, and after the charter was over, it sat unattended on the aft deck for several days. When the group departed, they left another gift—a cap which said, "If you ain't an oilman, you ain't shit."

Danny and I rode the Bomba Charger to Charlotte Amalie the next week, leaving the vase still sitting on the aft deck and, just for fun, stopped in at Little Switzerland to see if we could find out the value of our gift. The price was $750, and in the duty-free shops of St. Thomas, that meant it would sell for about $1,000 in the United States. After that, the vazzz was moved to a more secure location on one of the end tables in the salon, joining Mr. Foo in my bed when we were underway. The elegant crystal vase played a prominent role in weddings, anniversaries, birthday parties, and other special events on *Capricorn Lady* over the years; now it was a treasured accent piece for my Victorian apartment. Lauri placed it carefully in my bed, plumping the pillows all around to keep it safe.

After the surface was clear, Barbara and I lifted the ladder up, being careful not to disturb the two tablecloths, which were carefully arranged with the lace cloth underneath and a smaller one with roses on the top. I stepped on a straight-backed chair, then onto the table before starting up the ladder toward the ceiling.

The hatch wouldn't budge when I first pushed on it, but then I realized it was made in two parts, so it would fold back when moved. I shoved a little harder, then squealed as the hatch buckled, dodging the strange substance that rained down on my head. "Yuk, what is that stuff?" I yelped, seeing the pieces falling on my tablecloth.

The girls said it looked like insulation material to them, and I remembered the seller telling us the building had been redone several years before our purchase.

The sides of the wooden hatch were thick with cobwebs, and when I pushed it aside, I could see even more gossamer threads hanging from the ceiling over my head. I shivered fearfully, afraid to raise my head up any further into the space, but I inched my eyes to the level of the hatch. I couldn't see much as there was a plank sitting up on the left side of the hatch blocking my view.

"Be careful, Mom," Lauri cautioned—as if I were so elderly I might stumble and fall.

"I'm fine," I grumbled, remembering how Dan always worried when he saw me up on a ladder—as if I were a fragile flower to be protected rather than a sturdy adventurous woman who lived on boats for twenty-five years. He often cranked me up the mainmast on a swinging bosun's chair to repair the rigging on our sailboat, *Capricorn*, with the boat bobbing around dockside, or even out at sea, but let me climb a ladder in my store to replace a lightbulb, and it was "Watch out, babe, be careful."

"Give me that light," I demanded, taking it from Lauri's outstretched hand and turning it on, mustering up the courage to take a closer look from a higher vantage point.

My building is sixteen feet wide and fifty-five feet long—shorter than *Capricorn Lady*—but I was surprised to find the attic space was larger than expected. Pointing the light overhead, I searched the ceiling to see if I could see any area where water was leaking or daylight was coming through. So far so good. It seemed OK, and I was relieved, thinking I might get through another winter without a new roof.

I flashed the sides of the dormer with the light, first around the immediate area by my head, but there was nothing to be seen. Then I turned the light toward the rear of the building, sweeping the yellow beam slowly from side to side. Wispy webs hung everywhere, but the Mother of All Spiders did not seem to be present.

I did see two rows of round white ceramic knobs attached to planks on the floor. These knobs had wires running between them, and I wondered if they were from the time when my building housed the first telephone company in Florence in the early 1900s, but it was difficult to see anything past the old brick chimney that came up through the floor about thirty feet from the entry hatch. I don't mind confessing that I felt jittery and uncomfortable as I popped my head up into the space, then back into the living room, like some crazy jack-in-the-box. Loose insulation material was piled high in all the corners, and I imagined I saw something move in the shadows.

"It's impossible to see past the chimney," I announced breathlessly to the girls, "and there's no way in hell I am gonna crawl back there to look around.

"You need a better light," Barb advised. "That one is just too weak."

"Perhaps Danny has a brighter one we can use," I said, referring to him, as usual, as if he were still with us in the world, instead of in spirit.

I sped downstairs to the street, then around the back of my building, unlocking the door of the shed to take a look. I swept the crowded interior with the flashlight, trying to reach the pull on the light over Danny's workbench. It was difficult as the space was crammed with boxes of books, "stuff" from estate sales, and cases of large brown mailing envelopes, making it difficult to move around. Dan built the shed, then put up shelves around the interior, even though he was in the middle of an aggressive chemotherapy regime for his cancer and weak from radiation treatments. In retrospect, I feel he held onto life ferociously until he had completed certain projects he felt would make my life easier after his departure.

I was still emotionally unable to consider getting rid of any of Dan's tools, so metal boxes of odd and unfamiliar greasy engine parts and tools were stacked high on the floor. Electric sanders, drills, and woodworking equipment were piled on shelves next to large bins of plumbing and electrical parts so heavy the white shelving sagged under their weight. There were several enormous metal chests, with drawers full of mysterious metal implements, none of which I ever used and probably would never use. I kept one electric screwdriver in the bathroom of the store building, and a hammer, which seemed to deal with almost any problem.

Bingo, I thought, as I put my hand on a large droplight lying on the top of a square plastic bin.

"Thank you, Danny," I said out loud.

I grabbed the light, then raced up the alley to the front of the building, speeding through the hall of mirrors, glancing at my reflection as I went. *Danny would be proud I finished the project,* I thought as I climbed the stairs, seeing a few more open places on the wall where it might be possible to fit in another antique looking-glass.

Lauri plugged in the heavy yellow cord, and I remembered that Dan often hung this light from the ceiling in the machinery room of *Capricorn Lady* when he was working on the engines or at his workbench. That light had traveled a long way, from Nanny Cay Marina in the British Virgin Islands, to my building in Florence, Oregon.

The bright yellow beam gave a better view of the attic space which looked like the interior of a small pyramid. It was a little disappointing that the area seemed to be empty, as we had hoped for an exciting evening rummaging through boxes of interesting treasures and relics hidden away for safekeeping by past residents of the building.

"Still can't see anything past the chimney, girls," I said, "someone needs to go all the way to the back with the light."

I couldn't even imagine crawling on my hands and knees past all those creepy cobwebs, and the girls were as terrified as their mother, so we all agreed on the only possible solution. My sixteen-year-old grandson, Adam, could do it.

Lauri drove over to the bowling alley to pick Adam up that night after Rock-n-Bowl, saying he was needed to help Grandma do something important. When he arrived, it was almost midnight, but none of us had the patience to wait another day.

When we explained the task, the boy agreed immediately, but we insisted he wear long pants and a long-sleeved shirt for the adventure. I thought about setting off a bug bomb first but decided the spiders might not be as dangerous as the bug spray. I shivered as I remembered Danny complaining, "That stuff is gonna kill us, Judi," as I sprayed constantly to kill the crawling insects of the tropics on our boats.

Adam crept slowly through the attic on hands and knees, complaining all the way as he waved one hand back and forth overhead, swatting away dangling strands of cobwebs. "This is crazy, Grandma, ain't nothing up here," he muttered loudly, as he disappeared in the darkness behind the brick chimney.

Watching from the top of the ladder, I heard a loud tapping noise and the sound of wood splintering.

"What are you doing, Adam?" I shouted, "be careful, I don't want you getting hurt or tearing up anything."

"Found a loose board on the floor back here, grandma," he hollered, "looks sort of funny, so I'm gonna pull it up and have a look see."

A few grunts and male expletives rumbled forth from behind the chimney, and I wondered why we ever started this project. I could tell that more than one board was being pulled up, as it reminded me of the frightful sound I heard when the top four planks on the port side of the hull were torn back from the stem of Capricorn Lady as she surged back and forth on her lines on the dock at Nanny Cay Marina during Hurricane Marilyn.

"There's a cavity under the boards here," Adam shrieked, "I can see a box down there. Looks real old; I'm gonna lift it up."

"He's found something," I reported to the excited audience waiting below, "perhaps a treasure chest full of gold bullion and precious gems. Happy days are just around the corner now, girls."

A few minutes later I heard a loud triumphant whoop. "Got it," Adam announced proudly, "I'll bring it out, and go back to nail the boards down later."

"No problem," I said, thinking that I wasn't about to go back up there anytime soon.

Adam dragged the wooden box slowly toward the hatch, as I retreated down the ladder. We all clapped loudly as the bold explorer's feet dropped down from the opening onto the third rung of the ladder, followed by his upper body.

"Give it here," we three girls shouted, all hands reaching for the box as he came down the ladder, but Adam clutched the precious booty tightly.

"It's mine now," he teased, pretending to make a wild dash for the stairs leading down to the front entrance.

"Forget aboud it," I growled with my best menacing Tony Soprano imitation, "give it to Granny."

Barb hauled down the ladder, then pushed the table back to its proper place, returning the feet to the very same round indentations in the carpet. I placed the trunk on the table and Lauri handed me a cup of hot coffee.

The trunk had a lock, but Adam said he could easily break it loose with a crowbar from Danny's stash in the shed. For an instant, I felt we should wait, not break the lock, perhaps get an expert to open it without damage. But I must admit, I am an impatient woman who likes to make things happen.

The deed was easily done as the metal seemed to crumble when urged by the strong crowbar. The lock was so old it burst into several pieces, spilling small metal bits onto the carpet. We all held our breath as I opened the lid, hoping to see a stash of gold coins or jewels that would make us wealthy beyond belief.

I thought, at the very least, the box might hold something I could put up for auction on eBay.

Inside the wooden trunk was a smaller box with a faded gray leather covering. I lifted it out, then opened the lid.

Instead of precious gems, gold coins, or paper money stored by a miser who hated banks, we saw a thin book, with a faded and worn leather cover, and a large seashell. Underneath the book was a package wrapped in paper. Placing the book and shell on the table, I removed the folded tissue from the package. Despite my careful touch, some of the fragile textile disintegrated, falling into small pieces in my hand, revealing a pale pink dress with a long skirt and an underskirt of soft muslin.

Carefully I unfolded the garment, holding the dress in front of me, realizing its owner must have been short in stature, perhaps no more than five feet tall. The waist was tiny, and I estimated the dress would be a size 3 in modern apparel. The long skirt was finished at the hem with a border of lace about one inch wide, and the same lace trim appeared at the top of the high collar and on the wide cuffs, which also featured a row of six covered pink buttons.

I handed the dress to Barbara, who refolded it gingerly, placing it on the table. I picked up the book and opened the cover, hoping I would find a clue to its owner, wondering how many years it had sat forgotten in my attic. The girls were silent as I carefully turned the pages. Adam babbled about maps and treasure, but I could see the book was someone's personal diary or journal. Slowly turning the pages, I had a feeling that someone was watching, and Barb and Lauri felt the same. *Got the goose bumps,* I thought as my skin prickled.

"Are you there, Dad," Barb asked softly, but I didn't feel the same emotions that usually indicated his presence.

"No, it's someone else," I replied. "I feel someone is happy we found this book."

The pages in the journal were tanned and brittle from age, and I realized it would be difficult to read without damage.

"Perhaps I should take it to the Pioneer Museum up the street," I wondered out loud. "They could do some research, perhaps find who this belonged to." But a soft voice whispered for my ears only, "*NO, this is for you to do.*"

Inside the book, on the inside endpaper, in handwriting that appeared to be from a feminine hand, was written

Margaret Rose Lavell

The characters were graceful and elegant, and I traced my finger lightly across the name as if to feel something about the writer.

"I'll have to spend some time with this, girls," I said, "as I want to be very careful not to damage the interior. Don't speak of this to anyone please," I cautioned, "I want to do some research about the history of this building to see if there is any record of this person before we say anything about finding this stuff."

That was the beginning.

I am experienced in researching the value of antique books from the personal libraries of elderly people who have passed on, leaving their possessions to their heirs. Sometimes children and grandchildren have little regard for these bequests, preferring to dump or otherwise dispose of them. One day, one of these inheritors came to my store, asking if I wanted ten boxes of old books which had belonged to her aunt. She said she planned to take them to the dump if I didn't want them, so I gave her permission to put the load in my shed.

"I'll go through them carefully tomorrow," I promised. "Just give me a phone number where I can call you with an estimate of their value."

"That's OK," she said, "you can keep 'em. I'm going back to Portland today."

The woman looked relieved to be done with this job as she left my store, and I hoped I might find at least one valuable title in the lot.

When I closed my shop that night, I looked into the shed to see how many boxes had been left. The stack was almost to the ceiling, but I restrained myself from looking through them immediately. *Tomorrow will be time enough*, I thought, planning to go through each box carefully, removing anything that looked interesting or might be valuable. Then I would do an Internet search to establish a market price before listing them for sale in my online store.

I was lucky the Dumpster was empty as I filled it to the top the next morning. All of those cartons were full to the brim with wet and mildewed books. Black and green mold grew on the covers and in the corners of the cardboard containers, and I knew it would be dangerous to handle them. I coughed and sneezed as I lugged the heavy boxes out of the shed, puffing as I lifted them high over the rim of the Dumpster.

Bet they were stored in a damp barn or attic, I thought as I finally finished the job, vowing I would never be so stupid again. The contact number my benefactor left was not a working number, and I never saw her again.

On another occasion I accepted a load of books without checking the contents first and found the boxes infested with black spiders. A brave customer heard my squeals as several of the furry monsters crawled over the top rim of the box and down the side. She helped me pick up the cardboard cartons, and we fearfully carried them outside onto the back deck. I sprayed a whole can of bug killer into the boxes before fearfully relocating them to the Dumpster, vowing never again to take lots of old books directly into the store.

This commentary is to explain, dear reader, that I am careful in handling books with mold and mildew, and ordinarily a book like the one found in my attic would quickly find a new home in the trash. I dabbed away at the ugly spots of black mold inside the back cover using a damp tissue wipe which contained a disinfectant agent, knowing the fungus would spread throughout the book if it was not removed.

Eventually I read all of Margaret Rose's journal, but it was difficult as some of the pages separated from the spine when I turned them. The delicate paper crumbled when touched, and several pages had damage from moisture. On these pages much of the handwriting was blurred and unreadable.

From what I could read, however, I got a mental image of the woman who had written in the book, and I believed without a doubt she had experienced something so amazing she wanted to share it with others. I felt it was important to this woman to tell her story, letting people in the future know she had existed. Perhaps the book had been left for this purpose.

I started writing, using the journal as inspiration, but the words came easily. I dreamed about the woman almost every night, seeing events of her life, writing down notes in the morning when I woke.

I became obsessed with telling the story, ignoring shoppers in my bookstore, pausing my typing only long enough to collect payment for postcards and pirate flags. I am sure many visitors wondered why an employee in a shop would neglect her customers in this way.

The words flowed from my keyboard to the computer screen, and often when looking back at what I had written, I saw parts I didn't remember. At times it seemed like someone else was writing the story.

One day, a young man came in the store, asking if I had any books on the occult. I pointed him in the right direction as he loudly announced he was a student of the paranormal.

"Do you know there is a female spirit in this building?" he inquired smugly as another shopper stopped in her tracks to gawk.

"Yes, I do believe that," I said, obviously much to my visitor's surprise, "and when I bought this building, the past owner told me she believed the building was 'haunted'." I told him about the times when I personally saw books fly off the shelves, landing hard at my feet, and I also told him about the two separate unrelated people who have seen the ghostly figure of a petite woman in the place. Both ladies described the same strawberry blond hair piled high in curls and the old-fashioned pink frock with a long skirt, trimmed in white lace.

The journal of Margaret Rose Lavell is the inspiration for this fantastic tale of love and adventure, and in some places, I have quoted directly from her journal.

HECETA HEAD LIGHTHOUSE

Named for Don Brunode Heceta who surveyed the Oregon coast while on a Royal Spanish Navy Expedition in 1775 and noted a large expanse of shallow water off the headland rising 1,000 feet above.

The U. S. Lighthouse Service lit the wick of the original coal oil lamp on March 30, 1894. That light from five concentric wicks, magnified by a 392-prism British made lens, equaled 80,000 candle power. It was visible 21 miles from shore, limited only by the curvature of the earth.

Chapter 2

MARGARET ROSE LAVELL

Margaret Rose sat quietly in the wooden pew of the small church, her Bible clutched firmly in her hand. The woman's large blue eyes were downcast, seeming fixed on her tiny feet, which were clad in sensible black shoes with a small heel. The golden hair peeking from her bonnet was tied back neatly in a small bun at the nape of her lovely white neck, but a few curling tendrils escaped here and there, framing her pretty face like exotic tropical flowers. This disobedient hair seemed bent on escaping the restriction placed upon it by its owner, as if longing to be free. Margaret nervously raised her hand to the high white lace collar of her dress, pulling it away from her neck as if she were choking. Even though it was winter on the Oregon Coast, her body felt hot and uncomfortable most of the time. This sympton could indicate a woman experiencing menopause, but Margaret was a young woman, years away from this possibility.

Outside the wooden structure, rain streamed down from the heavens, accompanied by howling winds that lashed and whipped the steeple, shaking and hammering the walls as if some mighty creature were trying to enter. Tremendous ocean waves of up to twenty feet rolled toward the coast, pounding the rugged shore, tossing giant logs up on the rocks as if they were merely splinters, some as high as a hundred feet above the sea where they came to rest, tightly wedged into snug crevices where they would stay forevermore. Glittering droplets of salty ocean spray and plump marshmallow-shaped hunks of sea foam fell upon the gnarled stands of scrawny trees which grew along the coast, their branches permanently distorted and bent from the constant battering assault of the mighty winter winds which are a part of life on the Oregon coast in wintertime.

The raging north wind curled its icy fingers round crumbling tombstones in the old cemetery on the bluff, caressing the worn marble with tentacles of brine over the names of those passed over. "Motherrr, Motherrr, Motherrr," wailed the wind, its sorrowful keen oozing through the tightly sealed stained-glass windows of the simple log church on the hill. "Motherrr, Motherrr," came the whimpering cry again as Margaret Rose raised her eyes from the Bible.

Who is that girl with the strange sorrowful eyes staring at me through the window? she wondered, suddenly feeling the fair hair on her arms stand erect as her delicate white skin prickled all the way down her back. Margaret looked down at her Bible for a moment, then glanced back at the window, catching another quick glimpse of a girl wearing a hooded fur coat.

Tiny shocks and tingles danced over her body as she resisted the impulse to jump up and run out the door to have a better look. *Perhaps she will come inside,* Margaret thought, returning to her prayers, half expecting the heavy door to open at any moment. When that did not happen, Margaret turned once again to the window but saw nothing except the gloomy fog and the rain.

"Motherrr, Motherrr," the mournful howl came once again, but fainter now as Margaret dropped her eyes, an aching feeling in the pit of her stomach. *Perhaps it is only a figment of my poor sick mind,* she reasoned, forcing herself to sit more erectly to listen to the service underway. "Motherrr, Motherrr," she heard the pitiful sound once again, yet now it seemed far away and then no more.

At the lectern, Pastor William Stewart Coombs stood sternly, his gray eyes sweeping over the congregation. Only a few of the narrow wooden pews were filled with worshippers, most being elderly and infirm, as many of the younger parishioners had left the area to find work which would provide a better standard of living for their families. His wife, Margaret Rose, seemed like a bright star, out of place in these drab surroundings, and as he watched, he wondered what she was thinking. He frowned, seeing how her eyes wandered, darting back and forth between her Bible and the window, a sign she was unable to focus upon the sermon he had so carefully prepared for this day.

The night before, Margaret slept poorly, tossing and turning in their bed. Tears stained her pillow as they did so many nights since her mysterious appearance after a four-year absence from husband and home. Ever since her return home two months before, Margaret's slumber was disturbed by vivid dreams and nightmares, which left her drenched with sweat, crying as if her heart were broken. The reverend tried to give comfort by offering to pray with her, but Margaret turned her back, curling her body into a tight knot, knees to her chest, seeming unapproachable in her misery.

In the morning, as the reverend donned his white shirt and adjusted his necktie in front of the round dresser mirror, he watched the reflected image of his wife as she slept fitfully.

This unhappy woman seems so different than the cheerful young lady I married, he mused, remembering the first time he heard her name.

Several days after he arrived to take up his new appointment as pastor of the church on the hill, several of the ladies in his congregation took him aside, describing a beautiful young woman whom they felt would make the perfect wife.

"She's a lovely thing, so well behaved and prayerful," the ladies gushed, *explaining that the girl was the daughter of one of the assistant light keepers at Heceta Head Lighthouse.*

"She comes from a good family," they said. "But it must be lonely, stuck out there in the middle of nowhere."

Several weeks later, recalling this suggestion, the young minister hiked up the path to the impressive lighthouse, which sat on a thousand-foot bluff overlooking the ocean, hoping to see the girl they were speaking about. The ladies had told him a bit about the history of the lighthouse, explaining that the light keeper and two of his assistants lived in the little community of Heceta Head. Two Queen Ann-style cottages had been constructed for the keepers, the largest for the head keeper and his large family while the two assistants and their families shared the other.

The ladies said there was no school for the children of the keepers as the area was so remote, so most of the children lived with relatives in Yachats and Ocean Lake, returning home to Heceta Head for vacations and holidays. The minister found it interesting that Margaret Rose held classes for the children when they were home, teaching them about the history of the lighthouse as well as the flora and fauna of the area.

The view from the grounds around the lighthouse was breathtaking, but the sight the young minister hoped for was not available that day. Instead, he was greeted by one of the assistant keepers, who took him to the top of the structure, giving an enthusiastic historical commentary as they climbed. The man summarized the history of the lighthouse from its illumination in 1894 but seemed most anxious to share his feelings about life in this remote and lonely place. He confided that several assistants had lasted only a few months, unable to cope with the isolation, but assured the reverend he found life at the lighthouse peaceful and rewarding.

The man seemed overjoyed to have someone to talk to as he invited the minister to have a cup of tea and more conversation at his cottage.

"It's a tough job, it is, keeping the light flashing once every minute from sunrise to sunset," the man said.

"We have to haul the coal oil from the fuel house up the tower to keep the wicks burning. The smoke makes a sooty mess on the lens, it does, and it's a constant chore to keep the lens clean."

"How far out to sea can the light be seen?" the minister asked.

"Bout 21 miles they say," the keeper replied, "saved lots of boats from going down, not like the old days when they got in too close and went on the rocks.

*Have you heard the story about the ghost who haunts the lighthouse?"
the keeper asked as the two men sat on a porch overlooking the ocean.*

*"I believe I have heard something about that," the minister said softly.
"Isn't the presence rumored to be the grieving mother of a young child who
disappeared after falling off the cliff into the sea?"*

*"Yes indeed," his host agreed, "and there have been continuous reports
of other mysterious events. Several people have reported hearing strange
sounds in the night although I have never seen or heard any such in my
time here.*

*Do you believe in spirits?" the man asked the minister, who took a sip of
his tea, swallowing hard and taking a few moments to respond.*

*"We are God's children, and if we are faithful to his word, we will go to
heaven when we die," he answered, almost managing to dodge the question.*

*"But do you think a person can die, yet the spirit stay earthbound for
years and years?" the man persisted, as if looking for some confirmation.*

*"The human body is but a temple for the spirit, and perhaps God has a
reason to hold a soul here in the earthly realm after death instead of granting
immediate salvation and peace," the minister agreed.*

*"Perhaps the woman does not know she has passed over," the keeper
theorized, "and is experiencing her grief over and over through the days and
years, perhaps as a punishment for some transgression."*

*The minister's gray eyes looked sad as he promised to include this "entity"
in his prayers.*

*"The children love living here," the light keeper confided, moving the
conversation from spirits and God to more mundane everyday thoughts.*

*"Heceta Head is a wonderful place to grow up, with lots to explore,
including the many caves at the bottom of the cliffs along the shore, and
it's only a mile to the sea cave just south of here. We tell the little ones about
the ghost, hoping the tale will make them more careful in their play and
explorations around the area."*

*Minister Coombs asked where the other keepers and their families were that
day and was told they had gone down the coast to Florence for supplies.*

*"Don't expect em back until tomorrow, as it can take five to seven hours
travel time depending on the tides," he explained, "besides, it will be hard to
get Margaret Rose out of the general store. Heard they got a new shipment
of books, and that girl is a real bookworm. Always got her nose buried in a*

book, can't even talk to her sometimes, doesn't hear you. Makes her mother crazy. Had her way, that girl would spend all day, every day, reading and studying. Her Dad's got a huge library of books, inherited from his father I think, history and science, stuff I ain't got no interest in, whatsoever. Want to see it, Reverend?"

"Thanks, maybe some other time", the minister said, extending a hand to his new friend, "but I should get moving. I must get on home before dark." Hmmm, *he mused,* an educated girl, I like that.

"It's been great talking with you, and I thank you for the refreshment."

"Please return soon," the keeper begged, gripping the minister's hand firmly as if he were loath to have him leave.

"Of course, my friend, and you must come to church soon," the reverend suggested cheerfully as he headed down the path for the long trek home.

A few days later, the reverend was invited to dinner at a parishioner's home in the village, where he was introduced to the other assistant light keeper, Mr. Patrick Lavell, and his daughter, Margaret Rose. Her mother, Nellie, seemed excited to meet him, introducing him to Margaret's younger sister, Laura Leigh, and her brother, Frederick.

Margaret Rose and the minister were seated side by side at the dinner table where he was most favorably impressed by the young woman's intelligence and understanding of the world, even though at the tender age of seventeen, she was some ten years his junior. After dinner, Margaret entertained the company with several piano renditions, and although her sweet voice was untrained and tentative, listeners were charmed as she sang one of her own compositions.

In the months to come, the couple spent time together, usually in the presence of other friends or Margaret's family members, who obviously thought they would make a good match. Even though he was quiet and serious and she more sensitive and artistic, the reverend felt that with the help of the Lord he could guide her into more sensible ways.

Margaret confided to her suitor that she was an adopted child, and although she loved her mother and father very much, she always wondered about her birth mother. Talking about that seemed taboo, however, as any time Margaret brought it up, her mother's face flushed bright red and she immediately changed the subject. Margaret thought this reluctance to discuss her heritage might have something to do with the strange scars she had behind

both ears. She thought it best not to mention this imperfection to her beau, as her mom warned that boys wanted their girlfriends to be perfect.

Margaret loved her mother but felt they were not as close as a mother and daughter should be.

"My personality does not always agree with Mother," Margaret Rose confided to her suitor, "and I sometimes feel she is disappointed with me as a daughter."

Margaret's face looked sad as she thought how lovely it would feel to be enfolded in her mother's arms or have her face smothered with kisses. As the oldest child, she felt more was expected of her as her parents tended to be more flexible and understanding with her younger siblings—or perhaps it was because she was not really a true member of the family.

The reverend found it a bit difficult to understand why Margaret spent so much of her time singing and making up songs when she could be studying more serious subjects like the Bible. As she sat high on the cliffs above the sea, she wrote poetry, keeping a journal which was constantly on her person. She seemed emotionally unaffected by the often gloomy days of rain and wind, or the fog that crept up the mountains, shrouding the trees and dwellings with its thin gray fingers, but displayed a sunny disposition no matter what the weather. I will learn to deal with her frivolity, *the reverend decided, soon asking her to become his wife.*

Margaret's family and friends encouraged her to accept the reverend even though she did not seem to be head over heels in love, but he was a good man, with a secure occupation, which was unusual at the time.

After their wedding, attended by family and friends from north and south on the coast, the couple set up housekeeping in a modest cabin near the church. Margaret brought her own personal treasures to decorate the place and seemed delighted she was now mistress of her own home. Her parents, pleased their daughter was safe and secure with a dependable God-fearing husband, presented the reverend and his new missus with the piano that sat in the living room of their home at Heceta Head. Wedding guests brought generous gifts of china plates from England and crystal goblets from France. These were proudly displayed in a wooden hutch made from Oregon myrtle wood, handcrafted by the father of the bride. Everything seemed perfect.

Now Margaret Rose never sang, and the piano, once her delight, sat forgotten in the corner. Why was she so sad, and where had she been during the four years of her absence? She seemed to have no memory of anything after the day when she seemingly dropped from the face of the earth after one of her regular visits to the sea caves.

Before her disappearance, despite the difference in their ages, Margaret Rose had successfully learned to be the perfect wife for a man of the cloth, keeping a well organized and efficient house, happily lending assistance in all manner of duties for the church. This quiet gentle soul was loved and appreciated by the members of the small congregation, many of them ill and elderly, who looked forward to her visits. Often she brought warm homemade bread, sugar cookies, apple pies, or her special jams for their enjoyment. Margaret spent time reading to them, sometimes from her own writings, and lovingly performed small services which made their lives easier. In the summer, she brought roses from her garden or small cuttings of plants in clay pots to place by the window.

Margaret seemed tireless, and despite the periods of damp and inclement weather which were characteristic of the area, was in perfect health, not suffering the usual aches, pains, and complaints of other women. The only criticism which could be made was that she seemed distracted at times as she went about her duties, often leaving her chores to sit on her favorite bench for hours, staring out at the sea.

"Daydreaming again," the reverend chuckled when he discovered her there, her needlework tossed carelessly aside. Apart from this small flaw, the reverend's wife was the perfect example of a loving wife and a good, pious Christian woman.

God had not yet seen fit to bless the couple with children, but Margaret had faith she would be fruitful in the future, bearing offspring who would be well behaved and bring happiness to their lives.

Now, since Margaret Rose's return, she stayed in bed most of the day, staring at the ceiling of her room or gazing out the window. How lazy Margaret Rose had become, neglecting her husband and ignoring the mountain of dirty clothes piled by the washtub, so it was difficult for him to find anything suitable for Sunday service. How slovenly was her appearance, her hair in disarray and unwashed, pinned up this way and that, her clothing soiled and wrinkled. Even her favorite dress, the floral-patterned frock with lace at the sleeves and neck, was not fit for wearing.

Margaret Rose's garden, once her pride and joy, was now overgrown and tangled, with the constant Oregon rains nourishing obnoxious weeds and undisciplined wildflowers, choking the roses she loved so much in days gone by while ancient tree-sized rhododendrons, not needing the attention of humans to flourish, bloomed profusely in the spring, boasting giant blossoms of pink, rose, and white. Her husband suggested it might be good therapy to work in the soil again, but Margaret Rose seemed not to hear or understand his suggestion.

These days, it was difficult to engage this sad lady in conversation of any kind, although previously she was known for her sprightly sense of humor which seemed to find some good in any situation. Normally there was a musical sound to her lilting voice, which immediately caused people to draw near, wanting to share her company and know her better. Now there was only painful silence in the small house as the couple often went days without speaking to each other.

LIGHTKEEPERS' HOUSES

The classic Queen Ann-style houses were finished in 1893 at a cost of $80,000. The complex included the lighthouse with a 56' high tower, a house for the Head Lightkeeper's family, duplex for two Assistant Lightkeepers, a barn and two kerosene oil storage buildings.

Chapter 3

CHILDHOOD ON THE OREGON COAST

Margaret and her siblings, their cousins, and playmates grew up independent and strong, ranging far and wide on the Oregon coast with little supervision from adults. Shoes were worn only when it was really cold and wet, or on special occasions, and were passed down to the younger children in the family until the soles were worn and full of holes. Their feet were tough and calloused from walking on stones and trails to lush green gorges where blackberries and huckleberries grew in abundance. They learned which mushrooms were poisonous, gathered the good ones, climbed trees, and followed the rivers inland to dance under waterfalls that plunged into green gorges filled with wildflowers. Boys and girls wove chains of yellow dandelions, hanging them around their necks, matched with a crown of flowers for the hair.

The children fished for trout in the numerous streams which flowed down from the mountains to empty their sparkling fresh waters into the salty sea, and the occasional catch of freshwater crawdads was well appreciated as part of the families' diet. Even the youngest children wandered free along the rocky coast, plunging knee-deep at low tide into salty pools full of starfish and sea anemones, hunting for agates and the tasty mussels which clung to the rocks. They climbed high on the sandstone cliffs, searching for driftwood and shells, but no one worried about the danger. Once in a while, a child would be badly injured or even killed by a giant log hurled high on the beach by a sneaker wave in the winter months. Keeping your face to the sea in winter was the prudent thing to do, and it was a lesson parents tried to instill early on.

Long pieces of kelp drying on the sand became whips, and the empty shells of giant horseshoe-crabs were shields when playing warrior. Deer and elk were often seen in the forest and the backyards of homes, and it was not unusual to see a fat brown bear peering through a bedroom window in the darkness of the night. Mountain lions and cougar were respected as they prowled through the area, but sometimes it was necessary to hunt them down when they killed livestock or threatened humans. Sightings of elves and fairies were common, and some of the local folk claimed to have seen "Seehtiks," a massive hairy apelike creature who lived deep in the Cascades, avoiding all human contact even though he had characteristics of the human species. Most agreed the species did no harm, so they needed to be left in peace.

Kids and their dogs ran wild on vast stretches of sandy beaches, regardless of the weather, seeming not to notice the cold or rain even when their trousers were soaking wet. The dogs charged into flocks of gulls and sandpipers congregating near the freshwater runoffs from numerous streams flowing to the sea, but their barking was only a passing distraction, as the birds took flight in noisy white waves, then settled back down inches from their previous locations. Snowy plovers nested in the sandy dune areas while magnificent frigate birds hovered overhead.

The children of the light keepers at Heceta Head sometimes saw whales on their annual migrations north and south along the coast, often lying just offshore in the clear green water. Hundreds of gray whales called the Oregon Coast home and could be seen breaching and spouting a short way from the beach. An occasional orca was also spotted, and fishermen reported they sometimes entered the Siuslaw River at Florence, feeding on sea lions just inside the bar. Steller sea lions basked in lazy splendor on rocky offshore cays, sunning themselves on ledges where they mated and socialized, then sliding off into the sea to feed and play.

Best of all, from a child's point of view, were the numerous caves at the base of the cliffs, just waiting for exploration at low tide. Parents warned they must be careful not to get trapped by the incoming tide which crept up slowly at first, then quickly filled the caves, making escape difficult, if not impossible. In the depths of the caverns were bizarre forms of sea life living in tidal pools never exposed to the sunlight, and in some places, the shrill screeches of bats could be heard in the dark fissures where humans could not go.

Chapter 4

CAVERN OF THE SEA LIONS

A mile south of Heceta Head at the base of a high cliff, midway between Florence and Yachats was an enormous sea cave, and local folks said it was probably the largest cavern of its type in the world. A sea captain by the name of Cox had discovered the opening from the sea on one of his fishing trips in the late eighteen hundreds, later purchasing the land from the state of Oregon in 1887.

At the time the grotto was discovered, there were no roads along the coast, so travel was difficult. People moved around the area mostly by horse or mule, using rocky trails that ran perilously close to the precipice, where one wrong step could result in a disastrous plunge to a salty grave. There were other places where the wayfarer had to wait until low tide to ford rushing creeks and rivers in order to make his way either north or south. The slopes along the rocky headlands were used by farmers to graze their sheep, but there were many treacherous steep paths leading from these lofty pinnacles down to the sea. These trails were well-known to the native people who lived along the coast, as they gathered oysters and clams along the beach, gorging themselves with the sweet meat, leaving high mounds of shells behind.

Margaret and her friends often made their way down these tracks, climbing over piles of enormous rocks and logs deposited on the shore by winter storm swells to gain access to this subterranean cave. At the base of the trail, still hundreds of feet above the entrance, a series of heavy black fisherman's nets had been linked together, secured by heavy ropes tied around massive boulders, providing a means for the young and agile to descend the rest of the way.

The adventurous explorer lay flat on his or her belly, grabbed hold of the ropes, slithered backward until his knees passed the edge of the cliff, then dropped the feet, placing them securely in one of the square openings in the net. The climber had to be physically strong and unafraid of heights, descending slowly hand over hand, making sure of a good grip and foothold with every move. At the bottom, entry to the chamber was through a small opening in the rocks on the north side, and once inside, the climber was rewarded with a view of the picturesque lighthouse on Heceta Head, framed by the rock window. The return trip back up the net seemed easier, but because of the difficulty, the caves were seldom visited except by visionaries in the sea captain's family who dreamed of the day when the Sea Lion Caves would be a first-class tourist destination.

There were thousands of sea lions along the Oregon coast, but in this mammoth cavern, the viewer could see hundreds of golden Steller sea lions, some weighing as much as two thousand pounds. Through the wide opening of this cave, these mighty men of the sea rode in on the tops of immense cresting waves, much like surfers wearing shiny gray wet suits. Some made it up onto the slippery rock ledges in the dank interior on their first attempt, but others tried again and again without success. Once comfortably aground on the many craggy rims and stony seats, giant bulls and their harems staked out their territory, defending any attempt by an interloper to breach their secured ground.

The pungent, sour aroma of fish and sea life mingled with the dark interior of the cave assaulted the senses; it was revolting and exhilarating, all at the same time. On her first visit, Margaret Rose covered her eyes, peering fearfully through her fingers as these enormous creatures mated and fought, filling the air with loud barks, sighs, and a multitude of other frightening sounds which echoed off the walls and ceilings of the grotto. Even though she often saw the sea lions swimming just off the shore, she had never been so close to these animals.

In the morning, with the sun in the east, the cave was dark and bleak, but when the sun fell slowly in the west, it transformed the cavern into a magical place, illuminated in shimmering shades of pale green, icy blue, and rosy pink.

There were many bats in the cave, but most disturbing to the visitor was the unexpected appearance of a rat. Thousands of these scrawny creatures inhabited the caves in the early days, and a few deleterious lads made a game out of catching and killing them. They chopped off the tails, sometimes keeping the disgusting things as a trophy. Margaret Rose told her new husband how her older brother locked her into the woodshed one dark night, a prank made even more wicked as that was the place where he nailed the tails of his rat trophies on the walls.

**MARGARET ROSE LAVELL ON THE BEACH AT
DEVIL'S ELBOW, NEAR CAPE CREEK**

Chapter 5

THE MYSTERIOUS MERFOLK

Despite her fear of the rats, Margaret Rose loved the sea caves, nimbly moving up and down the net ladder quickly and easily, then spending hours by herself watching the sea lions at their play. Usually she took her sketch pad, journal, and a snack, returning home before dark. Though Margaret enjoyed foraging in the forests and fishing in the streams, her favorite place was the seashore.

She would find a comfortable perch on a suitable rock sheltered from the wind and warmed by the sun where she could gaze at the sea for hours and hours. *I wish I could swim with the whales and sea otters*, she fantasized, *playing in the salty green water, then pulling myself up on the warm rocks to sleep and dream.*

On stormy winter nights while the adults were playing cards downstairs in the kitchen, Margaret, her sister, and her cousins snuggled warm under the patchwork comforter on her bed, whispering about events they kept secret from their parents. They had often seen strange creatures swimming offshore, mingling with the sea lions and otters in the area where the whales spouted and fed. The children called them people of the sea, the "Mer" people, as they looked like men and women with the tail of a fish.

Sometimes the Merfolk came in close to the shore, gesturing with their webbed hands as if enticing the children to come and play in the surf, but their enigmatic smiles showed sharp, pointed teeth which looked evil and frightening. The males had muscular arms and torsos, the women smooth breasts and flowing hair, and on several sightings, they were clothed in dark smooth skins which covered their upper bodies. The garments had hoods which fit snugly over their heads, making them blend in with the sea lions.

Most of the children fled when they saw these extraordinary beings. They screamed and squealed as they climbed the cliffs back to the safety of the meadows on top, but Margaret Rose did not run. She stood quietly at the water's edge, listening to their melodic calls, hearing their voices in her mind. They seemed to be able to communicate telepathically, and Margaret Rose could hear them.

Come, come, they seemed to call, *Come with us.*

One summer day, a male creature who seemed particularly playful and friendly pointed a finger in her direction before diving deep beneath the surface. When he reappeared, Margaret saw a large shell in his hand, held high as if in offering. The sea man moved slowly toward the shore, then rose high out of the water with a tremendous thrust of his powerful lower body, heaving the shell toward Margaret. It splashed down in the shallow water, close to her feet, and she scrambled to retrieve it before the next wave broke on the beach.

The creature stared intently in her direction, and Margaret thought she saw him smile. *Good, good,* she heard in her mind, watching as he disappeared beneath the waves.

"Margaret, Margaret," the children shouted from the protection of the high cliffs, "come away, come away. Don't listen, or they will steal your soul." Margaret turned her back to the sea, the shell held tightly to her slender body, as she made her way up the hill to her friends.

From the journal:

Deep inside the caves they go,
Sheltered there from wind so wild,
Darkness hides their human faces,
Waiting for a special child.

He calls to me with songs so splendid,
smiles so sweet with hand extended,
voice so quiet, in my brain,
speaks of love and calls my name.

Chapter 6

THE LEAVING

On a summer day, Margaret Rose told her husband that she would visit the sea cliffs the next day.

"I plan to go down tomorrow, with your permission of course, taking a bite to eat and my sketch pad, but I will return early to prepare your supper."

"Again to the caves, Margaret," complained her husband. "Perhaps you should stay at home and spend your time in more sensible pursuits."

"All the chores will be finished before I leave," Margaret promised, "and you will not return home until after your visit to poor Mrs. McKinney. Please extend my sympathy on the loss of her husband."

"Well then, be very careful, my dear," warned Margaret Rose's husband. "You should not go down to the caves so often alone. It would be better to wait until I can come along to look after you."

"Don't worry, husband. You are so very kind, but I have been playing in the caverns since a small child, and know them well," said Margaret Rose with a sweet smile, touching his hand lightly with hers.

"I love to sit quietly in a corner, watching the kings of the sea, singing my songs, and thinking about you."

"Very well, my dear, say a prayer while you are there, for perhaps the dear Lord will hear you and bless us soon with a child," requested the Reverend Coombs as Margaret Rose poured his tea into a china cup adorned with tiny pink roses and rimmed with gold.

The next day, in the late afternoon, the reverend returned home, his mouth watering at the possibility of finding a warm berry pie cooling in the kitchen. He looked forward to the flaky golden crust, crimped ever so neatly around the top, purple juices oozing from the tiny slips so carefully placed in the middle in the shape of a flower, but much to his surprise no delicious aromas welcomed his arrival. Margaret Rose was always so dependable and efficient, having the evening meal ready to go on the square wooden kitchen table at 5:00 p.m. sharp, leaving adequate time in the evening for Bible study before retiring at 8:00. Tonight the stove was cold, and the table bare. *Where can you be?*

Soon the minister was pacing back and forth, his irritation replaced by worry. *Can something have happened to you, silly goose? Is it possible there has been an accident of some kind, or have you lost track of the time, singing your songs, drawing pictures, picking flowers and romping in the surf?*

To the shore he dashed, lantern in hand, calling Margaret's name as his gray eyes searched the horizon. Reverend Coombs was now running. Faster and faster he raced, his heart pounding loudly as he reached the cliffs overlooking the sea caves. He had never before climbed down the net ladder, having no interest in seeing either sea lions in a cave, or bats, and surely not rats.

Slowly he made his way down, carefully placing one foot after another in the square holes between the fibers of the net while holding tightly to the lantern. When he arrived at last at the bottom, Mr. Coombs was damp with sweat and dizzy with fear as he lighted the lamp, illuminating the entrance hole in the rocky cliff. He scrambled over some loose rocks by the hole, then stood on a large boulder so he could stick his head and upper body through the entrance. The yellow light cast eerie reflections and shadows on the ceiling, and shivers ran down his back as he caught glimpses of small dark animals skittering along the floor of the cavern. *God help me,* he prayed, having an inarticulate fear of rodents, as he pulled himself through the entrance and into the dark interior.

The minister danced across the floor of the cave on tiptoes, throwing one arm over his head, dodging and swatting at the air, squeaking with fright as bats swooped down from overhead. Finally he made it to the large opening where ocean waves broke just outside, sending shimmering salty fingers of green spray and foamy bubbles into the cave. There were only a few sea lions in the cave now as apparently most had gone back out to sea, but Margaret Rose was not there.

But what is that, that on the floor of the cave there, that white handkerchief with the lace trim, that sketch pad and pencil? What is that doing there, part of the crust from a sandwich, and where is Margaret Rose? Her clothes were scattered on the floor of the cave, her soiled white blouse in a pile with her flowered skirt and underclothing. The minister snatched at the blouse with quivering hand, recoiling in panic as he saw some of the covered buttons were gone—as if the thing was ripped from her body. *My God, what has happened?* he thought. *What devilish thing is this, where are you, where have you gone?*

Mr. Coombs was terrified. He did not believe his wife would intentionally leave her personal belongings in this dank, dark place. *Margaret is always so careful to take good care of her things. What terrible deed has happened here?*

The husband looked for his wife in every possible nook and cranny in the cave, crying her name, "Margaret Rose, please, please, answer me, please, where are you, my dear, oh my dear, where are you, where can you be?"

Tears streaked his face as he became more and more agitated, an awful gnawing feeling in the pit of his stomach. The pastor grabbed the sketch pad and Margaret's clothing as he quickly climbed back up the rope ladder to the top, then hurried to the village to find volunteers to launch a thorough search of the area.

Only a few men searched along the shore that night, casting the yellow light from their lanterns along the rocks and cliffs, looking down to beaches now awash as the tide came in high, but there was no sign of Margaret Rose. In the morning, at first light, men, women and children from all parts of the area joined the search, but Margaret Rose was not found. Rumors and gossip ran rampant as locals advanced various ideas about Margaret Rose's disappearance. Down in Florence, the ladies of the Wednesday sewing circle whispered shocking scenarios based on the finding of her clothing, buttons snatched clear off, and pantaloons on the ground. Everyone agreed that something terrible must have happened, and a few cast suspicious eyes upon the husband. The Reverend neatly folded his wife's clothing then buried it in the bottom of her trunk, but placed the sketchpad with Margaret's books and Bible. He never mentioned the sketches to local authorities, deciding the drawings were nobody's business.

Days turned into weeks, but no body floated to the surface or was found wedged in a slippery dark crevice in the rocks. Far and wide around the state, the word of Margaret Rose's disappearance was sent, but she was gone as if she were plucked off the shore and transported to another world. She was gone, and Minister Coombs finally had to accept that his wife had somehow departed from this life and would not return.

Margaret Rose's parents, despite their broken hearts, publicly stood in strong support of her embattled husband, telling all who would listen what a fine man he was. Many evenings he joined the family at the dinner table where they held hands and prayed for Margaret's return, but Margaret's mother privately felt a little uncomfortable because of his fawning attentions to her younger daughter. The minister's obvious interest seemed out of place and inappropriate for a husband who had so recently lost his wife. For a moment, she wondered if he was considering his options if Margaret was not found, as a preacher must have a wife by his side to be most effective in his job.

As the weeks and months passed, the minister found his changed status had affected his personal life in ways not expected. No longer did he receive frequent invitations to dinner at the homes of his parishioners, and even Margaret's family seemed uncomfortable in his presence. No longer did people approach with words of comfort. It was as if they were now embarrassed, not knowing what to say or how to feel, so they avoided the contact.

One night in the dimness of the small cabin, after the lamps were lit in the early evening, Minister Coombs opened his wife's sketch pad, hoping to find solace in her neat drawings of wildflowers and ocean waves, but he stared thoughtfully at the last sketch in the book, obviously unfinished, showing massive sea lions inside the cave.

What is that, what is that? he wondered, his bony finger wandering over the page, coming to rest on a strange figure in the corner just inside the cavern's entrance. *It looks like a man, he thought, but no, it is a sea lion, but the eyes, the eyes—they look almost human.* He stared and stared at the eyes, which were slightly slanted and mysterious in their intensity. There was a teasing quality to those eyes, almost a taunting feel to the image. *Come here, come near,* those eyes seemed to say.

The reverend looked closer, a perplexed look on his gaunt face. *Why would you draw that Margaret, he thought, how could you even conceive of a godless creature such as this? Look at him, staring out from the midst of those sea lions with that grin on his face.*

The reverend threw the book violently onto the table, then shuddered as he made the sign of the cross on his brow.

Several months later a service was held at the tiny chapel where candles were lighted and prayers were said for the soul of Margaret Rose. A square white stone inscribed only with her name and the date of her birth was placed in the cemetery as life went on without her. Now Minister Coombs was a lonely man, living by himself in the small cabin, immersed in his Bible and religion, becoming stern and thin as grief changed his character and personage. His gray eyes often appeared moist and sorrowful behind thick spectacles as he searched the Bible for inspiration for his sermons. In public, he said that grief was part of God's plan, but privately, he blamed his wife for not being more careful to avoid danger. He was now less, rather than more, understanding of the needs of his congregation, and he made it clear there would be no more discussions about his wife, the late Margaret Rose.

There were no steaming warm pies for the elderly now, no cheerful visits with reassuring words and loving touches. Attendance at his church was way down, with contributions almost nonexistent. The reverend's sermons lacked joy and optimism, but instead warned of damnation and retribution for minor sins, promising punishment for those who engaged in sinful activities such as dancing, drinking alcohol or playing cards. These distractions were the devil's way of luring the faithful away from the Lord, he felt, so services in the small chapel included only a few quiet hymns as worshippers sat quietly in their pews, eyes downcast, flinching as their pastor called them sinners who would go to hell if they did not repent.

The heart of the reverend seemed hard and cold, his disposition showing few traces of his prior kindness and sensitivity, as he settled into life as a widower. He covered the piano with thick blankets, now using it to hold piles of religious books and his sermons. *Why did this woman act so foolishly,* he conjectured, *wandering off by herself to sing and draw, when she should have stayed at home where she belonged.*

Once in a while, the minister considered calling on Laura Leigh, and in fact, one spring day she came to visit him, bringing a warm peach pie. Although she stayed only a few minutes, she was very friendly, seeming pleased when he insisted she take possession of some of Margaret's favorite clothes and female trinkets.

I wonder if the girl would accept me, he mused, feeling church goers were more comfortable with a pastor with a wife and children.

Chapter 7

CATCH OF THE DAY

The town of Florence, Oregon, nestled along the scenic Siuslaw River, was about twenty miles south of the church on the hill. According to an old legend, a French schooner named Florence wrecked in 1875 near the mouth of the Siuslaw, and months later the wooden nameboard washed ashore. The board was salvaged from the beach, and the place where it came ashore was named Florence.

In 1902, Florence had a population of about three hundred and was the largest town on the Siuslaw River. The town was prospering with several lumber mills, a cannery and a thriving shipyard, so fishing and logging were important occupations for the populace. 1908 was an exciting year as the town held the first Rhododendron Festival, which featured the crowning of a queen. Visitors came from around the state, and the celebration was so successful it became a yearly event.

The dense forests and seaside basalt cliffs of the central coast stop just north of Florence where they are replaced by sand dunes and wide beaches which run to the Siuslaw. On the south side of the river, the giant dunes continue fifty miles south, being intersected by the Umpqua River at Reedsport and the Coos at North Bend.

Early one morning the forty-foot sailing gillnetter *Daniel T.* left the wharf, passing by the towering sand hills along the south side of the river. Captain Dan waved to the captain of the ferry as it crossed the river from Florence to Glenada, then headed west toward the Pacific Ocean despite warnings about heavy seas and strong winds from the north. The captain knew the boat's wood-planked hull was built strong, and with her wide beam, the *Daniel T.* would be able to handle the weather conditions that were expected. The vessel was named after the captain's father, one of the toughest sea dogs in the coastal fishing industry. The old man went "over the bar" at the age of 47, as much a casualty of the hard wet drinking days of winter as the heart attack that killed him.

In the early nineteen hundreds, practically all "purse seiners" were powered by small five to seven-and-a-half-horsepower engines, the most popular being the Frisco Standard gas engine, but only a few years later, most owners had invested in the new twenty-horsepower model. These engines were extremely temperamental and difficult to start, and most crews did not know how to do repairs to keep them running smoothly, but this new invention changed the face of the fishing industry. Owners could now have larger boats, which meant the potential for a bigger catch. Before these engines were available, boats used only sail and oars, restricting them to work areas close to port, with the result that these places were overfished and exhausted. Captain Dan knew his twenty-horse was tired and cranky, but his dream was to work hard and save enough money to own a fifty-five to sixty-five foot vessel with a forty-horsepower engine one day.

The *Daniel T.* had a mainsail, a foresail, and a clubfooted jib. The sturdy vessel was painted dark green, a color which portended good fishing, but her taff rails were shiny, having just recently received a fresh coat of brown paint. The vessel carried a double-planked skiff which was used to set the nets in a circle around a school of fish, but at the moment, it was tied down securely on the aft deck, covering piles of net which had recently been repaired and restitched. Once safely outside the inlet, Captain Dan planned to sail northwest to his favorite fishing ground where the crew would drop the skiff in the water and start fishing.

With treacherous swells already building across the inlet, the vessel took green water over the bow and decks as the captain made his way carefully across the shallow sandbar and out to deeper, smoother water.

The engine smoked and choked as if to protest the inclement weather, but once outside the inlet, the captain turned up into the wind so the mate could crank up the mainsail, before manually pulling up the jib. Falling off, he set his course in a westerly direction, broad reaching, rushing along with the fresh breeze on the starboard side. When the boat felt stable on her course, he turned the helm over to his mate before killing the engine. The *Daniel T.* was a stiff boat, and her degree of heel was slight, so she felt very stable in the water despite the heavy swells. It would be several hours until the vessel reached the planned destination, so the mate took the first watch while his captain went below for a nap.

Captain Dan got comfortable in his berth, shoving two pillows along his body to prevent an unplanned roll onto the floor. As an owner/operator, he spent most of his profits keeping the *Daniel T.* repaired and in working condition. The fishing season was short, and when the enormous swells of winter arrived, some as much as forty feet high, he would face a long gray winter with no income. Some of the fishermen worked in the lumber mills off season, but the captain planned to spend his time mending the sails and repairing the rigging. Normally, he would spend most evenings at his favorite tavern on Front Street, trading stories with other fishermen and loggers, but since he had recently given up drinking alcohol, it just didn't seem the same.

His petite blond wife was at home, with their two children, but often she accompanied him on his trips, being comfortable in any type of weather. Her parents understood her need to be by her captain's side as much as possible so were always happy to look after the children while she was gone. With Laydie at the helm, the captain could work with the crew on deck, making these trips more productive and profitable. This time, however, one of Captain Dan's daughters was feeling ill, and the grandparents were visiting relatives in Eugene, so she helped provision the boat with stores, catching the dock lines as he left for sea. *I'm a lucky man*, he thought. *I must tell her so on my return.*

Captain Dan had barely closed his eyes, or so it seemed, when he heard the excited voice of his first mate.

"Captain, Captain," shouted the mate, "come up, hurry, there are fish everywhere."

Captain Dan threw himself out of bed, grabbed his heavy jacket, and headed for the helm, finding that the crew had already dropped and furled the sails. The *Daniel T.* was drifting in the middle of an enormous school of baitfish, and the surface of the sea was slick with the oil from their bodies. Seabirds hovered overhead, occasionally diving down to grab a snack, while several large gray sea lions floated up and down on the lazy swells. The captain thought this was a little unusual as he did not usually see these animals in that particular area.

Already the young deckhand was getting the skiff untied in preparation for setting the nets while the mate prepared the net to go overboard. The three men hoisted the skiff into the sea, put the oars into the oarlocks, and then secured it alongside the *Daniel T.* with a bow and stern line. The mate hopped into the boat, tying the first part of the gill net to the stern of the small craft, then rowed in a broad circle around the school of fish, letting out the net as he went. Returning to the *Daniel T.* the three men worked together to bring in the heavy rope along the bottom of the net, cinching it in tightly to create a purse.

Once the purse was sealed at the bottom, it trapped the large fish feeding on the baitfish at the surface, so the crew could winch it up onto the deck using a ramp with a row of heavy rollers set close together. When the net was brought up on the deck, the net would open, spilling the fish onto the deck.

As the net came up onto the rollers, there was a noisy commotion in the water. Several of the sea lions had come in close to the *Daniel T.*, and were throwing themselves violently against the sides of the net. Their screams seemed to have almost a human quality as they attacked the webbing, butting it with their heads, then diving underneath. *What the heck is this?* the captain wondered, heading for his shotgun. *I'll kill the sons of bitches before I let them destroy my nets. Just a few rounds fired in the air should scare them off.*

Bam, bam, the noisy blast seemed to do its job as the sea lions scattered in all directions. They surfaced a short distance from the boat, watching as the crew brought in the net.

"What's that, what's that?" the mate cried, pointing to a part of the net just ready to come over the rollers. "Stop, stop," he demanded, "there's a goll-darn sea lion in the net."

The captain left the winch, making his way carefully across the slippery deck, past struggling salmon as they fell into the hold. But as he reached the rail, a large wave crashed broadside onto the port side of the boat, throwing the net and its contents hard against the hull.

The animal in the net, previously struggling and moving, now lay still. It seemed to be dead, or badly injured.

"Careful now, careful," warned the captain, "move it up off the roller, we don't want to damage the mesh. Take it easy, easy now. Get that damned thing out of there and pitch it in the sea."

As the mate and deckhand opened the net, the motionless animal fell to the deck, seemingly dead or seriously wounded. *My God, what kind of beast can this be?* the crew wondered. The creature was wearing a leather hood, and escaping from underneath appeared strands of gleaming golden hair.

As the three men watched, the animal twitched, then rolled over on its side, exposing the face of a woman to full view. She was wearing a skintight suit made of sealskin which entirely covered her body, including her head, leaving only the eyes exposed. Her legs were held tight together by the bottom part of the suit, which flared out at the bottom, almost like the tail of a fish. This suit was definitely made for swimming, not walking as it would prevent the person from standing on two legs.

The two crewmen moved to the other side of the vessel as far away as they could possibly get without jumping overboard. Captain Dan had seen many strange things during his years on the sea, but he had never seen anything like this. Despite his fear, he moved close to the creature, crouching at her side, tentatively stretching out his hand to touch a curling tendril of heavy hair.

Had Captain Dan's attention not been diverted by the woman on his deck, he might have noticed one of the sea lions swimming in frantic circles around his vessel. It came close alongside the hull, then dove deep, reappearing behind the vessel. Suddenly it seemed to charge, bellowing loudly, as it soared out of the water heading for the transom. The first mate, acting instinctively, grabbed a heavy wooden gaff with a steel hook. Drawing his arm back, the man hurled the weapon with all his strength at the animal, hitting it on the upper left side of the body, near the neck. Just a few more feet and the animal would have crashed over the stern of the vessel, but it fell short, splashing down hard. The crew instinctively covered their ears as a horrific scream of pain filled the air.

"Why the hell did ya do that," Dan complained in an extremely agitated voice, "we've lost a perfectly good gaff there; it's coming outta your share of the catch."

"Got em, I did," the mate bragged, "Worth it, it was. Hope I killed the bastard."

The woman raised her head for a moment as if she heard the cry, then fell back, seemingly unconscious. The top of the strange garment shifted as she moved, clearly showing a womanly shape inside the suit. *This is indeed a woman,* Dan realized. *What is she doing here?*

"Clean up this mess and prepare to get underway," the captain ordered as he scooped the woman up in his strong arms.

"I'm taking this lady down below to get these wet skins off and get her warm."

Captain Dan carefully laid the woman on his bunk, then pulled the leather hood away from her face, revealing her exquisite features. He felt embarrassed and uncomfortable as he slipped the suit down off her shoulders, exposing delicate white skin and voluptuous

53

full breasts, then finding she was wearing no garments under the leather suit. He hesitated only for a moment before peeling the tight suit off past the woman's tiny waist and shapely long legs. Fine tendrils of silky hair between her legs hid the lady's feminine parts, but there was no doubt in the captain's mind that this was indeed a lovely young woman. Her skin was very cold, and she seemed to be breathing ever so slowly.

The captain covered the woman warmly with the patchwork quilt on his bunk, then folded the leather suit neatly, placing it on the chair beside the bed. Dan's patient seemed to be resting easily now, but the large bruise at her temple was swelling and turning purple. The woman's eyelids fluttered for a moment, revealing the deep blue color beneath, then closed as she sighed softly. Captain Dan moved to the doorway, glancing quickly behind as the woman stretched, throwing off the covers, exposing her naked body to the chilly sea air. He closed the door quietly, then taking a ring of keys from his pocket locked it securely.

"We're going in," Captain Dan announced to the crew, "get the dinghy up on deck fast." The circumstances of this woman's appearance were so strange he knew he could not continue as planned. Where did she come from? Could she have fallen off a passing schooner, or perhaps one of the lumber ships which worked the coast from California to Portland? How could that be, in view of the strange suit she was wearing. Dan knew that a person falling overboard in icy Pacific waters had little chance for survival, even if wearing sealskins. There were too many questions to be answered, and Captain Dan wished his wife was aboard this trip. She would know what to do.

The crew hoisted the mainsail, then the jib, as the vessel sailed back to the mouth of the Siuslaw, making an easy seven knots. It was an easy run over the bar with a slight following sea, but Captain Dan always seemed to know the best way in and out of his home port. His arrival would be unexpected, but it was just a few steps from the wharf to his home, and he planned to send the mate to tell his wife to come to the boat as quickly as possible.

Several times on the way in, the captain unlocked the door of his cabin to check on his passenger, but she seemed to be sleeping soundly. It was dark when the vessel finally tied up to the quay and the lines were secured. "Go get Laydie," Captain Dan shouted. His mate hurried to comply, making a mad dash across the street toward the captain's house. He pounded on the door to the upstairs apartment of the narrow two-story building, and almost instantly, heard a response.

"Who's there?" a quiet feminine voice requested.

"It's Martin from the boat, ma'am. Come quickly, the captain needs you."

"What's wrong?" the captain's wife cried as she threw open the door, dressed in her slippers and evening robe. "Has something happened to the captain?"

"No, Laydie," the mate assured, "but there is something you have to see."

"Wait a moment. I'll throw something on and be right back."

Speeding up the narrow stairway, the captain's wife took a quick look at the children sleeping soundly in their beds, then called down to the mate, "Come upstairs, Martin. You must watch the children while I'm gone."

Within minutes, the captain's wife reached the wharf where the *Daniel T.* waited, and her husband paced anxiously back and forth on the deck. Assisting his wife onto the boat, the man wrapped his arms around his lady, holding her tightly.

"What's wrong, Danny?" Laydie asked lovingly in a quiet voice as if she could solve any problem which might arise.

"Come with me, love. Come down to my cabin, there is something you must see," the captain begged as he took her small hand, leading her below.

The captain fumbled for his key ring, then turned the key in the lock, slowly opening the door so his wife could peek inside through a narrow crack. The captain's wife put her face closer to the door then bolted back quickly, not believing the sight before her eyes. On her husband's narrow bunk, on top of the quilt she hand-stitched, was a beautiful naked woman with a mass of tangled hair. The woman's body was curled in the fetal position, knees almost to her breasts as she slept.

The captain closed the door quietly, glancing at the woman at his side. Her face was frozen in disbelief, blue eyes wide and face flushed.

"My God, Daniel, what is that woman doing on your bunk, naked as the day she was born?" the captain's wife gasped.

"I swear by the good Lord, darling, we found her out there, in the sea," the captain blustered, looking embarrassed and ill at ease. "She wore nothing but a suit made of sealskin. It's there in the cabin, on the chair by the bed."

"I must sit for a moment," Laydie murmured, as she took a seat on a small wooden stool. Moving to the small iron stove in the middle of the room, the captain poured strong black coffee into two mugs. Knowing how dearly his wife loved the hot, steaming brew, he hoped it would calm her nerves, so she could decide what to do next.

In the next hour, Captain Dan related every detail about the finding and rescue of the lady in his cabin, but he never mentioned the sea lions or the strange reaction of one animal after the discovery of the lady in the net. In the excitement of the moment, he put aside the memory of how the wounded beast howled as the vessel sailed back toward home port. The sea lion followed for a while, his blood staining the surface of the sea, but then disappeared behind the horizon. Obviously, Dan did not connect this strange behavior with the presence of the woman in his bed as he searched for some reasonable explanation.

"We must wake her," the captain's wife declared as she rose from her chair, heading for the door to the cabin.

The couple quietly entered the room where the captain's lady picked up a corner of the quilt, discretely covering the woman's body.

"Wake, my dear, wake up," Laydie whispered, gently stroking the woman's hair where it fell in a tangle near the bruise on her temple. "You are safe with us. Wake, my dear," she repeated, noticing a slight tremor in the long fingers on the girl's hand. And then an eye slowly opened, the blue interior fringed with long black lashes. Two eyes opened wide as a look of fear and astonishment took over the previously relaxed face. The woman struggled to sit up, then fell back as if exhausted. The captain's lady plumped up the pillows beneath her patient's head, stroking her hair once again, hoping her touch would relax and calm.

"Danny," Laydie said in a low voice, "this girl is very young, perhaps no more than twenty-one or twenty-two years of age.

Who are you, dear?" she asked in a quiet voice, "where have you come from, and what is your name my poor child?"

Confusion was evident as the woman's eyes darted around the room, searching every corner.

"Can you speak?" asked the captain's wife, wondering if the lady spoke a foreign language and had perhaps fallen from a passing ship from a far-off port. "Can you speak, my dear, and tell us your name?"

"I don't know it," the woman replied, tears suddenly flowing from her eyes, as she began to sob.

"Where am I? Where is this place, and what am I doing here?"

"She's in shock, Danny," said the captain's lady, "or in a state of amnesia due to the bump on her head. We must get her dressed in some suitable clothing, then take her to the house and get her to bed. I don't think we need to rush her to the doctor, but we'll see how she feels in the morning. After that, there'll be time enough to go to the authorities to see if anyone can identify her."

Laydie helped the weeping girl into a woolen shirt and a pair of the captain's trousers. Captain Dan wrapped her in a blanket, then easily picked her up, carrying her off the *Daniel T.*, across Front Street, and up the stairs of his home. It wasn't long before the girl was snoozing in one of the children's small beds while the girls slept together in the other.

In the morning, a brilliant sunrise gilded the placid waters of the Siuslaw with orange and yellow reflections. Seabirds perched on the pilings alongside the wooden docks on the river, resting on roofs of several decrepit fishing boats abandoned by their owners. At the captain's house, the children woke early. At first they were timid and surprised at the presence of the beautiful lady in their home but they soon climbed up onto her bed, ready for play.

Laydie brewed a pot of strong coffee, bringing a cup to her guest as she sat up in bed. The fear seemed to be gone from her lovely face as she accepted the coffee, sipping it tentatively as if it were the first coffee of her life. "Good," she said, smiling.

Later in the morning, the girl dressed in the pretty pink frock she had selected from Laydie's chest of clothing, and with her hair washed and combed, tied into a proper bun at the back of the neck, looked like other gentlewomen of the time. *Much better,* the captain's wife thought, *than the disgusting suit of sealskin clothing she was wearing when she was rescued from the sea.* Laydie made a mental note to show her the suit, in hopes it would restore her memory. But that would be for later, after they had made a visit to the police department.

The short walk seemed to invigorate and excite the girl, but she seemed a bit shaky on her feet, taking the arm of the captain for better support as she walked. It was difficult to convince the girl to accept the high-laced shoes with small heels, and now she walked in them clumsily—as if they were the first pair of shoes she had ever worn.

By now, word about the rescue of this mysterious woman had spread like wildfire, and the police chief was waiting behind his big wooden desk. He stood to greet the trio of visitors, but seeing the girl's face, smiled in instant recognition.

"I know this girl," he announced in a gruff voice, a fat wooden pipe protruding from between his clenched teeth. "She has been missing for almost four years."

"Bring me the photo of Margaret Rose Coombs," the chief called to his secretary. "She has been found at last."

Captain Dan and his wife glanced at each other in disbelief. *Can it be true?* they wondered. *Can this really be the girl who went missing four years ago from the sea caves up the coast?* She was the wife of a minister, they recollected, and was pronounced dead a year after she disappeared.

The secretary produced a faded photo of a smiling young girl dressed in a long gown with a high lace collar. Her hair was tied back, but several ringlets curled around her face, and long tendrils of hair curled around her neck and hung down over her breast.

The girl grimly glanced at the photo, then hid her face on the Laydie's bosom. Shaking with fright, she burst into sobs.

"Poor lamb," the secretary said kindly, dabbing at her own eyes with a hankie, "she is completely without any memory of her past. It will take care and love to make her well once again."

"We must send word to the reverend," the police chief directed his secretary.

"Tell one of the deputies to saddle a horse and go up the coast immediately. It will be a terrible shock for the reverend to hear his wife is alive, but he is a lucky man to be so blessed with her safe return."

Laydie stood with her arms round Margaret Rose, comforting the girl, who seemed hysterical to hear she was married, with a husband.

"No, no," she moaned, shaking and weeping as the captain's wife assisted her outside onto the street, motioning for Dan to follow.

"We'll take care of you, dear," Laydie said, "until you feel ready to return to your old life. Let's go home now, cause I know a cup of hot tea with one of my ginger spice cookies will make you feel better."

OLD TOWN FLORENCE, CIRCA 1905

Chapter 8

THE HOMECOMING

Later that day, the sheriff's deputy arrived at the little church near Yachats. His horse was lathered up and exhausted from the ride, having been pushed hard by the excited deputy. On the way, the man practiced what he would say to the reverend. The news would be a dreadful shock, so he intended to say it in a careful way which would not give the man a stroke or make him faint dead away. *What a tragedy that would be,* he thought, *first finding the wife, but then losing the husband. And what could be said about her finding? The woman was found offshore, no other vessel in the area, wearing only a strange suit made from sealskin, with no apparent memory of anything that happened during the last four years. In fact, no memory of her past at all, including her marriage. How could the man deal with this? What strange or evil things could have happened during those years?*

A prayer service had just ended at the little chapel on the hill, and the pastor was standing on the stairs, bidding farewell to his parishioners. The deputy approached on foot, having tied up his horse near the cottage, steeling himself for the task ahead. He remembered the day he told a young mother that her son had fallen off the rocks on the north jetty of the Siuslaw into the icy water, drowning before the eyes of his playmates. And another time, it was his duty to tell a young woman her logger husband had been killed when a tree fell on him after a bad cut.

This job seemed harder though, because he couldn't think what answer he could give to the questions that would obviously be asked. Where had the woman been, and what had she been doing for four years? That was the question, but there was no logical explanation.

Pastor Coombs finished shaking the hand of the last person coming from the service, just in time to see the deputy approaching the steps of the church.

"Hello, sir," the deputy said. "I have some news for you."

"Oh, and what is that?" asked the reverend.

"Can we go inside and sit in one of the pews?" the deputy suggested, shaking his hand.

"Surely, and welcome," Reverend Coombs said, a quizzical look on his face.

Suddenly all the sensible words practiced became forgotten as the deputy was overcome with the excitement of the moment.

"Your wife was found, sir," said the deputy. "She is alive and well."

For a moment, it seemed as if the minister had not heard what was said as he sat frozen in the uncomfortable wooden pew. But then he jumped to his feet, grabbing the deputy by the front of his shirt, shaking him until he turned red in the face.

"What kind of cruel joke is this?" the reverend gasped, his voice quivering with anger.

"My poor wife, Margaret Rose, is long dead, perhaps lost in the sea, four years ago. How can you torture me like this? Me, a man of God, who spends his life trying to help others, despite the grief and sorrow I have suffered."

"It's true, it's true," the deputy stammered, "she was found, pulled from the sea by the crew of a boat fishing out of the Siuslaw. She has absolutely no recollection of any part of her past life, including her name, or anything about her marriage.

"Please believe me, good sir," the deputy begged. "We must go back to Florence so you can be reunited with your wife. Perhaps the sight of your face will ignite some spark of memory."

Hearing that, the reverend fell to his knees in the aisle in the small church, facing the altar as he prayed out loud.

"Dear Lord, if you have returned my Margaret Rose, I promise to be a good husband and work for your glory every day of my life. Whatever she has done, whatever the events of the last four years, I will forgive her and accept her back as my wife."

"I'll get the horse and buggy, my good man," shouted the reverend as he dashed off toward the cabin. "Just give me a moment to grab a few toiletries and a clean shirt, and we'll be on the way."

As he shut the door, the reverend paused for a moment, sweeping his eyes around the interior of the small dwelling. Not much had changed since his wife's departure, but the clutter indicated this was the home of a bachelor who did not spend much time with housekeeping matters. Several days of dirty dishes were stacked on the sink board, the uneaten remains congealing on the surface. A kettle of cold beans sat on the stove, and a pile of unwashed laundry was tossed in the corner. The bed was rumpled and unmade. *If Margaret Rose has really returned,* he thought, *she will have this place tidy in no time.*

The northern portion of the trail along the coast from Yachats to Florence was narrow and winding, with treacherous drop-offs on the west side. Often during periods of heavy rain the hillside collapsed in this area, burying the road under piles of loose rocks and mud. In some places, the road was more than a thousand feet above the sea, so any misstep could result in a disastrous plunge down the cliffs to the rocky shore below.

As the two men came down from the mountain just north of the city, the topography changed, bringing breathtaking views of miles and miles of wide ocean beaches glowing in the sun. The tide was out, so they made good time on the hard packed wet sand, traveling along the wide bright golden ribbon of shore that flirted with the foamy waters of the Pacific Ocean. In this beautiful wild place, seabirds wandered through the shimmering shallows while

whales, sea lions, and other inhabitants of the sea ruled the deep
waters just offshore. Here the relentless wind created endlessly
changing and shifting rills and ripples in the sand, a constantly
changing natural sculpture, while gently waving spires of sea grass
blanketed the dunes along the beautiful shore. These spectacular
sand mountains ran along the shore all the way to the mouth of the
Siuslaw River, where the trail turned east along the river, running
into the main part of town.

The deputy planned to go directly to Captain Dan's home even
though the hour was late, feeling any delay would only make the
situation more difficult. He pounded on the door, and in a few
minutes heard footsteps coming down the stairs. Reverend Coombs
reached up to straighten his windblown hair, stroked his mustache
and short beard, then gave his necktie a tug. He was anxious to make
a good impression on his wife and steeled himself to be charitable,
regardless of her appearance.

Perhaps she had gotten plump or, because of her mental state, no
longer took pains with her appearance. Margaret's peaches-and-cream
complexion, with only a few freckles on her pert nose, would easily
burn in the sunshine, so he always insisted she wear her bonnet. He
hoped the activities of the past four years had not left her tanned and
leathery like some of the other coastal women he knew. He prayed for
the strength to face whatever trial or tribulation was ahead, feeling
sure when Margaret arrived safely home where she could resume her
wifely duties, her memory would return, and all would be well again.
With the help of the Lord, he believed, he would get through this
thing and perhaps one day would have the family he wanted.

Captain Dan cracked the door slightly, and when he realized the
identity of his visitors, stepped outside, looking nervously behind
him and up the stairs.

"This man is Minister Coombs," the deputy announced quietly,
"and he is anxious to see his wife."

Captain Dan took the reverend's proffered hand, grasping it
firmly in welcome.

"Very glad to make your acquaintance, sir. So sorry it has to be
under these unusual circumstances."

OHNALEE

"How is my wife?" the minister inquired, his calm demeanor slightly diminished by the presence of one small tear that appeared at the corner of his eye.

"Is she well? Has she been injured?"

"No, sir, not seriously," the captain replied, "but she did receive a hard bump on her forehead when we rescued her from the sea, and the doctor feels this could be the reason for her loss of memory. Doc says that physically she should be fine in a few days and will recover fully. As for her memory, we can only pray for the best. The doctor hopes she will slowly start to remember bits and pieces of her past life, but it will be difficult."

"I must hear the details of her finding, in the fullest of detail," the minister declared. "As I understand, she was recovered several miles offshore."

"Yes indeed," the captain responded, "but we can chat later about these matters as I know you are anxious to see your wife. I warn you, though, it would be unwise to upset her by asking questions she seems unable to answer. She seems to have suffered a great ordeal, with no memory of the circumstances that landed her on my boat.

My wife has tried to prepare Margaret Rose for your arrival, by informing the lady of a few events of her past, but I know the meeting will be difficult for both of you."

"I understand, and I thank you for your kindness, Captain," the minister said softly. "I would not want to risk her future, so I will do my very best to let my wife have all the time she needs to be restored in mind and body."

The deputy, having done his best to assist, said goodnight and left as the two men climbed the steep, narrow stairway, one slightly behind the other. At the top of the stairs, the captain's wife took the minister by the hand, leading him to the parlor where Margaret Rose sat by the window. She looked up, an anxious look in her bright blue eyes as the man approached slowly, stopping a few feet away.

"Margaret, dear heart, this man is your husband," Laydie declared, reaching for the girl's hand, placing it in his. The minister raised the hand to his lips, then kissed the fingers gently, gazing in

65

awe at the slim figure before him. *It is really her, my wife is really alive,* he thought, *thank the Lord.*

Margaret's face was flushed, her eyes misty as she contemplated the man standing before her. *It cannot be true, it cannot be,* she panicked, turning her face away. *There is no way I can be married to this man. He does not look even a little bit familiar.* Seeing her distress, the captain's wife sat down beside her on the window seat, putting her arm around her shoulders.

"It's all right, my dear," the captain's lady whispered, her mouth close to Margaret's small ear.

"Your husband is a good man, whose only desire is to care for you until you are well again. You must not worry about the future. He will be patient until you are feeling better. It will happen slowly, but soon, bits and pieces of memory will return, and you will be as good as new."

Margaret Rose fidgeted as she sat in her seat by the window. Her clothing felt tight and restrictive, especially the tight corset the captain's wife insisted she wear, the stays of which cinched in her tiny waist and pushed her bosom high in the pink dress.

Hurry, hurry, you must go quickly, she thought, *I must be free of this dress and tight shoes, so I can breathe.*

Captain Dan, seeing his wife's intense glance in his direction, realized it would be best for the minister to leave, as the hour was late, and everyone was tired. Margaret seemed totally overwhelmed by the emotional meeting and looked ready to collapse. Her heart fluttered so frantically in her small body, she felt it might take wings and fly away.

"Why don't we go over to the boat, sir?" the captain suggested. "We can sleep on the *Daniel T.* tonight, leaving the ladies to talk and rest from the events of the day. In the morning, we can meet for breakfast. Everyone will be more relaxed, and you and Margaret can become reacquainted as we stroll."

"Good idea, and thank you for that," the minister agreed with a sigh of relief, seeming all too ready to flee the crowded apartment into the fresh coastal air outside.

"I thank the Lord for your safe return, my dear," the minister said, bowing to his wife and the captain's lady as he turned to go.

Next morning, the two couples strolled along Front Street for an early breakfast at one of Captain Dan's favorite restaurants, but it was hard to ignore several rude and uncultured people who gawked, pointed, and whispered as they passed. Word of Margaret Rose's puzzling return had now spread through the town, fired by an announcement in the *Siuslaw Oar*.

"*Woman Found after Four-Year Disappearance*," the headline blared, with details describing the strange events leading to her rescue from the Pacific Ocean by the vessel *Daniel T*. Much to the chagrin of Captain Dan, his first mate had provided a minute-by-minute description of the finding, with lurid details about the form fitting leather suit the woman wore and the fact she wore no underclothing beneath it.

The newspaper's art department, had provided a shocking drawing, depicting a buxom woman, breasts partially exposed, wearing a revealing skintight outfit. The caricature's wild hair streamed out in every direction, and her eyes had a come-hither stare. "Goodness gracious, no decent woman would go about dressed like that," huffed one of the shopkeepers to her clerks. "What a floozy."

Speculation was rampant as locals met on the street and gossiped at their various places of employment. Where was this woman for four years? Had she been abducted by one of the Chinese laborers in the area then imprisoned in one of their camps, perhaps subjected to the most lurid sexual indignities? When they were done with her, did they just dump her offshore like so much rotten garbage?

Or maybe the Indians captured her, treating her as a member of the tribe, teaching her to fish from one of their dugout canoes. That would explain being dressed in animal skins. Whatever the answer, most agreed she definitely would be a different woman than the innocent girl who left four years before.

One woman offered the theory that Margaret Rose fled from the minister because she was beaten or abused. Possibly she was forced to endure strange sexual hungers no proper lady would tolerate.

Down on Front Street at one of the local pubs, a logger said he heard that a friend helped Margaret stow away on one of the lumber ships that ran the coast back and forth between San Francisco and Seattle, stopping in at Florence on the way. When discovered, she agreed to serve as the ship's cook until she reached California.

By the time she reached California, he speculated, Margaret might have discovered that life aboard ship was a pleasurable way to travel and see new places, and perhaps she even had a relationship with the handsome captain. It was certainly a more exciting life than living in a tiny cabin on the Oregon Coast.

"The girl fell off the ship as it passed the mouth of the Siuslaw," the man announced loudly to his mates as the barkeep drew off another stein of dark ale from the wooden cask behind the counter.

After a fine breakfast of fried eggs with a thick slice of ham, accompanied by hot biscuits, marionberry jam, and white gravy, the two couples returned to the waterfront. Mr. Coombs then announced he was in a hurry to recover his personal belongings from the *Daniel T.* as he planned to leave for home as soon as possible. Hearing this, Margaret Rose turned white as a ghost and squeezed the hand of the captain's lady so tightly the good lady gasped.

"Is that such a good idea, sir?" Laydie questioned. "Your wife is in such a delicate state that it might be safer for her to stay a few more days, so she will feel stronger and less confused."

"Thank you for the kind suggestion, madam," said the reverend, shaking his head from side to side, "but I must be back for Bible study tomorrow."

Margaret Rose's eyes darted from the face of her hostess, then back to the captain, looking for all the world like a prisoner just sentenced to death.

"Please let me stay, sir," she pleaded, tears flowing down her cheeks.

"No, my dear," replied the reverend firmly, looking Margaret directly in the eye with a penetrating gaze. "When you are mistress of our home again, you can start healing, with my help and that of the Lord."

In less than an hour, after the reverend picked up a few supplies at the local grocery, Margaret Rose was assisted up onto the seat of the buggy, just as meek as a lamb.

With no personal belongings to pack, still wearing the pretty pink frock provided by her hostess, the departure took little effort.

"I will return your dress one day, dear friend," said Margaret Rose as she waved farewell.

"The dress now belongs to you, sweet Margaret," answered the captain's lady. "Please God, we will see you soon again in Florence."

The reverend gave his horse a light touch of the whip as the buggy's wheels turned slowly, following the winding river, then heading north along the sea.

After a few attempts at conversation, the couple was silent, and every once in a while, the reverend placed his hand on the hand of Margaret Rose. At first, she pulled it away quickly but then seemed content to let it stay. *That's a very good sign*, he mused, humming as he drove the horse along the trail toward the cabin.

After a few hours, the reverend opened the package given to him by the captain's wife as they departed. His eyes twinkled at the sight of two delicious sandwiches of cheese and homemade bread and several delicious spice cookies. *What a kind woman she is*, he thought, as he handed Margaret a sandwich, quickly finishing his in several large bites. Margaret picked at the cheese listlessly, then handed the remainder to the minister, who finished it quickly, brushing the crumbs from his moustache.

Margaret's face seemed fixed on the sea as they traveled, her eyes staring out at the horizon until at last she dozed, her head lying lightly against the reverend's shoulder.

"We are here, dear," the reverend said softly as he reached the cabin. "You are home."

Blue eyes, fringed by long dark curly lashes, opened wide with a questioning look as Margaret Rose stirred, stretching her body, then leaning forward to gaze at the cabin now in her view.

"Let me help you," the reverend offered, reaching up and taking her hand. He put his hands round her tiny waist, easily lifting her down to the ground. Leading her up the wooden steps to the porch, he unlatched the door, motioning for her to wait until the lamp was lit. Margaret followed closely behind, standing just inside the entrance as the light illuminated the interior of the cabin.

"Oh, sorry for the mess, my dear," apologized the reverend. "It's been quite an ordeal trying to fend for myself, but I'm sure you can get the place in order quickly.

Why don't you put the kettle on for tea?" he suggested, not imagining this would be a chore which would puzzle and confuse his wife. It was as if she had just arrived in a new world, without a clue about how to accomplish small tasks. Seeing her bewilderment, the reverend wiped off the table, pulled out a chair, and when Margaret was seated, lit the kindling in the stove.

In a few minutes, the kettle was boiling, and he poured the water into the pot, letting the tea steep until it turned a golden shade of brown. Margaret Rose seemed to relax as she sipped the warm brew from a delicate china cup from the wooden hutch, cautiously glancing around the room at the jumbled disarray. Suddenly she stood up, then moving toward the corner, removed the blanket from the piano. She pulled out the bench, perching tentatively there, poising her fingers over the keys, then began to play.

Minister Coombs was overcome with emotion, hoping this was an indication that some small bit of memory had returned, but in a minute, her body tensed, and the fingers were still. With a blank look on her face, Margaret Rose returned to the table as if the event had never happened. Idly she stirred the tea with her spoon, eyes fixated on the closed window. The wind had come up since their arrival, and in the distance, crashing ocean waves could be heard. Margaret seemed to be fascinated by this sound as she stood, going to the window, then opening it wide. Her sad blue eyes seemed riveted to the west as tears appeared on her cheeks.

"Come away from the window, Margaret," her husband begged. "We must close it to keep out the cold, damp air. You'll catch your death."

The minister pulled down the window, then putting his arm around his wife, led her to their bedroom.

"It's late, my dear, and you must rest now," the reverend urged as he opened a trunk at the foot of the bed.

"Here are your things, Margaret. I kept them all these years, hoping against hope that one day you would return. I'll give you some privacy now to find a nightgown and make yourself comfortable before I return."

Closing the door behind him, the minister waited a respectable amount of time before returning to find Margaret sound asleep, lying on top of the bed quilts. In the darkness, the man quietly removed his outer clothing, then crawled into bed in his underwear. His attempt to pull a corner of the coverlet over Margaret Rose was to no avail as, after a couple of minutes, she violently kicked it off.

I hope she doesn't freeze like that, the minister worried, but soon he was snoring loudly.

Chapter 9

THE EPIPHANY OF DREAMS

So at last, the lady Margaret Rose was returned to her husband, but she seemed not the same person who left four years ago. There was a listlessness to her person, and a sadness to her voice, which was seldom heard. In the days following her return, the reverend's hopes were dashed as it appeared a quick cure to her melancholy was not to be. Margaret Rose was depressed and sad. No longer did she sing or write poetry. Her beautiful eyes were often filled with tears, and she displayed little interest in her home or the church.

Minister Coombs urged Margaret to accompany him to services, but she often refused, and when she did go, seemed entirely in another world. Parishioners brought covered dishes, pots of soup, pies and hot homemade breads as Margaret seemed unwilling or unable to resume her housewifely duties.

The minister longed for a return to the previously satisfactory relationship they enjoyed as husband and wife but, being a gentleman, decided he would not push the issue or insist on his rights. Despite this good intention, Margaret's nearness in their marital bed was almost unbearable. The soft aroma of her hair and body, the curve of her breast under her flannel nightgown flavored by the fragrance of talcum powder, tempted and distracted him from sleep. One night, despite all good intentions, the minister lost control.

He climbed roughly on top of Margaret as she slept, hiking up her nightgown, and before she could resist, had penetrated her most private parts, spending himself in seconds. Margaret struggled out of her slumber, crying out in terror and surprise, throwing him off of her body.

"Forgive me, forgive me," the man blubbered, adjusting his nightshirt and pulling down her gown, but Margaret just lay there on the bed motionless, staring at the ceiling. Large tears welled up in her sad eyes and ran down her cheeks, but not a word was said. In a few minutes, she turned over on her side, and after a few muffled sobs, the sound of her breathing indicated that she slept once more.

The minister said a prayer for forgiveness, and in his heart, he believed one day Margaret would be well again, welcoming him to her body as before. *I'll not let that happen again until she begs me*, he thought.

Margaret's parents and her siblings were overjoyed at her return, but she seemed confused and distracted, wondering, *Who are you? I don't remember.* Her mother visited often, putting her arms around her shoulders, looking deep into the face of her child, recounting events from her childhood, and Margaret Rose was polite as if she were speaking to a stranger.

"Where did you go, dear? Please remember," her mother begged. "I need to know. I missed you so very much, sweet child."

Weeks went by, and still the nights were filled with the sounds of Margaret's weeping. There seemed to be no respite from the vivid nightmares that disrupted her slumber, and she was constantly exhausted. Only in the daytime did her sleep seem normal, free of these dreams, so Margaret spent much of her day in bed, heedless of the chores that needed to be done.

One night, Minister Coombs opened the trunk which held Margaret's clothing and personal belongings. In the bottom of the trunk was her Trumpet Trident shell and leather journal. He placed the shell in the center of the table, and oh joy, almost instantly Margaret's eyes lit, with an intensity he had not seen since her return. *Perhaps,* he thought, *some memory connected with that shell has been received in her poor head.*

"Margaret, dear, I have a wonderful idea," the minister exclaimed. "Here is your journal, only half filled with poems and childhood memories. There are many pages remaining, so you could use the book to record the nightmares that so trouble you. Perhaps in the writing, you can capture the phantoms of your imagination on paper, the better to understand and conquer these fears and hallucinations. Every morning, when you rise, while the memory of the dream is vivid in your troubled mind, you must write the details before they are forgotten."

The man frowned, feeling regret that he had destroyed the one clue which might have been useful in jarring his wife's memory. One night, after Margaret left, he felt particularly disturbed and depressed. Margaret's sketch pad was sitting near the table as usual, and he knew it contained the hateful drawing of the sea cave. Every time Reverend Coombs looked at the picture, the eyes of a beast stared back at him, taunting, teasing, suggesting something so unspeakable he could not dwell on the thought for another moment. *I'll fix you,* he screamed, grabbing the sketch pad then throwing it in the fireplace. The pages curled as the orange flames licked their corners, turning the paper brown before bursting into flames.

On the one hand, the minister was happy the sketchbook was gone, but on the other hand, he knew it held the clue to Margaret's disappearance. The answer lay in the smile of the beast, and even though the drawing had been destroyed, the image was burned into his mind as though intensified by the heat of the fire.

She must never know about that drawing, he decided, trying once again to chase the hateful image from his mind.

Margaret glanced through the journal, reading of childhood adventures, her first kiss, and schoolroom accomplishments. There were numerous childish sketches of plants and trees, ocean waves, birds, seals, and sea lions, but nothing she saw triggered the memory she so dearly wanted to find once more.

"I will do that," Margaret Rose agreed, "but I must ask you to respect my privacy. Please promise that you will not pry into the contents of this diary as I fill it with my memories. I fear that recollections of these dreams will be disturbing and repulsive, the result of my damaged mind, and I don't want to trouble you any more than I have already."

"Good enough. I promise that," replied the minister, "and I pray the good Lord will agree with this plan and bless us with a healing."

"You are a good and generous man, husband, and I don't deserve you, but I appreciate your patience and kindness."

In the days to come, Margaret Rose hopped out of bed at first light, grabbing the journal off the bedside table, even before she emptied her bladder. If she waited to use the china pot conveniently waiting under the bed, the memory of the dream would flee, not to be recovered, no matter how hard she tried. With her favorite quill pen in hand, Margaret filled page after page with her neat handwriting, often weeping as she wrote. Her husband, true to his word, did not interrupt, and despite the temptation, did not touch the journal or attempt to discover its contents.

With each day that passed, however, Margaret Rose seemed more upset and out of touch with reality as she became immersed in the dreams that flowed from her mind to the journal.

What is this? she thought as she read and reread the journal. *In my dreams, I travel to a realm far different than this one, a place where I am loved. I feel like my dreams are reality, not just dreams. Am I losing my mind? Can it be I am totally insane?* she wondered. *And why, why, when I wake, do I feel as if my heart has cracked into two separate pieces, one searching for the other. There is such a feeling of loss and tragedy in my soul I feel I cannot live in this world anymore. I wish I could sleep all day, every day, and never wake. I long to live in the world of my dreams, with* him.

One morning, Margaret Rose woke feeling even more agitated than usual. This was the strongest and clearest vision she had ever experienced, and it seemed inexplicable by the laws of nature. But finally, there was conviction and a sense of awe in her soul as she understood that her dreams whispered recollections of an experience that could not be explained but was absolutely true.

She wrote down the details of the dream, remembering the day as if it were yesterday—*doing her chores, finishing preparations for supper, preparing a sandwich of bread and cheese, packing her sketch pad and pencils, then making her way down to the sea by the sea lion caves. It was a beautiful day, this summer day, with a light wind and gentle seas. No blustery, foggy Oregon day this, but a day to dream, an awesome marvelous day, a day to sing and draw and see friends, friends who often visited in the sea caves.*

Down to the cave she hurried, knowing it would still be dark as the sun was in the east, but in a few hours it would be overhead, then in the west, when it would light the interior of the cavern with wondrous colors of pink, lavender, and green. There were hundreds of sea lions in the cave this glorious day, basking on the rocks as if they were families living in different neighborhoods. The dominant males barked and bellowed as other males tried to horn in on their territory, rudely pushing the intruders back into the water.

Margaret Rose waited patiently, sitting on some flat rocks at the side of the cavern. She was not in a hurry, and hopefully they would come soon, as they had so many times before. There would be time in the day to draw and laugh as she thrilled to their melodious voices and sweet songs. He would come, she knew, he would come eventually, if not today, then another day, to speak to her softly and tell her sweet things heard only in the privacy of her own mind.

He would come as he had done many times since she was a child. She remembered the shell he gave her when she was only ten, that very same shell which was presently sitting on the dining table in her cabin. He was a young man then, when he told her that life in his society was about three hundred years, a statement that seemed too fantastic to be plausible.

Margaret Rose wrote frantically, the dream now flooding her senses with memories of something so incredible no one else would believe it. Memory returned as she wrote, and tears flowed freely from those stunning blue eyes, as she *remembered everything that happened on the day her life was changed forever.*

MOKEEMA IN THE CAVERN OF THE SEA LIONS

Chapter 10

REMEMBERING

*F*inally they came, the women first, riding the gentle green waves into *the cave, the frothy white salty caps undulating and curling around their sleek bodies, breasts full and white, wavy hair flowing about their shoulders, fiery dark eyes laughing, filled with mischief like the fun-loving imps they were. There were three of these sprites, and as they pulled themselves up onto the rocks from the sea with their strong arms, their lower bodies glistened, the iridescent green scales reflecting the light.*

"He comes, he comes," they trilled, pointing to the wide rocky opening as Margaret's eyes searched the horizon beyond the waves.

Margaret's fingers quivered as she wrote these words in her journal. She could almost smell the dank green odor in the caves and feel the salty air on her skin. She remembered how clumsy she always felt when the sea people arrived, wishing she could look like them and join their play as they chased back and forth, leaping and skipping through the waves, calling to each other in their strange language.

These people were not required to sit on hard wooden benches, reading from a book as they sat for hours at church, Margaret Rose thought, as she remembered that day. No meals to prepare, no pots and pans to wash, no piles of laundry to soak in boiling water, beating it clean on a hard board of metal and wood. No soap to make, no house to clean, no one to complain they were frittering away their time, being playful and lightheartedly silly. Margaret remembered how she felt at the end of each visitation when her friends left, and sometimes she cried as she waved goodbye, watching as they swam back out to sea and over the horizon to their world.

"He comes, he comes," shouted the females, pointing at Margaret and grinning from ear to ear. "He comes for you."

Margaret held her breath as through the opening of the cave, a large figure surfed in on the top of a clear green swell. With a flip of his powerful tail, the creature easily lifted himself out of the water, joining the females on a large flat rock. All of the Merfolk wore cloaks made of gray leather with hoods which fit snugly over their heads, but the male was also carrying a large leather bundle, which he threw down on the rocks near the garments of the females.

This handsome male radiated energy and bold sexuality, and it was clear from Margaret's face that she was intrigued and fascinated by his presence. His upper body was smooth and hairless, the muscles firm and sculptured, with not an extra ounce of fat anywhere. His golden tawny skin looked as if he had spent most days toasting in the sunlight, and there was no sign of any facial hair. Long dark wavy hair cascaded from his finely shaped head, falling below his waist.

The creature's eyes were dark and luminous, and he grinned, showing his strong slightly pointed teeth as he pointed his finger in Margaret's direction. "Ohnalee, Ohnalee," he called, using the name he had given her when she was a child.

The females settled down on their perch, seeming to enjoy the rays of sunlight that now splashed into the cave as the sun continued on its western trek. They lolled lazily in their usual fashion, combing each other's hair and chattering incessantly, but the male seemed fixated on Margaret as she sat sketching.

"Ohnalee, Ohnalee, you come now," the creature called, almost *impatiently. "Come close, and we can go."*

Margaret knew she should be frightened at this invitation, but rather than alarm, she felt a fluttering excitement that tempted rather than frightened. Could she really go, go with these people and live in the sea? Was it possible? she wondered, hearing his voice clearly.

Ohnalee, Ohnalee

Come with me,
and you will see,
another world beneath the sea.

Come with me,
and you will feel,
the splendid joy of being free.

Margaret threw down her sketch pad, kicked off her shoes, and moved closer to the male creature, so near she could see his heart beating in his strong chest. She extended the index finger of her right hand, touching him gingerly, tracing down from his chin, down his neck, and down the center of his chest, down to where his lower body was green and glistening. His glowing eyes watched intently, the dark pupils flashing with green jets of light as she moved her hand over the muscles of his strong arm and down to his hand. It looked almost like a strong human hand, except for the small transparent pieces of tissue which connected one finger to the next. Margaret's heart pounded as she took his hand, raising the upturned palm to her lips. For just a second, her lips brushed the skin as her eyes met his, and the reaction was electric.

His hands reached toward her face, one finger tracing from the center of her forehead, down the middle of her nose, then to her mouth. His hands were cool, his touch gentle as he gently slid that finger slowly into her mouth. Margaret's face grew flushed as desire grew, and she could not resist the temptation to touch that probing finger ever so gently with her moist tongue.

Margaret stopped writing for a moment, sitting at the table in the middle of her kitchen, feeling that desire now, the excitement building, a delicious fiery feeling between her legs as she remembered everything. Now it was not the dream remembered; it was the actual moment remembered, the moment when a human woman decided to take a chance and go with her heart, wherever it led, no matter how forbidden or dangerous the voyage may be.

"How can I go, Mokeema?" Margaret begged, saying his name out loud. "I am human and cannot breathe as you under the sea."

"Oh, my sweet Ohnalee," Mokeema responded, "now you must know the truth of your heritage. You are half-human and half of the sea people, sometimes called the 'Mer.'"

Margaret Rose was shocked and confused. What could he mean? There was no way possible she was not human, was there?

"I don't understand," she stammered as Mokeema drew her close, putting a fingertip behind each ear.

Margaret Rose struggled to pull away, her face beet red and her heart beating fast. She was embarrassed and worried he had discovered this flaw.

"Ohnalee must listen," Mokeema insisted, his persistent finger tenderly massaging the scars.

"There are several different tribes of the Merfolk," Mokeema explained, "and many moons ago, a human woman was taken by a man of the Dragon Mer. The woman was entranced by his songs and strength, thinking she would live for three hundred years by his side, but she was treated as a slave by the warrior and his people.

When the woman died bearing a child, the child was not accepted because of her dominant human characteristics. It was weak and could not live beneath the sea, so the ruler demanded the infant be destroyed, but one of the women who had befriended this human carried it away before the deed could be done.

You are that child, Ohnalee," murmured Mokeema, still stroking the strange scars behind her ears.

"You are a child of the Dragon Mer, and you will be able to breathe under the sea as we do, with these."

Mokeema took Margaret's small hand, placing her fingers on the small flaps of skin behind her ears.

Margaret was still, remembering the many times she had touched these small slits with her finger. She believed these were injuries of some kind, perhaps not repaired properly as she was able to insert just the tip of her finger into the openings.

Now she understood why her mother refused to speak about her birth mother and why she was adamant these scars be hidden.

"When you come with me, these will open, and you will breathe as I do," Mokeema assured Margaret. "You must have faith that this is true as I will never lie to you."

"I will go," Margaret replied, looking deep into Mokeema's dark liquid eyes, knowing if she followed this man, she would leave family and friends perhaps forever. Life would never be the same again.

"You will be safe with me," Mokeema promised, his strong arms cradling her body against his chest.

"I have waited many years, always knowing one day you would come. Soon we must leave this area, traveling south to the land of warm water and endless sun, not to return until the winter has gone, and you will come with us.

I will prepare you for the journey my darling," Mokeema said as he removed Margaret's gauzy blouson so quickly that a few buttons fell off.

Margaret Rose felt no shame as he removed her skirt and undergarments as many times she had played in the waves with this man of the sea before, sometimes throwing all her clothes in a pile on the beach, returning home soaked and sandy. These free spirits had no understanding of the word "shame," so it seemed natural to be naked in their presence.

The females crowded near, giggling and tittering, giddy with excitement as they stroked Margaret's fair skin and golden hair.

"Ohnalee, Ohnalee," they sang, "you are coming with us, at last, at last."

Margaret stood shivering in the sea cave as Mokeema reached for the large bundle, then carefully unfolded a suit made of soft sealskin.

"These garments were constructed especially for you, my Ohnalee. The leather came from one of the oldest and bravest of the sea lion people. He was a brave warrior who died in battle with the Dragon Mer, and his spirit will protect you from danger. Magdalena Meda, beloved wise woman of our people, has blessed this suit, and when you wear it, you will not be cold."

Margaret allowed Mokeema to help her step into the soft gray suit, which held her legs tightly together, then flared out at the bottom in a shape resembling the tail of a fish. The top molded tightly to her full breasts, and the bodice was laced with leather ties. The front of the suit was decorated with small golden coins bearing strange markings.

Mokeema pulled up the hood over her hair, tucking in a few rebellious tendrils which refused to be covered.

Margaret Rose clung tightly to this man of the sea as he took her into his arms.

"Close your eyes, beloved, and I will give you breath for the journey," the male whispered as he placed his mouth over hers, breathing into her lungs, filling them with air.

Margaret was weak with fear, but the intensity of her emotion overcame all reluctance. Mokeema's closeness was overwhelming, his strength all consuming as she felt his power filling her lungs.

"I will swim with you close to my body," he murmured, his melodic voice heard clearly in her mind. "You must relax and trust me, as it will be natural for your human side to fight for the air it thinks your body must have to live.

Dream and sleep as we travel, and when you wake, you will be in my world, where you will be safe and well.

Now, now, my love, we go," Mokeema whispered as he plunged into the incoming waves and headed west. The women followed, swimming hard to keep up.

Margaret trembled, her body tense, but Mokeema's strong arms held her tightly, and she felt reassured by his strength. At first she tried to hold her breath, but after a few minutes she relaxed and did not struggle. Sleep came as she was carried deeper and deeper, past the dead zone where there was little oxygen and only a few small fish, then over mighty forests of kelp, swaying below in the deep.

At times she was aware that a mouth had again covered hers, filling her lungs with warm moist air as they descended slowly, far behind the horizon, where the sun sets.

OHNALEE AND THE SEAGOAT

Chapter 11

MER, FOR SURE

Margaret Rose Lavell closed her journal and slowly walked out onto the porch. Passing up the comfortable wooden rocking chair, she sat down on the steps. She shivered, even though the day was warm, and tears flowed down her cheeks, as the memories came now quick and clear.

"Ohnalee, Ohnalee, wake," whispered melodious voices as Margaret Rose stirred from her slumber. "Wake, Ohnalee, it is time to wake," the voices requested sweetly as soft fingers caressed her forehead and wound through her hair. That feels so good, *she thought, stretching luxuriously, reluctant to wake and leave her erotic dream. In her dream, she had been swimming through the sea in the arms of a handsome creature whose soulful dark eyes were fixed on hers, but she knew that when she woke, there would be breakfast to prepare and laundry to do.*

Margaret opened one blue eye slowly, then closed it in disbelief. Was she still dreaming? This was definitely not the interior of her cabin on the Oregon Coast. Both eyes flew open wide as her vision cleared. Taking in the scene around her, Margaret saw she was reclining in a soft nest of silky green oceanic vegetation. The plant's lacy tendrils swayed in the current, curling ever so loosely around her body, caressing her as gently as a lover. She felt very comfortable and was not cold.

Her blue eyes fluttered as they searched the area from side to side, then overhead. Margaret Rose tried to sit up, but quickly fell back, overcome with emotion. She was in a vast underwater cavern with a myriad of stalactites and stalagmites hanging from the ceiling, reflecting light filtering through the entrance. The leafy couch seemed to be covered by a metal canopy, the interior of which was encrusted with thousands of pieces of mirrored glass decorated with small seashells and sparkling stones of many colors. Can those stones be diamonds, rubies and emeralds, *she wondered, her image reflected clearly as the mirrors and stones cast twinkling prisms and jets of light and color in every direction.*

"Ohnalee, Ohnalee, we love you," Margaret heard, finding her couch now invaded by several female sea sprites, who boldly settled themselves at her side and by her feet. "Sit, sit," they requested, taking her hands and pulling her up to a sitting position, then dropping necklaces of gold coins and seashells around her neck. On her head, they placed a tiara made of delicate gold mesh, studded with precious stones.

Margaret remembered her astonishment when she realized she was not dreaming.

"You must come, Ohnalee. He waits," commanded the sea sprites, "Hurry." Margaret Rose complied, quivering with excitement, passively letting herself be draped in a cloak embellished with intricate swirling stitched patterns that resembled the spiral curls of her Trumpet Trident shell. She was still in disbelief at what she saw and was amazed by her ability to breathe easily underwater. The leather suit proved a great benefit as she quickly grasped how to undulate her body, swimming like a dolphin, thrusting her legs up and down in a smooth liquid motion, which propelled her easily through the water.

"Come, Ohnalee, follow us," her companions called. Margaret swam after them, enchanted with this new feeling of complete freedom. Her body felt totally weightless as she glided through the water. I feel like I'm flying, *she thought, placing her arms alongside her body as the thrust of her strong legs pushed her effortlessly through the sea. She was enthralled, charmed, and thrilled, thinking,* I'm a fish. I think I've always been a fish at heart.

"I belong here, I belong here," she shouted out loud to her companions.
"Ohnalee not fish," they giggled. "Ohnalee is Mer."

Her companions stayed close to her side, pointing out interesting details as they traveled, and Margaret Rose noticed many of the caverns were marked with piles of shells and golden pillars encrusted with gems. "Where do these beautiful stones come from?" she asked as they passed a particularly lavish and artistic entrance.

"We take what we need from the ships that fall to the bottom of the sea," her sea sisters explained, "and nothing is wasted." About that time, Margaret saw the broken hull of a wooden ship lying on its side at the bottom of a large crevice. Although the discovery of gold in California in 1848 spawned the birth of regular coastal shipping, and schooners such as the Star of Oregon were being built by local pioneers, Margaret Rose had never seen a vessel such as this before. The beamy ship had a high stern and a small transom, and Margaret could see a gaping hole in the bottom of the hull. The large cabin had small doors on the port side, and the two masts which once supported the sails and rigging were broken off at the deck.

When Margaret and her companions passed close to the ship, she could see large chests of gold coins and precious jewels with their lids standing open. Several of the sea people were digging around in the treasure boxes, filling leather pouches with colorful stones and coins. One strong male tipped one of the chests on its side, carelessly dumping the contents out onto the seafloor. Margaret gasped, seeing thousands of priceless black pearls lying on the sand.

Margaret could see that the gold coins were inscribed in an unknown language, perhaps Japanese or Chinese, she thought, unable to make out the meaning of the symbols. They were like the coins on her suit.

"The pretty stones of the sailors are nice to find," remarked Margaret's companions, "but the people do not like the black ones. They prefer the shiny ones for buttons and decorations for the body."

Then she described how the people found other materials they needed inside wrecks like this, including spools of string and wire.

"Many of the people have tasted the liquid contained in jars and flasks in the fallen ships," the sprite said, "but it makes some feel dizzy and silly, while others, especially the males, get mean and want to fight. If a large amount of this liquid is consumed, the personality seems to change. Gentle males become

hateful and cruel, particularly to their mates. The Queen no longer permits anyone to partake of this drink, but a few disregard her law. These outlaws search for bottles to use in trade for other forbidden substances.

Ohnalee wondered what these other outlawed substances might be, but her guide seemed reluctant to continue discussion of this topic. Ohnalee grinned, thinking that alcohol could never be banned in the taverns along the river in Florence; there would be a riot for sure.

"Mokeema has taken the reclining bed from one of these ships for your use, lady, which you will soon see," confided one of her new friends. "It is decorated with beautiful carvings of birds and flowers, so unique we believe it was made for a queen or empress of those people."

This vessel is very strange indeed, *Margaret mused,* not at all like the ships I saw carrying cargo back and forth along the coast, or any of those rotting hulks cast up on the rocks along the shore.

"Ships like this come from far-off lands over the horizon," one of the women explained, reading her thoughts.

Margaret remembered hearing about a mysterious swift warm black current that captured disabled vessels, sweeping them far from their traditional trade routes along the shores of Taiwan and Japan, carrying the helpless crew toward the northwest coast of the United States.

"The ancient ones have said the ruler of those lands was the descendent of the great goddess of the sun," the sea woman said. "We know the people are small, with eyes of a different shape than yours as we have seen many who did not survive the long journey across the sea. When we find these ships, we do not disturb the mortal remains of the crew, leaving them entombed for all eternity in their boats."

"I have heard stories about sailors who were rescued by the Indians who lived along the coast" said Margaret, "and it is believed that some were eventually accepted by their captors as members of the tribes while others worked their way south to warmer areas of the United States. Some people think they established communities that resembled the ones left behind far across the sea to the west."

How sad, never to return to your home, *Margaret thought, experiencing a sharp flash of regret about leaving her parents and siblings behind.* What were they doing, *she wondered,* and what were they thinking. I didn't mean to hurt you, *Margaret brooded for an instant, realizing they would think she was dead.* I'm OK, I'm OK, *she repeated, concentrating on the thought of her mother's face.* Think of me, Mother, and know I am safe, and will always love you.

"So sad, your face, my lady," one of the most beautiful of the nymphs trilled, her dark eyes gleaming with pleasure as she placed a comforting arm around Ohnalee. "Be happy, my sister," the sea woman whispered in her ear, "you have a new family now."

For some reason, Margaret felt a special kinship to this particular woman, and she wondered about the ugly jagged scars across her back. The woman seemed to sense this curiosity, saying, "It was a long time ago, lady, and I do not think of it."

"What do they call you?" Margaret asked, feeling soothed and strengthened by her presence.

"I am Jade," the woman replied, bowing slightly, "I beg only to serve you and be your friend."

Margaret Rose noticed this woman looked slightly different from the other ladies who were guiding her. Her dusky skin was almost translucent, and the brown scales on her tail gleamed with glittering dots of black and gold. She had an exotic, almost Oriental cast to her features and a thin straight nose. Around her right arm, just above the elbow, was a tattooed bracelet about four inches wide. The ornate dragon design was done in shades of brown and black, and Jade explained its significance before Margaret could even ask the question.

"My marking is the tribal symbol of the Dragon Mer people," Jade explained.

"When a female is ten years old, a marking ceremony is held to celebrate the passage from childhood to maturity, forever binding the individual to the tribe." Jade shuddered as she described the painful process, saying the child was not permitted to protest, flinch, or cry out, as this was a sign of weakness, and such an inferior specimen would be ostracized and ignored by other members of the tribe.

"Even when I was cut for disobedient actions, I did not cry out," Jade said, strength and intensity streaming from her body as she took Margaret's hand.

"I will tell you of this, one day, my lady."

Margaret knew instinctively she could depend on this woman's support and friendship and looked forward to the time when Jade felt ready to explain more.

As the women continued on their way, Margaret saw this part of the ocean floor was not peopled with thousands of fish and other sea creatures as one would expect, and the ones she did see were strange colorless beings with unseeing eyes.

Her companion seemed to know the question instantly as she explained that most fish were unable to live at this depth. "Soon we will go up to the more shallow parts of the ocean to hunt and play," said the sea woman, "and you will swim with the whales and dolphins."

As Margaret and the women sped along, she noticed an area where several males seemed to be fighting. They were all massively built and obviously well trained in the martial arts as they struggled for domination of their partners.

"They are training to be 'Guardians'," Jade said, knowing Margaret was confused about what she was seeing.

"Only the very best can qualify to guard the royal family, and they must dedicate their lives to this profession."

Jade said it was a great honor to be a Guardian, but the life was difficult, and many were not accepted. Strength, loyalty, honor, and intelligence were expected, but candidates must also promise to be celibate, which was a pledge not easily kept.

Jade pointed out the dark entrances to several caves near the area, saying this was where the men lived communally, waiting to be called to service.

The females now sped up a steep incline, and as they crested the top of the hill, Margaret saw a vast plain that stretched out as far as she could see into the distance. Ruins of enormous buildings, their foundations cracked and crumpled, assaulted the tranquility of the ocean floor, creating visions of a disaster too immense to contemplate.

"According to the legends of the ancient ones," Margaret's guide explained, "this was the capital city of the Motherland."

The sea sisters explained that long ago, the spirits of the fathers spoke to their ancestors, telling of a glowing star that plummeted from the sky, smashing into the earth, bringing death and devastation. The terrified inhabitants of this civilization tried to flee, but there was nowhere to hide, as the explosive force of the collision bathed the earth in a fiery shroud, melting even the golden gates of the temples. Wave after wave of strong tremors undulated over the land for days, rupturing the earth's crust, cracking and pulverizing the shining cities, reducing most man-made structures to piles of rubble. The oceans spilled out of their beds, sweeping the wreckage from one end of the planet to the other, scattering the remains so that almost no trace of that highly enlightened culture remained. Finally, the sea gave a loud belch as its open mouth consumed even the highest mountains of that ancient land, sending all to a watery grave far beneath the sea.

Certain virtuous uncorrupted dwellers of that universe who were well loved by the gods were given the holy gift of advance warning about the coming cataclysm. Falling to their knees, they prayed day and night for seven days and seven nights, begging for protection. Because of their sincerity and faith, these honored ones were blest with a new form and swam away safely, flipping just under the surface, as the hungry sea devoured the earth. These special ones learned to survive under the sea, developing a rich culture which valued love and civility, evolving over the eons, with no memory of the lost civilization. Only a few wise ones carried the strands of knowledge in their DNA. They were able to communicate with The Makers *through visions and dreams, passing on sacred information about what was required to satisfy the gods and live a virtuous life. This power of knowledge was passed from one generation to the next, with each oracle choosing his successor, seeing and identifying the proper recipient through divine inspiration.*

Margaret listened intently, feeling a bewildering sense of deja'vu as information about the ancient race was transferred from her new friends in gushing torrents of words. Clear images flashed across the landscape of her mind as the women seemed anxious to share everything they knew. They constantly interrupted each other with colorful details, but seemed content to let Jade play the prominent role in Margaret's education. Jade said the influence of the Shaman was strong and important to the society, and often a replacement was identified when the child was still very young. Such a child was revered and sheltered. He or she lived in the wise one's household and was instructed in all the arts of healing and magic, so when the elder passed over to the land of the fathers, there was an easy transition.

As the days and years passed, strong undersea eruptions forced parts of the crust up above the sea's wild white horses, creating terra firma once again. Some sea people were attracted to the newly dried areas, so pulled themselves out of the sea and onto the land. Their amphibious features were a hindrance which eventually disappeared through the evolutionary process in much the same way as humans lost their tails.

Margaret learned that some humans, probably descending from these ancient ones, could learn to breath again beneath the sea. When these people were recognized by the sea people, they were approached gradually and encouraged to return to life beneath the ocean's surface.

"The human who agrees to live in our undersea world will be blessed with many more years of life than could be expected on land," the sea sisters explained.

"Our normal life span is about three hundred years, but a human returning to the Mer could share our world for about a hundred fifty years."

THE LEGENDARY POCAMPI

94

Chapter 12

FOREVER—THE PROMISE

Margaret stirred from her reverie, smiling at the sight of several green hummingbirds hovering over a large stand of fuchsia bushes by the fence. The tiny birds seemed suspended in mid-air over the multicolored blooms, their brilliant feathers reflecting the sunlight, but only for a second was her attention diverted from the deluge of memories which now overflowed into the salty Oregon air. A ripple out on the sea caught her eye, and she stared, eyes wide open, as she returned to the land of the Mer.

Margaret and the sisters continued past the ruins of that lost ancient land until presently on the horizon, she saw a gleaming golden spire.

"We are almost there," Jade explained, "to the place where the Queen Mother waits."

Soon the small troop of swimmers stopped in front of a large stone structure that appeared undamaged. At the four corners of the building stood tall columns, each with a golden globe at the top. The two columns guarding the entrance were also decorated with a large scallop shell inscripted with the letter M. Her guides said the scallop was an ancient symbol representing the ebb and flow of life, and the M symbolized the Motherland from which their race originated.

"We place the scallop shell on our dwelling places to show our love for life and our families," Jade said. "The shell signifies that our people are travelers who journey to far-off places and lands beyond the sea."

Margaret instinctively reached for the small scallop shell she had worn around her neck all her life, feeling its comforting shape with her fingers. She thought her mother gave her the shell when she was very young, and she remembered when the gold ribbon was replaced by a thin gold chain on her tenth birthday.

Passing through the gateway, Margaret entered a large open enclosure. There was no roof, so light from above settled on the occupants of the temple, bouncing off the spectacular throne in the center. This throne was topped by a statue of a large golden fish, walking on legs. The sea women explained this image represented the time of the long ago when the gods gave humans the tail of a fish and gills so they could breathe under the sea, escaping the great inferno when the Motherland was destroyed.

When she spotted the regal figure sitting on this dais, Margaret trembled and shook. She had never seen a more frightening being.

The female was obviously of high rank as the others attending her, both male and female, were seated on lower levels in deference to her position. Margaret's heart pounded as she spotted Mokeema reclining at the right side of the throne.

"Stop now," Margaret's guides cautioned as they grabbed her arms firmly. "Do not proceed until the Queen gives permission."

Margaret waited, floating in the clear water, hair fanning out around her face as the woman on the throne stared at her with luminous black eyes. The Queen's eyelids were painted silver, and each eye was lined with black. The woman's dark hair hung almost to the bottom of her shiny red tail. The luxuriant mane was streaked with glossy silver strands, which added to her powerful and electrifying appearance. On her head was a crown made entirely of diamonds with a golden fish in the center. Ohnalee had no doubt that the eyes of the fish were large emeralds.

The Queen wore a long red cloak made from soft leather, and Margaret could see a hood hanging down behind. Although the woman clutched the garment close around her body, as if she had suffered a bit from the cold, Margaret could see her upper body was naked underneath. Her breasts were no longer firm, but the nipples were pierced with a slender gold bar, with round diamonds at each end. At the side of her nose was another diamond, and when she smiled in Margaret's direction, sharp, pointed black teeth glittered with shiny stones.

"Come forward," the Queen commanded, crooking a long finger in Margaret's direction. With this gesture, Margaret saw her nails were long and curled with a small diamond on each tip.

Margaret glided to the dais, then attempted to curtsey as she came near the Queen. It was not a very elegant gesture as she was not entirely at ease in her new circumstance. Bowing when one had legs to stand on was certainly not as difficult as bowing with only a fish tail for balance.

"I am Maru, Queen of the Merfolk, Ruler of my Tribe, Mother of Mokeema," the woman chanted in a strong but silvery voice. "I bid you welcome to our world and pray you will be happy dwelling with us."

"I see you, Ohnalee," said the Queen, "beloved of my son, Mokeema, Guardian of the People. One day he will be Sakima, the king, and you will be at his side."

Margaret's mouth fell open, and for a second she lost her composure, gawking almost stupidly at the Queen. She was shocked and dismayed at this announcement as she had no idea that Mokeema was of royal blood or would be leader of his people. At that moment, Margaret felt inadequate, insecure, and afraid. She cast her eyes downward, looking at the suit of gray leather which seemed very ugly when compared to the sleek fish tails of the others around her. Why would this handsome prince choose her, when there were so many other beautiful exotic sea women who would have gladly shared his couch? I am weak, *she thought,* not fit to be the consort of this prince of his tribe.

"Be not afraid," said the Queen, reading her thoughts, "you are strong and brave; you have proved that already. Our ancestors were human, and with you by his side, Mokeema will have a mate who can help him understand

the needs of his people in this new and changing world. You will be as two halves of the same being, your human traits blending with his. Mokeema and I welcome new fresh ideas from your world that will make life better for our people."

The Queen smiled broadly, saying, "I pray your union will bring grandchildren who will possess the best attributes of both races."

Hearing that pronouncement, Mokeema came forward, taking Margaret's hand to stand before his mother, the Queen. The moment his fingertips touched hers, Margaret felt a tingling sensation, almost like a jolt of electricity. Tiny goose bumps rose on her arms and down her back, and she shivered, not from the cold but from the excitement of his presence. She thought this man was the most wonderful and fascinating creature in the universe, and the most miraculous thing of all was that he felt the same way about her. Margaret could see the love in his eyes, those beautiful, soulful eyes that looked so intently into hers, making her heart pound fiercely as it had never done before.

Mokeema pressed Margaret's hand to his lips, and she quivered as the tip of his warm tongue touched the center of her palm. Margaret pulled her hand back quickly, embarrassed his mother might have seen this intimate caress. So mischievous, and so very sexy, she thought, with that cocky grin that makes me laugh and feel better, no matter what my problems may be.

"Be good," Margaret whispered, and the message came back loud and clear. I am good, good for you, my Ohnalee. *Mokeema threw his head back and laughed, and soon everyone in the assembly, including the Queen, was laughing with him. It was obvious everyone adored Mokeema. His personal magnetism and dynamic personality were so strong and appealing no one could resist.*

And this man is mine, *Margaret thought joyfully, and then she heard the word that made her heart sing.*

"Forever," *Mokeema said.* "Forever."

Then the Queen motioned Jade to come to the throne. The woman prostrated herself on the ground at her feet as the Queen spoke to the assembly.

"This woman has served me well in all the days since her escape from the Dragon Mer. She was friend to Ohnalee's mother, and now, I wish her to stay close to the daughter she saved from a cruel death. This woman suffered much when the Dragon Mer discovered she took the child, Ohnalee, ashore,

and even today they would kill her instantly if they could find her. Ohnalee is the daughter of the cruel ruler of the Dragon Mer, and his queen does not know Ohnalee lives.

Despite terrible torture," the Queen continued, "the maiden Jade resisted her interrogators, never admitting the child survived. If she knew the truth, the Dragon Queen would come against us with all her warriors as she would see Ohnalee as a challenger to her daughter as the next ruler of the Dragon Mer."

The Queen motioned for Jade to rise.

"You are truly one of our people now, and I place you under the protection of my son."

Mokeema smiled, taking Jade's hand. "Welcome devoted Jade," he said, I accept you into my household, and I wish you to be the companion of Ohnalee, helping her in all things."

Jade bowed low to Mokeema, signaling her acceptance of his protection.

"I dedicate my life to you and your family," Jade said solemnly. "You can count on my love and loyalty always."

Margaret's mind raced as she was bombarded with all this new and unbelievable information. She realized that Jade could tell her about her birth mother and was responsible for the safe and loving life she had experienced on the Oregon Coast. She was excited at the thought she could talk with Jade for hours, learning about her mother and the cruel and vicious man who demanded her death, then tortured the woman who disobeyed this order. This was her father, but she could envision his cruel character from the deep scars visible on Jade's back.

"You will be my best friend, Jade, and I welcome you as my dearest sister," Margaret said, staring intently into Jade's soulful eyes.

The Queen raised herself from the throne with a flip of her tail, coming toward her son and his new bride. Queen Maru raised her hand, and immediately a servant came forward bearing a silver case. The Queen opened the lid, removing a silver pendant with an exquisite scallop shell mounted on the face, holding it high for all to see. The shell was crowned with a spectacular white stone that glowed as if a candle were lighted and hidden within.

Queen Maru dropped the pendant over Ohnalee's head, then gave her a kiss on both cheeks.

"We call this stone of the moon the 'Traveler's Stone'," the Queen said.

"Our people have always cherished the moonstone as a protection against the perils of travels to distant lands. I believe this beautiful stone can help your spirit adjust to this new beginning while infusing your body with the strength necessary to deal with the fulfillment of your destiny.

Wear this pendant, my dear Ohnalee, as a token of our love and affection. If you stare deep into the milky depths of the crystal, you may hear the voices of your loved ones even though they are far away."

The Queen grinned at Ohnalee, looking exactly like Mokeema at that moment. Her eyes gleamed as she continued, "It is said the stone enhances fertility and brings happiness to the environment in which it is held, so I wish that for you, dear Ohnalee.

It is done, my son," said Queen Maru with a smile. "This woman pleases me well, and all is as I promised you many years ago when you were just a young boy. Ohnalee has come to you of her own free will as a grown woman, and your patience has been rewarded."

Margaret looked confused, wondering what this meant, but she knew that now was not the time to ask for an explanation. She bowed low, putting her forehead almost to the ground, then looked directly into the face of Queen Maru, her mother-in-law.

"I thank you for your kindness, and I will keep this pendant close wherever I go."

Queen Maru stretched her hand toward Ohnalee, and this seemed the perfect opportunity to place a kiss on the back. The Queen smiled as Ohnalee's lips brushed her skin; then she waved Ohnalee back to Mokeema's side.

"Take your Ohnalee to the dwelling you have chosen, my son. Make her welcome and happy, then teach her our customs and ways."

The Queen then turned and left the assembly, followed by her impressive entourage of guards and servers. Her cape billowed out like a red cloud as she departed, and Ohnalee was enchanted when she saw the Queen's carriage waiting just outside the temple.

The silver carriage was shaped like a large scallop shell, had no wheels, and was pulled by a team of the most amazing creatures ever seen or imagined. Six exquisite small white horses were hitched to the buggy, each one snorting and pawing the ground as they waited impatiently. From the top of their heads, past long flowing manes which ran down the center of their necks, they were perfectly shaped stallions with strong front legs and spade-shaped hooves. At the midsection, however, normality ended and fantasy began as instead of hind legs, each animal had a coat of luminous silver white scales that covered the body, then flared out in the tail of a fish. The strong tails swished back and forth, stirring up the sandy bottom beneath, much like a misty fog on a gray November morning in Oregon.

When the Queen was comfortable with a young handsome male attendant cuddled on each side for warmth, the carriage master gave the team a gentle flick of his slender whip. The horses soared off the seafloor in a swirl of sand and tiny shells, their strange round eyes gleaming, shooting beams of silvery light that lit the dim waters as they carried their queen home.

"They are the Pocampi," Mokeema whispered reverently, "the only remaining of this species in the entire universe. They have served the rulers of our people from early days, and we think they have the ability to live forever. We guard them well, as they are a treasure that cannot be replaced."

As the newlyweds turned to depart, Margaret noticed an exceptionally attractive female sea person who seemed to be extremely unhappy with this turn of events as she displayed a definite look of distress on her face. The woman wore a small jeweled tiara, the mark of high position, and her seat near the Queen marked her as a member of the nobility. Her dark almond-shaped eyes seemed fixed on Mokeema, and when he took Ohnalee's hand, the lady scowled, actually baring her sharp teeth, a loud hiss showing her hatred.

Margaret wondered the reason for this show of anger but did not dwell long on the issue as Mokeema put his strong arm around her body, then guided her out of the temple, leaving quickly with a powerful swish of his tail.

FOREVER

Chapter 13

INTO MYSTIC REALMS

Margaret Rose Lavell blinked her eyes, and for a minute, came back to the present. Her face felt hot, and she was thirsty. The sun beat down on her pale skin, and she realized she had not thought to put on her bonnet before coming outside, but a potential sunburn was not enough to distract her from this particular memory. She stood slowly and moved to the rocker, sitting gingerly as if any quick or abrupt motion might disrupt the flow of the vision that flooded her mind. It was as fiery as the sun, as hot as her skin, as moist as her hands. She was sweating, crystal drops of perspiration oozing from beneath her arms and between her breasts. Margaret looked nervously around, her eyes searching the surrounding area. She felt embarrassed and agitated, as if an onlooker might somehow be able to read her thoughts and discover the depths of her arousal. She shut her eyes and returned to Mokeema.

Words were not required as Margaret Rose glided alongside her man of the sea in this strange new world. Holding her pale hand tightly in his, Mokeema seemed unable to take his eyes off her face.

Beautiful Ohnalee *his eyes seemed to say as he smiled lovingly, leading her to an area she had not seen before. On this part of the seafloor, gardens of strange exotic plants swayed rhythmically back and forth in the gentle current, bending their tips to the ground, then to the surface as if reaching for the sky. Margaret did not know it was possible to have so many shades of white, as these plants were in tones of grayish white, pinkish white, greenish white, bright white, silvery white, iridescent white, and all variations in between. Stands of coral, looking like shiny spirals of precious metal, wound and twisted in gorgeous arrangements, and Margaret could see transparent jellyfish of every size and shape, bobbing and quivering over the top of the reef. Numerous species of strange unseeing creatures hid in the crevices and small caverns, popping out and standing at attention on their tails, as the royal couple passed by.*

Seeing her amazement, Mokeema told her, his silvery voice ringing like a clear bell in her mind, that the plants and fish and other sea life she saw were unknown to man and unimagined in the world above. Humans had no idea such species even existed, believing survival would be impossible at those depths.

This was a mysterious but beautiful world, and Margaret thought if she had to describe it to a human, the best comparison would be with the landscape in the frozen regions of the earth, such as Antarctica, Alaska, or even the high mountains of Colorado, at altitudes of twelve thousand feet on the Continental Divide. There, at icy vistas high above the tree line, even the trees were stunted and thinner because of lack of oxygen. These areas were also devoid of wildlife and plants, and humans found it difficult to breathe in the thin cold air.

Margaret decided she must now always think of herself as Ohnalee, since she was leaving behind her old world and human identity. She had chosen this new life to be with Mokeema. She wanted to be a "belonger" in this new sphere, no longer a stranger from another world. This was not a visit, not a vacation to be enjoyed before returning home to normal life, and she felt ready to accept every gift and challenge this new land offered.

"Ohnalee, very brave," Mokeema said softly, as if reading her thoughts.

Ohnalee found it difficult to take her eyes from Mokeema's face as she was filled with love and desire, yet slightly fearful of what was to come. She remembered the first night she bedded with the reverend, a responsibility to be endured as a wife, yet as a "good" woman, not one she was expected to enjoy.

Mokeema came to a halt in front of a large concrete structure that was in perfect condition. Obviously, this building was constructed in ancient times but had survived the cataclysm of long-ago days without damage. The ground outside the structure was decorated with shells and coral, and Ohnalee saw piles of driftwood, hard as steel, sculptured by wind and waves into fantastic shapes and forms. It looked as if someone with an artistic eye had carefully twisted and intermingled these pieces into a spectacular underwater sculpture.

Large glass spheres in shades of purple, green, and blue rested comfortably on piles of yellow and black fishing nets, looking like enormous precious gems. Ohnalee smiled, thinking she would feel at home here as her cabin on the Oregon coast was also decorated with pieces of driftwood she had dragged off the beaches and up the steep trail to her home. She had created a border of seashells along the path to the house, adding to the collection on every trip to the beach.

One of Ohnalee's most prized possessions was a gigantic cobalt blue handblown Japanese float, complete with the original netting, found on the rocky shore beneath the lighthouse, but she had never seen so many floats in one place, with so many different gorgeous colors as the ones decorating her new home

Hundreds of Trumpet Triton shells, Pacific murex, and splendid pink Pacific scallops were arranged in colorful gardens of coral and sea fans, with lush borders of green and black sea urchins, their sharp spines warning the visitor not to pick the flowers.

Ohnalee giggled as she realized this arrangement might change from day to day as the shells seemed to be moving about. These shells were not empty abodes like the ones she found on the beach but contained living creatures, free to relocate at any time.

The most splendorous feature of the structure was the wealth of heavy gold coins, black pearls, and diamonds that were wedged into every crack and crevice in the walls. The gems radiated light which turned the surrounding area into a magical fairyland of shimmering color. So lavish and elegant was this unique dwelling that Ohnalee was charmed and delighted.

"For you, my Ohnalee," Mokeema breathed, easily lifting her in his arms, then swimming through the wide entranceway of the dwelling.

The interior was small, but bright as there was no ceiling, which allowed the silvery light from the world above to shine down and illuminate the structure. In the center of the room was a bed for a queen.

"How beautiful," Ohnalee gasped as she ran her hand over the surface, feeling the cold dark marble under her fingertips. The bed was carved in the shape of a scallop shell, with a border of gold. Margaret loved roses, and when she saw the intricate bouquet of roses carved in the stone at the foot of the bed, she thought about her gardens in Oregon for the first time since her departure. Mokeema grinned proudly as Ohnalee swam around the bed, her finger tracing the flowers and leaves that were carved into its surface.

Easily reading her thoughts, Mokeema told Ohnalee that the bed came from a ship bearing a strange insignia he had never seen before.

"The ship carried the image of the sun," he said, "and was heavily laden with chests full of shiny stones and coins. One container was filled with green stones of different shades, sizes and shapes, and some of our people have learned to carve designs into the smooth surface, making decorations to wear on their bodies. We believe the contents of this vessel were meant for an empress in the land of the rising sun, but it drifted far from those shores as so many have done before."

"Thank you for this beautiful gift, my prince," Ohnalee whispered, giving no indication she had known in advance of this present. "It is the most beautiful piece of furniture I have ever seen in my life."

Mokeema's eyes twinkled with pleasure at his bride's reaction, and then he directed her attention to a large circular device sitting on a pedestal in a corner.

"When we took it from the ship, the shiny cover gleamed as bright as gold," Mokeema said, "but the water of our world has caused the metal to fade, creating this beautiful green color.

I prefer this more subtle color to the other," Mokeema said.

Ohnalee agreed, knowing the salt content of the ocean had caused the patina of the device.

"We call this device a compass," Ohnalee said. "It was invented by the Chinese centuries ago. The floating needle points north and south, helping mariners navigate from one place to another."

Mokeema was excited about this revelation, realizing the knowledge could be helpful, but he knew the Mer had a built-in sense of direction, a kind of internal compass that helped them find their way from one place to another the same as their brothers and sisters of the dolphin tribes.

"We will talk more of this ship and its contents at another time, dear Ohnalee, as my heart is spilling over with love, and my body shakes just looking at your face."

Ohnalee noticed the bed was cushioned with white sea sponges stacked at least four feet high, then covered with more of the soft green lacy plants which were piled beneath her body when she wakened after her arrival. It was a bower fit for an empress.

Mokeema's eyes grew misty, their usual piercing black coloration now changing as flashes of dark green light glowed in the depths. Ohnalee heard his sweet sensuous secret voice singing as he held her close, running his fingers tenderly up and down the center of her back.

Touch me, hold me, tenderly enfold me,
See me, feel me, let your love reveal me,
Hear the passion of the music that dwells within my soul,
And we'll share the special sweetness of the sound,
Dear one, I am yours forevermore.

Mokeema picked up Ohnalee in his arms, and laid her most lovingly on the soft silken leafy bed. After a while he peeled the gray leather suit from her body, flinging it to the ground. Jade appeared instantly, as if she was hovering just outside, grabbing the suit then quickly retreating in a swirl of bubbles. Mokeema's fingers moved gently over the curves of his mate's body, exploring the marvelous mysteries of her form, and later, when she was ready, she was instructed in the art of making love as practiced by the sea people. The couple joined both body and soul and, after a while, held each other close as the light of distant stars celebrated their joining. And later when the stars faded away, and the light of the early day filtered down to the land of the sea people, Mokeema and Ohnalee swam among their people.

Members of the tribe came from far and wide, anxious to see the human who had come to live among them. Mokeema wrapped his bride in a new red leather cloak like the Queen's and carried Ohnalee proudly in his arms.

He explained that he was proud to carry her among his people, the better to show her beauty to all.

"When I am with you, I will often carry you as I would the most priceless treasure," Mokeema said, "and as my lady, you will never need to swim by yourself. I have assigned Guardians to your service, and they will always be nearby to accompany you anywhere you want to go.

When we go to the upper lands of the sea to hunt, we will both wear the leather jackets and hood, to protect our bodies from the beasts who are our enemies," Mokeema warned, holding her even more tightly. "No one will ever hurt you, my Ohnalee," he promised. "But I must warn of a danger you must understand."

Mokeema's sculptured features were solemn as he told Ohnalee that no other human must ever possess her leather suit.

"Your suit has great power," Mokeema warned, "the knowledge of which has been passed down from our fathers. It enables the wearer to adapt to life under the sea, and if a human captures this suit, they might find the remote areas of the sea where we live safe from interference, perhaps bringing evil to our people or stealing those treasures we possess."

He warned Ohnalee to keep her sealskins close, particularly when she was visiting sheltered coves along the shore.

"There will be times when it feels safe to remove your garment, to let your lovely skin feel the warm rays of the sun as you relax in the shelter of rocky ledges and coves away from the sting of the wind. These days will make you happy beyond belief, but you must remember my words."

Mokeema's face was stern as he warned she must always be watchful.

"If a human creeps up on you as you sleep," Mokeema continued, his face dark with emotion, "he could do you harm and then take the suit, so be always watchful, never letting the garment out of your sight."

Ohnalee promised, terrified at the prospect of such a terrible event.

Chapter 14

LOST LADY OF THE ORIENT

Margaret Rose remembered how happy she felt as Mokeema curled his body next to hers, loving and sleeping, talking and sharing thoughts and plans in the darkness of the nights, in the morning of the days, when she lived by his side in the deep of the sea. Thinking about her lover's strong sharp teeth and how gently he used them to excite her, made her pulsate with excitement.

"Bite me, bite me," she begged, shivering with desire as Mokeema held her down tightly, nipping and nibbling at the side of her neck, then moving down each arm toward her fingers. One by one he licked and gently chewed those fingers, then rolled her over on her stomach so he could work on her back, gently teasing and biting, now softly, now a little more agressively, the sharp points of his teeth harmlessly caressing her flesh all the way down to her feet.

Margaret closed her eyes once again, and returned to the land of the Mer.

"Tell me about the boat that carried the scallop shell bed across the sea", she begged Mokeema, remembering his promise to continue the story. His face was animated as he continued the tale.

Mokeema told Ohnalee how the crew of the junk was weak from starvation as they approached the coast of Oregon, so several of the sea people attempted to help by bringing gifts of fish and edible seaweeds. But when the sailors saw the Mer approach, they went crazy with fear, thinking they were under attack by monsters or demons.

"The little yellow men screeched curses at the people who had no intention to harm them, and before they could descend safely beneath the surface, the wicked men pointed a long shiny device in their direction.

It was a tiny thing, Ohnalee, no larger around than a piece of tubular coral, but the people heard a noise louder than the roar of thunder, and then they saw a flash brighter than the sun or the bright zigzagging fire that comes from the house of the gods when they are angry.

Then the evil fire came again, striking one of our women in the shoulder. The wound was deep and the blood spilled out like a dark red cloud, sending waves of pungent fragrance to the attention of our feared enemy, the Great Shark. Her mate gathered his woman in his arms, fleeing to the depths, but she had no life fluid left and expired before they reached safety.

We are not a warlike people," Mokeema continued, "but the small band of women and warriors could not let this evil act go unpunished. They raised their voices to the heavens, calling down the spirits of our ancestors to do battle at their sides. Within minutes, the sky grew dark, and the wind swept the seas into mighty curling breakers so high the ship disappeared from view. Swirling black clouds hid the bodies of these mighty spirit warriors, but when the sea calmed again, the ship had slipped beneath the surface to a watery grave."

Ohnalee was fascinated by the story as she fervently believed in the existence of the spirit world. Prayer is the same in any culture, *she decided.* If we want anything bad enough, we can humbly entreat God or his angels for assistance, and if we are worthy, we may receive our heart's desire.

"There was a woman on the ship," Mokeema continued, telling Ohnalee about the small female they found locked in a luxurious cabin. Mokeema described how the people found the craft settled on the bottom in a coral *garden and broke open the door to a small lavish room in the center of the boat. It had no portholes and must have been an uncomfortable prison for its occupant.*

The tiny woman had shiny black hair, arranged with jeweled combs that held it in place in an elaborate coiffure. She was attired in a ruby-red garment made from a smooth, glossy fabric, embroidered with tiny stitches in a design with peacocks and flowers. Her painted fingernails were so long and curved, it would be impossible to eat without assistance. Around her neck was a necklace of rare black coral, which grows only in the deepest parts of the ocean.

The lady's feet were wrapped tightly with long pieces of fabric, covered by a short stocking with a red background and black border around the top. When the people carefully removed these bandages, they found her tiny feet were deformed and distorted, with the toes of these useless feet curled almost to the heel. The toenails cut into the soles, and some were imbedded deep in the flesh. Mokeema said they wondered how she could have stood or walked.

In the corner of the room was an ornate chair, with a heavy handle on the back and one at the foot. Perhaps this was used to carry this unfortunate woman up top to the deck, where she could get some fresh air, Mokeema surmised.

Ohnalee was sad, thinking about this girl, knowing the pain she endured from childhood as the bindings were made ever tighter, torturing her feet into this cruel position.

"That girl was of the highest class," Ohnalee told Mokeema. "She was destined to be the wife or concubine of a wealthy lord, trained from childhood to please a man in every aspect, but never expected to feed herself or walk unassisted. She would have been intelligent as well as beautiful, educated in the arts and music, skilled in flower arranging, able to read and write. She was probably being delivered to her new family with a rich dowry suitable to her position and family."

Daughters were considered inferior to men in that society, Ohnalee explained, but they were useful in making strong political alliances or obtaining the favor of powerful leaders or wealthy landowners.

"This woman was imprisoned in a silken cocoon, with everything in the world she wanted, except the right to be free."

Mokeema looked melancholy. "I would rather die than be confined like that," he whispered, and Ohnalee agreed.

"We have left her in the golden chair in the room," Mokeema said. "Her spirit is free now, at peace in the home of her ancestors. She can never be confined again, and no one will disturb the resting place of her mortal remains."

Chapter 15

TRANSITION

Margaret Rose remembered the days after her arrival in the kingdom of the sea when she slowly came to know and recognize members of the community. *She learned Mokeema's name meant "guardian of the people," and her name, Ohnalee, meant "pearl of the sea." All the people were kind and gracious, bringing gifts salvaged from the many shipwrecks scattered over the ocean floor. Only one person in the community seemed to wish Ohnalee ill, and that person was the princess Stephania.*

Margaret Rose remembered the maiden's hateful glance on the day of her joining to Mokeema, and later, she learned the reason for this reaction. Stephania was the daughter of the leader of a tribe of sea people who lived far to the north, and one year, during the annual migration to the land of the sunny islands, her people stopped at a group of small rocky islands off the coast of California. These islands were a place where sea people stopped to rest on their long journey south. At these gatherings, young people engaged in pleasant flirtations while the elders discussed more serious concerns, and often members of one clan would leave to travel with new friends afterwards.

Smitten with Mokeema's gentle nature and knowing the power he would hold in the future as ruler, Stephania asked her father's permission to leave her people to serve as a handmaiden to Mokeema's mother. After that, the sea-maid traveled close to Mokeema, brushing her breasts against his skin, flipping her sleek green tail back and forth in a sensual way, stroking his strong back and arms, and massaging his tired muscles. Princess Stephania was certain he would choose her when it was time to mate, so she hated the human woman when she came to join the people.

Margaret Rose remembered scrumptious banquets at the Queen's palace where the food was as beautiful to the eye as it was delicious on the palate. The Mer feasted on lobsters and other shellfish, as well as sea urchins, seaweed and kelp. Ohnalee squealed with delight as Mokeema tore a lobster apart, breaking the shell into pieces so he could easily pick out the delicious pink flesh. "More, more", she demanded, opening her mouth wide like a baby bird, as her lover fed her with his strong hands. Never did Ohnalee crave the hot berry pies of olden days, roasts of venison, or steaming soups made with clams and oysters. No more cooking, *she thought happily, not missing her kitchen or the many household duties that used to fill her days. Ohnalee found the new cuisine delicious, fresh, and healthy as her body had now totally adapted to life under the sea.*

Memories of life on the Oregon Coast grew fainter as the days passed, and sometimes it seemed that Margaret Rose Lavell was a fictional character, not flesh and blood.

Mokeema was the perfect mate, choosing to spend his days swimming leisurely by Ohnalee's side or carrying her in his arms. Most males of the sea people left their females alone to entertain themselves, preferring to hunt with the other males or engage in various sports. Mokeema declined numerous invitations from male friends to come along on their hunting expeditions, which included visits to other communities where, it was said, voluptuous, promiscuous females were anxious to service the sexual needs of the hunters. Although Mokeema seemed content in his new role, the elders of the tribe chuckled, wagering he would soon tire of his human spouse and return to his old habits.

JADE

115

Chapter 16

JADE

Total recall of the past now placed Margaret in a trancelike state where the present was not real, but was altered and transformed by the reality of her experience. The soft whispers oozing out from the vast dark recesses of her mind grew louder and louder, begging to be free, roaring as loud as the pounding hoofs of the white horses of the sea as they came galloping onto the shore.

Some days Ohnalee, Mokeema, and Jade ascended to the upper levels of the ocean, swimming with whales and sea lions, floating lazily on the surface of the water or sunning themselves on the rocks close to the shore. Mokeema told Ohnalee that his people believed whales and dolphins had lived on the land in ancient times, but chose to return to live beneath the sea.

Several times, Ohnalee saw humans in the distance, but she trembled at the sight, diving under the water, begging for Mokeema to come down, come down with her, to home. Being seen or recognized might bring searchers in boats, she thought; they might even have guns.

"No one will do you harm, my lady, as long as I live," Jade growled. Both Ohnalee and Mokeema smiled, pleased the woman was always near, ready to help with anything needed.

For a long time Ohnalee was embarrassed to ask her mate about the identity of his father, but Mokeema brought up the subject himself after a conversation when Ohnalee was telling about her childhood.

"In my world," Mokeema began, "highborn women take lovers whenever they choose. They may have more than one male at a time, selecting only the strongest and bravest, but often do not know which of these pleasant enjoyments produce the gift of a child. My mother honored many males with her favor, but sharing power with anyone is not required or desired by our Queen."

"I will never take another lover no matter what the custom," Ohnalee whispered, "you are the only one for me." Mokeema smiled, and held her close.

One October day, Jade convinced Ohnalee to swim with her toward the Oregon Coast. Ohnalee longed to feel the warmth of the sun on her skin, so put her fears aside and agreed to go.

"I know a safe place where we can toast our bodies on a warm ledge, and you can observe the flowers and trees of the land," Jade said, "and perhaps my lady would like to learn more about the Dragon Mer tribe."

Ohnalee agreed as she had been waiting for the right moment to ask Jade about her birth mother.

Mokeema sent a contingent of sea lions to watch over the ladies, warning Ohnalee, as usual, to keep a good eye on her suit when she took it off to sunbathe.

When they reached the coast, just north of Florence, the two women flipped their bodies up onto an outcropping of rocks with the Heceta Head Lighthouse in view. Their Guardians stayed a short ways out from the beach, bobbing up and down in the swells, and within a short time they were joined by several of the Steller sea lions who lived in the vicinity.

This is a perfect spot, *Ohnalee thought as she folded her clothing, placing it safely in a dry pocket beneath a large rock before stretching out in the sun. The ledge was protected from the wind by several large flat boulders, but she had an unobstructed view of the lighthouse.*

"Be careful not to burn your beautiful white skin," warned Jade, always worrying about her like a mother hen. It had been several weeks since her last tanning session, so Ohnalee knew it was good advice.

"There is the place where I put you on the shore when you were just a wee baby," said Jade as she pointed toward the long white beach just south of the lighthouse.

"Will you tell me about that, dear Jade?" begged Ohnalee.

"You were only a few days old, with a head of unruly yellow hair and large bright eyes blue as the color of the water in the deepest part of the ocean. Those mischievous eyes looked at me with curiosity and intelligence, delving deep into my soul, probing my purpose as if to say, 'Watch out, I am not the puny weakling you think.' I knew immediately you would survive, against all odds.

I wrapped you in a covering of soft seaweed to protect your soft skin from the sun, then placed a perfect small scallop shell on a cord around your neck."

Jade smiled at the recollection, but hesitated for a moment as if she didn't know where to begin.

Ohnalee waited patiently as she longed to know every little detail of that day. Then Jade turned on her side, facing Ohnalee, and it was easy to see the pain in her eyes as she struggled to summon up the past and let the memories flow into the open. Jade's golden body glowed in the sun in stark contrast to Ohnalee's white skin, which was already starting to turn pink. The two females were totally different in almost every way, yet despite their exterior appearance, they had developed a strong bond that made them feel more like relatives than friends.

"How old are you, Jade?" blurted Ohnalee, wondering why that question suddenly seemed important.

"I'm sorry, I shouldn't have asked that; don't know why I did," Ohnalee said, feeling a little embarrassed. Since she joined the Mer, she found it strange that no one spoke about their ages, and they never celebrated birthdays as humans did. It was difficult to tell much about anyone's age as they attained their full growth quickly, then seemed to coast along in splendid shape and health without any visible signs of aging.

Elders such as the shaman Magdalena Meda were revered for their wisdom, and Ohnalee had heard she was very old, but she looked strong and agile, with smooth skin and glossy hair. Mokeema said his mother had lived a long full life, but even he did not know exactly how old she was. Age didn't seem to make much difference anyway in the social structure of the

Mer as females and males mated without any consideration of age; it was attraction that mattered most.

"We do not keep track of the years, dear Ohnalee, but I was birthed in the land of the Dragon Mer about one hundred years ago. When your mother came to live with the tribe, she was just a child, perhaps only fourteen in human years, but she was very brave and beautiful."

Jade stroked Ohnalee's hair and nuzzled her cheek as she continued her story. "You must soon go into the shade, my lady," Jade said worriedly, "your skin is getting redder by the moment."

Ohnalee moved her body into the shadow cast by a large boulder, and Jade moved with her. Jade turned over on her back, positioning her head on a flat rock, then stretched out her arm so Ohnalee could come closer. Ohnalee felt warm and protected as she cradled her head on her friend's shoulder.

"The Dragon Mer were once part of Big Maru's tribe," Jade explained, "but split off after a fierce battle that pitted brother against brother, and father against son.

To understand this separation, you must know more about the family history of Queen Maru."

EIRE KERRY

Chapter 17

EIRE KERRY

Margaret Rose stood, feeling stiff and uncomfortable. She rubbed her eyes, and walked down from the porch to the edge of her garden where she had a good view of the lighthouse at Heceta Head. Finding a shady spot under a tree, Margaret Rose stretched out on the grass and closed her eyes once again.

Jade explained that Maru's mother, Kerry, was the daughter of the Muiroigh tribe from the "land beneath the waves," near the emerald green shores of Eire.

"The females of this clan wear a red cap made from feathers,"Jade said. "The hat is called 'cohullendruth' and has magical properties that assist them to travel through the water at extremely fast speeds. The Muiroigh dress in clothing made from sealskins as we do when traveling in northern waters, taking on the characteristics of seals to any curious human eye watching."

Jade said the Muiroigh women were shape-shifters, able to go ashore after hiding their capes and cap, and on one of these visitations to a seaside town, Kerry fell passionately in love with a sea captain who was about to leave on a journey that would take him to far-off places around the world.

She was fabulously wealthy, with a fortune in gold plundered from sunken ships, so the liaison enabled the captain to dress his ship with new sails and rigging, then provision it with stores to last for months, with funds left over for the future.

It was dangerous for a woman of the sea to let a human know of her lineage as the human could control her forever just by the possession of her cap and cape, but Kerry's lover knew and accepted everything about his beautiful mate, often kissing the thin webbing that ran between her fingers. The cap and cape were hidden away in a special box on the ship, kept safe in case Kerry needed to go below the waves in search of more gold to continue their wandering.

Jade said that Kerry and her captain roamed far and wide around the globe, having many adventures on land and sea. They often left the ship for months in a safe anchorage under the watchful eyes of their crew, once traveling across South America to the Caribbean and back. During this trip, they met an Aztec warrior priest who became enamored of Kerry, offering her gifts of gold and jewels to follow him to his kingdom deep in the green jungles. It was obvious that the Aztec tolerated the presence of the captain only because of his fascination with Kerry, but he made it plain that he considered himself a more appropriate candidate for her hand. The couple traveled with his army for several months as he conquered village after village, plundering their wealth and murdering all who stood in his way.

The sacrifice of captives was common, and black-robed priests, their hair matted stiff with human blood, sacrificed three, four and five indians every day. Life flowed from death, they believed, so the blood of their victims was plastered on the walls of the temple. The hearts were offered to nourish the deities and thus sustain the world.

Kerry was sickened at this practice of gruesome ritual human sacrifice, which seemed more about instilling fear into the people rather than appeasing the gods, so she decided to return to their ship. The Aztec lord was enraged at her decision to leave but pretended to agree, wishing her well. To convince her of his goodwill, he told her about a vast network of secret caves and caverns which ran from the Pacific, under the earth, all the way to the warm waters of the Caribbean.

"These places have deep pools of glowing green water and stalagmites of blood red limestone which seems to ooze from the ceilings and walls of the

caverns," he told Kerry, as he stared at her with hard, piercing black eyes. To further impress her, he drew a crude but easily read chart, showing the entrance on the Pacific side and where the traveler would emerge on a sunny Caribbean beach.

"Hidden in the depths of the earth are mountains of treasure hidden by ancient peoples," he bragged. "If you go there, you can take what you need of this bounty," he said, still hoping to convince Kerry to stay. He boasted that the caves contained not only gold and precious jewels, but hoards of stockpiled weapons of every description. Kerry knew, from probing the poisonous depths of his mind, that he planned to ambush them on the trail, killing the captain, then keeping her captive as his slave.

As Kerry prepared to leave, the Aztec appeared in full regalia. He was richly dressed and even his sandals had soles of gold. His goodbye gift was a large crystal skull carved from a large block of solid quartz. Kerry saw that the skull had a moveable lower jaw, and the Aztec said it took more than three hundred years of carving to create this masterpiece.

"I would prefer that you stay with me, lady," he stammered, not used to pleading his case before any woman. "You will share my position, wealth, and power.

I can give you more than that 'sea rat' ever will," he scowled, pointing a long finger in the direction of the captain.

Jade said that Kerry extended her hand, shaking her head firmly from side to side, her eyes holding his captive. Then the man bowed, kissing her fingertips lightly.

Kerry and the captain had shown their digust at the vile treatment of captives taken by the Aztecs, and their plan was to free as many as possible.

Jade told Ohnalee how, silently and carefully, under cover of night, Kerry and her captain made their escape with several prisoners. Just as expected, they were followed by at least one hundred fierce Aztec warriors who hoped to surprise the couple when they stopped for the night. The men waited until they thought all were sleeping, then crept into the camp as the fire dimmed, leaving only glowing embers. They struck with knives and swords, slashing hard at the shapes they thought were sleeping by the fire. Suddenly, from behind, dark forms appeared, silently swooping down upon the attackers, taking them by surprise. Silver steel flashed in the dim light as the defenders *lopped off heads and limbs until the Aztecs were destroyed. After the fight, several of the defenders swore they saw a strange apparition arise from the bed of blazing embers in the midst of the battle.*

"It was as tall as a tree, with glowing eyes," one of the men whispered while others agreed that the beast breathed fire from its fearsome mouth, roasting the warriors as they fell.

Kerry and the captain appeared not to have seen such a creature, and when the sun rose in the morning, there was no indication of its presence. Kerry would say little about the incident, except to reassure the captain that they were protected by the spirits of her ancestors.

The Aztec lord had let others do his dirty work, but Kerry knew that his days were numbered. Soon after the attack Kerry learned in a dream that he suffered a horrific death at the hands of a powerful rival who ordered that his heart be ripped from his body as a sacrifice to the Gods. Despite her knowledge of his cruelty and the murder and sacrifice of thousands of victims, Kerry whimpered in her sleep as she watched two minor priests cover his naked body with bright blue paint, then hold him down over a stone table which arched his chest upward. She heard his hideous wail as the head priest used a sharp stone to make an incision under his right rib, and she quivered and shook in her bed as she saw the priest hold his still-beating heart in his bloody hands, holding it up to the sky before burning it in a bowl on the altar. A large warrior then came forward and lopped off his head, which was thrown down the 365 steps of the temple, followed by the headless body. The crowds below set upon the corpse like a pack of wild dogs, tearing the remains to pieces, tasting the blood and rubbing it on their faces. It was a bloody end to a bloody life.

Ohnalee covered her eyes and shuddered at Jade's story. She found it hard to believe that human beings could perform such unspeakable acts in the name of religion, and the vision Jade was painting with such vivid details would not be easily forgotten.

"I'm going to have nightmares about this forever, Jade," she warned her friend.

"I am so sorry, my lady, but I want you to know the past that made Kerry the miraculous person she was, so you will understand some of the wisdom and knowledge she passed on to her child, Maru the Queen. Kerry told these stories over and over when she came to the Mer people here as if she wanted

them instilled firmly in our memory, to be passed from mother to son and on and on forevermore."

"Go on, go on, dear Jade, I must know more," Ohnalee begged.

Jade continued the story, saying that during the time Kerry had the crystal skull in her possession, she dreamed about it several times, finding it had been passed down from father to son for hundreds of years. Each artist spent thousands of hours polishing the surface of the crystal by hand after the basic features were roughed in, as there were no tools at the time that could be used for this project. When it was finished, two members of the family of carvers were on their way to the ancient city to place the skull on the altar of the gods in the Temple of the Warriors as an offering, but they were murdered in an ambush by the Aztec lord and his army.

Kerry and the captain were led to the ruins of the old city by the spirits of these carvers, and when the skull was finally in its destined hiding place, the creators rested, finally free and content. The city was buried deep in the jungle, almost completely covered with centuries of thick vines and dense vegetation, so Kerry believed no human would ever find the place again.

When at last Kerry and the captain neared the harbor where they left their vessel, they gave the map of the underground caverns to their friends, who promised to use the knowledge only for the good of their people.

The warriors promised to explore the network of caverns from ocean to ocean, passing the knowledge of the secret route down to their children and their children's children.

"Our families will keep your memory sacred," they promised, "as your generous gift of knowledge will change our lives forever."

Then one of the men stepped forward with a square silver box in his hand. "This gift is a token of our friendship and everlasting thanks, revered lady."

Kerry and the Captain listened quietly, but suddenly Kerry closed her eyes. Her slim body swayed, and she staggered for an instant, almost falling. The Captain put his strong arm around his mate, being familiar with her ability to pass into an altered state of reality.

At first a dark red curtain blocked her view, but suddenly it lifted, revealing purple flashes of light on the horizon. The explosions of color grew larger and brighter, then broke into small wispy tangles of silvery dust. Kerry saw an elderly man sleeping on a hard pallet. He tossed and turned as his soul left the body, traveling fast, then nimbly jumping the barrier, crossing the threshold from the dream state into a fiery landscape of death and destruction. The earth shook and the sky was alive with zig zagging bolts of lightening that struck the ground nearby. He screamed, opening and closing his eyes in terror, seeing nothing but a bright blueness that concealed all. I can't see, I'm blind, *he thought, rubbing his eyes and staggering in the darkness. Sobs and pitiful cries emanated from all directions, begging, pleading for help, but the shimmering blue glow obscured the sufferers from his view.*

Kerry grimaced, her face contorting, as she hovered in the dwelling of the priest. She saw the man clearly as he struggled to return to consciousness. "No, no," he muttered, arching his back, waving his arms and throwing his legs from side to side. His body was drenched with sweat, and his muscles ached as if he had done battle with a thousand demons. When he opened his eyes, escaping at last from the horror of the vision, the electric blue haze was gone, but clenched tight in his hand was a large blue turquoise.

Kerry knew that the stone had come from the Motherland in the last days of the great upheaval. It must have been left behind by the honored ones when they fled.

Quiet voices brought Kerry back to the present, and she saw the assembly standing respectfully, waiting for her return.

"Please continue," she requested.

The warrior opened the box, drawing out a spectacular silver necklace. "The medallion was made by one of our most talented silversmiths many years ago. The head priest had the stone incorporated in the design. He said it was very powerful and came from another world, one far different than this.

After the holy man died," the warrior continued, "the necklace was guarded by his followers and kept in a secret place for many years. The master foretold that you would come one day. In visions he saw you many times. He said you possessed not only great courage but also miracle—working powers that would be enhanced by this gift. This pendant is not only to bless you with long life and happiness, but is destined for another in your line. Only she can unlock the secret of the stone.

Kerry gasped with pleasure as she accepted the exquisite silver pendant suspended from a heavy silver chain with round and oblong beads. In the center was a perfect scallop shell in a heavy silver mounting. A large turquoise stone was placed at the top of the pendant, and every part of the piece was hand shaped and hammered until it fit perfectly.

The captain placed it around her neck, fastening the heavy clasp as the pendant settled snugly just above the hollow between her breasts. A great chant went up from the crowd assembled, and Kerry beamed as she accepted the homage of her friends.

"You must return one day, dear lady," the warriors begged, "and when that day comes, we will welcome you as a queen."

Kerry's eyes misted as she knew she would never travel in this part of the world again, then speaking perfectly in their language, Kerry promised she would treasure the gift forever.

"I have no children now, but I will pass this pendant along to my eldest daughter, and she will bequeath it to her daughter and so on, and perhaps one day, your daughters will meet mine, finding their connection when they see the pendant. Tell your sons and daughters to send down the word to their children to look for the pendant, and when it is seen, no matter how many years have passed, let them greet the wearer with the same love and courtesy you have given to me and the captain."

Jade told Ohnalee that the captain and Kerry returned to their travels, and after many years, Kerry and the captain replaced their original ship with another larger vessel when the hull sagged from dry rot and worms made their home in the planks on the bottom. Sadly, it is the destiny of the long-living Mer to outlive their beloved human companions, and Kerry's beloved Captain grew old and very tried. One night at sea, the Captain was at the helm when his big heart gave out. He crashed to the deck, dying instantly, leaving Kerry alone, in charge of the ship and crew.

"Kerry was heartbroken without her captain, and wanted no part of life on a boat without him. She knew it was time to return to the sea when she heard the songs of our people in the distance as the ship sailed north in the cold waters off the Oregon Coast," related Jade.

"One night as the ship passed offshore of Heceta Head, Kerry donned her cloak and red cap, then plunged over the rail into the dark water. She watched as the ship continued on without her, finally disappearing over the horizon."

They will believe I took my own life, *she mused as she dove deep,* just another silly weak woman who couldn't live without her man.

"Kerry made her way to our lands," Jade said, "and found the Merfolk in the area hospitable. She was strange and exotic, regaling everyone with tales of her adventures. The males were feverish in her presence, and after her first summer with the people, she birthed a female child in the enchanted islands. The shaman named her Maru, but it was difficult to say who was the father."

"Did Maru tell you this, Jade?" asked Ohnalee, totally fascinated with the story.

"Queen Maru said her mother related the story over and over, turning it into a long ballad which she and Kerry sang together. Kerry knew her daughter would never forget her Muiroigh heritage as the song of Kerry's life and people was woven firmly into her heart and mind.

After the birth of Maru, Kerry caught the eye of King Davide. He was a notorious flirt, known to pursue any beautiful sprite who caught his eye. His first mate had died in childbirth, and the baby quickly followed her mother to the land of the ancestors. People thought Davide would never settle down with any one female as most women could never accept the continued questing of his roving eye.

Kerry found King Davide charming and funny. He was a good companion and listener, able to provide the wealth and status she required. His dalliances were an insignificant fact of life that did not affect her position as his mate and queen. Their open relationship enabled Queen Kerry to take lovers of her own, but a special part of her heart was reserved for the life and love she shared with her captain.

One day, when Kerry was very old, she gave the red feathered cap to her daughter Maru, asking that she keep it safe and pass it along one day to a worthy woman of her choice."

"The cap is the proof of our tie to the Muiroigh Clan," Kerry said, "and perhaps one day it will be returned to my home off the coast of Eire."

"What happened to the silver pendant," Ohnalee asked, thinking Maru had never mentioned it to her.

"I don't know where it is," Jade admitted, "but I assume Kerry gave it to the Queen with the feather hat, or Magdalena Meda is keeping it safe in a secret location."

Jade told Ohnalee how one morning, Maru swam to the dwelling of her mother but found her gone. As she wailed in despair, she heard a quiet voice *speaking in her mind, saying,* Be brave and calm, my daughter, as I go with the great whales to a place where I can rest in peace and wait for the ancestors to come.

Wiping away the tears, Maru felt her mother's gentle hand on her hair, proving she had already descended to the ancestors.

Cry not, my child, as we will be together again after you have done your duty to your people, but continue to sing our song to remind you of your Muiroigh ancestry.

Ohnalee interrupted, wondering if Jade knew the words and melody of Kerry's song.

"Yes, I do, Ohnalee, and one day, if you like, I will teach you the words and melody. But for now, I want to finish the story of the creation of the Dragon Mer tribe."

Ohnalee nodded, but her stomach was growling. "I'm starving, Jade," *she complained, rubbing her gently swelling belly,* "should we stop and get something to snack upon?"

"In a while, Ohnalee," *her friend agreed, knowing exactly how she was feeling.*

"I am just getting to the interesting part."

Chapter 18

DRAGONE

Margaret Rose sighed and turned on her side. A yellow dandelion brushed against her check, and she grimaced, slapping at the offending weed, then sinking back into her reverie.

"Dragone was the son of King Davide and a tawny gypsy traveler the ruler met on one of his journeys," Jade continued. *"She stayed for a while after Dragone's birth, but left the child behind to wander forth as her nomadic people have always done."*

Jade explained that even though the King treated his son well, Dragone always felt his father preferred his stepdaughter Maru. Imaginary slights made him seethe with resentment, which festered through the years.

Ohnalee wondered why King Davide chose his stepdaughter as his heir, rather than his son, and Jade immediately gave the answer, saying,

"From early childhood Maru showed the mark of leadership. Kerry came from a noble line of women; the gift of sight and magic was in their blood. Maru inherited her mother's strength and wisdom, and was never interested in childish pursuits. Rather, she studied hard to learn everything

that would be required to rule, even though she understood her brother was the heir apparent.

On the other hand, Dragone seemed to attract trouble and he disagreed with his father on almost every issue. He was disobedient and stubborn, hot-blooded and irrational, and he tested his father's patience in every way.

Jade told Ohnalee that as he grew older, Dragone grew weary of his father's domination and devised a plan to overthrow him. The scheme was detected by the Guardians, and the other plotters were locked in a dark dungeon where they would never see the light of day again.

"King Davide was merciful to his son," Jade said, "deciding to banish him rather than imprison him with the others."

"Go from my lands, and never return," the King bellowed, his cold dark eyes flashing, "you are not my son from this day forth."

"It was at that point, Lady," Jade said, "that Davide named Maru as his successor."

"Dragone fled far from our lands," Jade explained, "but Davide warned Maru to be strong and vigilant, as he knew Dragone would never accept his exile peacefully."

Davide grew weak and weary of life. He was very old, and prayed for the 'gods' to call him home and one night the moon looked down through the water to where Davide rested. A bright finger of light descended to the land of the Mer, and Davide smiled. He left quickly, following the spiral of energy to the place where loved ones waited.

Although Dragone was cruel and ruthless, many thought he would be a better ruler than a female, and even before Davide's Remembrance Ceremonies were finished, dissent fermented in the kingdom, creating a poisonous brew which threatened peace and tranquility.

Although Maru wore the crown, that did not put an end to the unrest as some members of the tribe stayed loyal to Maru while others pledged allegiance to Dragone. Stories of his brutality and ferocity spread through the kingdom, but many joined his armies as they thought he would easily unseat his sister, and they wanted to be on the winning side.

Just the name Dragone brought followers to his banner, as the Mer believed their ancestors could change into fierce dragons in battle. Many thought the name indicated Dragone was favored by the ancient ones, so when he roared into their valleys and undersea dwellings followed by his entourage of warriors, the Mer joined his ranks without protest. If they did not, his warriors slaughtered the males and took the women to be slaves.

In spite of his brutality, women seemed mesmerized by his presence, and when his army left an area, seeds were left growing in the bellies of his conquests. Dragone decorated his dusky buff body with symbols carved into the flesh, and designed a a brown and black marking that was placed on the upper arm of each and every member of his new tribe as proof of their allegiance.

After months of training and fighting, Dragone assembled his army in the Queen's Valley, planning to attack at daylight. They carried long spears with stone points and hatchets made from sharpened rocks tied with leather thongs to handles of strong carved petrified wood. The warriors were exhausted from their travels far and wide recruiting for their army, so they were overjoyed when several women arrived carrying casks of refreshment recovered from some of the sunken ships in the area. This liquid had been forbidden to the Mer for many years as just one sip convinced the taster to have another, and then another, and soon more smiling females arrived with even larger casks of the delicious drink.

Dragone knew nothing about the arrival of these women as he had disappeared into a dwelling in the area where he tied up the two female occupants after killing the male. Pleasuring himself with the two females seemed a great way to prepare for battle in the morning. And besides, *he thought*, it will bring more babies for my tribe.

"I am the conqueror, I am the conqueror," he bellowed, grinning as he thought about how many would die under his sword in the morning. Bloodshed and sex were his vices, and just thinking about combat made him excited. "I'll fix that big mouth fang-tooth witch," he gloated, "make her pay for all those years when she treated me like dirt. By tomorrow I will be supreme ruler of all the Mer, and then I'll decide whether to display her ugly head on my pike, or just put a harness on the hag and make her pull my chariot."

The elder of the two woman was silent as he pounded her body ferociously, while the daughter hid her eyes and mewed quietly.

When Dragone was done with the women, he pushed them away, then fell into a deep slumber.

The older of the two scowled at the sleeping Dragon Lord, showing her sharp pointed teeth as they fled away from the area.

"*I could kill him right now but don't worry my sweet,*" *the mother whispered,* "*we will have our revenge; the monster may not survive to see another sunrise.*"

By midnight, Dragone's warriors were satiated. They had gorged on food stores confiscated from terrified farmers in the area and entertained themselves with the horde of willing females who followed the army. Sleeping bodies were scattered around the landscape and all the casks of liquor were empty but the generous female purveyors had disappeared into the darkness.

"*That was when the Queen's forces struck,*" *said Jade,* "*it was a massacre, a bloodbath so terrible it must never be repeated. Hundreds of warriors died that day as the Queen's fighters crept up on the drunken soldiers. They came in fast and quiet, slashing and stabbing their spears into the hearts of the sleeping warriors and their followers, without so much as a single whoop to announce their arrival. They chopped and slashed, hacking off heads and tails in a savage explosion of pent up hatred. The carnage was unspeakable, and when it was done, only a few wounded were left alive.*"

"*Show no mercy,*" *commanded Queen Maru when she sent her army to the killing fields, so those who survived did so only because they were hidden beneath the bodies of their downed comrades.*

"*Dragone slept through the pandemonium as if drugged, stirring only after the butchery was finished. Hearing a strange swishing sound outside, he reluctantly pulled himself out of an erotic dream where he was having sex with two females at the same time, then stumbled out the door of the dwelling place into a nightmare. The bodies of his dead warriors had attracted the attention of every shark in the area, and they tore at the remains, ripping them to pieces. The water was colored a dark red, and pieces of skin and bone were everywhere.*"

"*What happened next?*" *begged Ohnalee,* "*I am feeling sickened and disgusted at this story, but I must know more.*"

Jade said Queen Maru's warriors returned to her palace, rejoicing over their victory.

"*You are safe, my Queen,*" *her Commander assured his sovereign,* "*but the coward Dragone was hiding during the killing and has escaped, followed by a few miserable maimed and weak survivors.*"

Jade said the Queen was merciful, deciding not to give chase, but she vowed she would kill him on sight if he ever set foot anywhere near her kingdom again.

As the years passed, Dragone's little band grew in size. Evildoers from Queen Maru's kingdom were often banished as she did not believe in sentencing her subjects to death, so they took shelter with the band that came to be known as the Dragon Mer.

Dragone had many children, but life was hard for the outcasts, and they struggled to survive. This struggle made them fiercer and more cruel as Dragone put his imprint on the character of his people. The weak were killed, and only the strong survived. Dragone lived with only one thought in mind, and that was his obsession to seize control of the kingdom of Queen Maru one day. If he couldn't do it, it would be left to his son or heirs to finish the job.

DRAGONE & MIKO

135

Chapter 19

THE SPIRIT OF THE LIGHTHOUSE

Margaret Rose sat up for a moment, gazing at the lighthouse in the distance. The sun was in her eyes, and she blinked, then shielded her eyes from the glare. After a few moments of contemplation, she returned to the grass, curling her body, knees almost to chin.

"How did my mother go to the Dragon Mer?" Ohnalee asked. *"What would possibly make her go? Did they take her by force?"*

"Dragone was hunting along the coast one day," Jade said, *"when he saw the girl playing on the cliffs. He called to her, using his most erotic and sensual song, and she came, walking slowly down until she reached the beach. He said she was very beautiful, and he curled his finger, gesturing her close to the water's edge.*

Dragone is a very attractive male, with dark skin and flashing eyes. His song is impossible to resist, and any human woman would be enthralled by his attention.

Dragone reached out his hand, and she responded as if in a trance, wading out into the water until it was more than waist deep. He took her then, moving quickly before she could resist, carrying her out into the deep water in his arms.

He said the girl did not cry out as he placed her up on a rocky ledge that could not be seen from the shore. There he wooed her with a soft voice, saying she would be a queen, ruling by his side for more than a hundred years. He placed her hand on his strong chest and kissed her fingers, mesmerizing her with his charm. When he took her, she did not protest, and after he had made her his own, he put his finger behind her ears, feeling for the mark of the Mer.

How is it that we know the children of the Mer, even when they have human blood, you want to know, Ohnalee?" Jade smiled. "We can smell them."

"What do you mean, smell them?" Ohnalee wanted to know. "You think we smell funny?"

"Smell of the sea, you do," Jade chuckled. "We can hear your thoughts, and we can smell you.

Your mother's name was Agnes," Jade continued, "and she was given to me to care for when Dragone brought her home to the tribe. She was very sweet and innocent and missed her mother but was enchanted with her lover. She did not struggle when he placed the tattoo on her arm even though it was very painful."

"Did he really love her?" Ohnalee asked.

"In his own way, I guess he did. But after a while she became pregnant, and he tired of her, casting her from his presence. Agnes was heartbroken, and I hoped she might choose to return home after the child was born.

I tried to help her adjust to life with the Dragon Mer, but Agnes was a gentle soul, not used to hardship or strife. The warlike attitude of the Dragon Mer was terrifying, and she made not a single friend among the women, most of whom thought her weak and useless."

Ohnalee started weeping as she got a mental picture of the woman who had birthed her.

Jade said it became obvious that Dragone planned to keep the child after it was born and give Agnes to one of his warriors as a trophy for good service. She would be no more than a sex slave, the lowest of the low, forced to do her owner's bidding at all times.

"The girl often cried for her mother," said Jade, "and when the birthing time came, she was tired and weak. She lived just long enough to see you take your first breath, and you smiled as she held you in her arms."

137

Ohnalee was sobbing now, and Jade covered her body with the sealskin cloak as the sun sunk beneath the surface of the sea, and the temperature dropped.

"Don't cry, my sweet, Jade will always love you," the sprite whispered. "We'll stay here tonight and keep each other warm while I continue the story.

There is one sad thing I must tell you before going any farther," Jade said.

"A few months after your mother was taken, some of our men were hunting close to the cliff where the lighthouse stands. They saw a woman throw herself off the bluff, screaming a name as she fell. That name was Agnes.

I never told Agnes that story," said Jade, "as I thought it would only add to her misery.

I think the mother thought her child had fallen into the sea, and was so consumed by grief she jumped."

"Did Agnes tell you her mother's name?" asked Ohnalee.

"It was Ruby," Jade said, "Ruby was your grandmother."

Night had fallen, and the stars filled the sky over Ohnalee's head. The Seven Sisters of Pleiades smiled down on the two friends, and every once in a while, a shooting star streaked across the sky leaving a silvery trail of dust. The moon was only a white sliver in the heavens that night, so every star and planet was clearly visible.

"You were very small," said Jade, "born with human characteristics rather than Mer, so I knew you could not survive for long under the sea. Dragone came to see you, and I saw he was disgusted rather than filled with pride."

"Get rid of the thing," he ordered, "I never want to see it again."

"I knew what he meant," said Jade. "He wanted me to kill you as was the usual practice with infants who were weak or deformed. He considered your human traits a deformity, so you were not acceptable.

I was afraid to argue with him, knowing he might kill you instantly, so I agreed to do it."

"Fine," he said sarcastically, as he turned his back to leave, "don't wait, do it quickly."

Jade was usually strong and stoic, but she wept as she told how she wrapped Ohnalee in a sealskin blanket, hiding her under her cloak as she left the enclave of the Dragon Mer under cover of darkness. She knew that *humans often came to the beach near the lighthouse, so she determined that would be the best place to go with her small bundle.*

"You were so sweet, so very sweet," Jade remembered, telling Ohnalee how she kept her on the rocky ledge for a while, cuddling her close. "I sang to you, Ohnalee, and I promised I would watch you as you grew. I told you to be a good child, and one day, we would be together again.

When I took you to the beach, you clung tightly to my neck as I found a safe place high above the waterline."

Ohnalee turned on her other side, and Jade curled her body close, her breasts pressing on Ohnalee's back. Ohnalee's skin felt warm, and she realized she was a little sunburned. Jade wrapped her arms around Ohnalee, kissing the back of Ohnalee's neck, stroking her round belly as she continued the story.

"A woman with a white animal came down the trail from the bluff," Jade remembered, "and I saw her throw a round ball at the beast. She shouted 'Catch, Jupiter, catch,' and the creature made a noise similar to our sea lion friends as he chased the ball into the tall grass near where I left you."

Jade said she heard the woman call, "Come, come, Jupiter," but he refused to leave his position in the grass.

The woman ran through a field of daisies to get to the white animal, and then she shooed the dog away, bending to pick up the tiny bundle.

"She held you close, Ohnalee, looking up and down the beach, calling 'hello, hello,' as if searching for the person who left you. After awhile the woman carried you up the path toward the lighthouse, and when she disappeared from view, I went back to the Dragon Mer."

Jade whimpered, but Ohnalee wiped away her tears and kissed her face as she continued the tale.

"Dragone had me followed, and when I got back, he sent one of his men to bring me to his dwelling place. He was furious, screaming and raging that I was a liar and a traitor. I promised I would never do anything to hurt the tribe, but he said I was disobedient and had to be punished."

Jade shook as she told how Dragone tied her wrists together with a heavy cord. He hung her from a large hook in the roof of his dwelling place, then cut her back with a sharp scallop shell. Over and over again, he slashed her tender flesh until the water ran red, and when he was done, he gave her to his men for their pleasure.

139

"I am so sorry, so sorry," Ohnalee cried, but her friend whispered, "It was worth it."

Ohnalee and Jade fell asleep, and when the sun rose, they woke, and Jade was ready to talk some more.

"One of the males was kind. He left my hands free and pretended to sleep, so I could escape. I knew he was sympathetic but had to keep his mouth shut in fear of retaliation. If anyone knew he helped me, he would be killed."

"I hate him, I hate him," Ohnalee interrupted, thinking of her father. "I will never forgive him for hurting you."

"I ran far," Jade continued, calming Ohnalee with her quiet voice, "and Queen Maru took me in. Her people treated my wounds and made me well again. I felt I could trust Maru with my life, so I told them about you, whom I love as a daughter."

Jade told Ohnalee that Mokeema often accompanied her to the beach below the lighthouse after the shaman Magdalena Meda's vision that she was meant to be his mate.

"He loved you from the first moment he saw you," Jade said, "but he knew you must be grown and come to him of your own free will, so he was patient, watching as you walked on the sand and played with your friends."

"Sometimes I heard a voice calling." Ohnalee remembered. "It made me want to go to the beach or the sea caves, but I thought it was only my imagination."

Jade swung her tail over the edge of the rocky ledge, then slid off into the water as Ohnalee watched.

"Gonna get us some breakfast," the sprite promised as she disappeared beneath the surface. Ohnalee knew her friend would return with as many oysters as she could fit in the leather bag she carried, so they would feast on the tasty creatures inside the shells until their bellies were full. Ohnalee could see a stream of fresh water rushing down from the bluff nearby, so she looked forward to a freshwater bath afterward.

Ohnalee sat cross-legged on her rocky perch, meditating on the story she had just heard. She closed her eyes, feeling entirely at peace, now even more certain she had made the right decision. Ohnalee stretched her arms overhead, then uncurled her legs, moving closer to the edge of the ledge. She dangled her feet over the side, her toes wiggling as they skimmed the top of the water.

"Ouch," she cried in surprise, feeling something nip at her big toe.

"Gotcha," Mokeema said with a grin as he captured both white feet in his hands, placing a kiss on each toe before pulling himself up onto the ledge.

"Couldn't be without you another minute," he announced as he curled his body around Ohnalee's.

"Told Jade I'd wait until she told you about your mother, but she's had you long enough."

Ohnalee beamed as her mate stroked her back and ran his fingers through her bright hair. The feeling was electric as his fingers massaged her neck and tickled her ears.

"Stop that," Ohnalee teased. "Jade will be back any moment."

"I'll bet you were out there all night, waiting," said Ohnalee with a knowing smile.

"Not out there," said Mokeema pointing to the sea lions a short ways out, "right over there."

He pointed to another rocky ledge close by, one so near Ohnalee knew he had probably heard every word of Jade's story.

"Didn't have to hear, knew it already, Ohnalee, but was worried you might be sad and need me.

Ha ha, here she comes," shouted Mokeema as Jade's head popped above the surface. He reached down to help, hoisting the heavy sack up onto the ledge.

"Enough for all," he grinned, looking around for a heavy rock to break the shells.

The three sat on the ledge for a long time, talking while they shucked the oysters from their spiny outer case. Mokeema loosened each oyster for Ohnalee, pointing to her mouth with a mischievous, sly grin on his face. Ohnalee closed her eyes then opened her lips so Mokeema could slide the delicious morsel onto her pink tongue.

"Ummmmm," she murmured as she sipped the salty nectar from the shell.

When they were satisfied and couldn't eat another bite, Jade swept the ledge clean, throwing the shells into a large pile nearby. Soon flocks of noisy seabirds descended to pick at the remains of the feast.

"My father must be very old," commented Ohnalee, thinking back on the story of his banishment from Queen Maru's kingdom.

"He is old and strong as ever," said Mokeema, "but one day another will take his place. His queen believes her child will rule, carrying on the evil practices Dragone has instituted, but we will see. Perhaps the gods have *their own plan for the Dragon Mer as the image of the Dragon is sacred to our ancestors, and Dragone has desecrated their memory by his actions and the doctrine he preaches.*

He has perverted the old stories we honor, changing their meaning to justify his quest for power."

Jade and Mokeema exchanged a knowing glance, but Ohnalee did not notice, seeming more interested in the light keepers' houses on the bluff. As she watched, she saw a flash from an upstairs window, then a shadow which lingered for a moment behind the glass.

You must go, Ruby, you must go, *Ohnalee thought, sending her inner voice toward the shore.* Your daughter waits in the land of the spirits, and you must go.

The shadow disappeared as a gust of cold wind raced down from the mountain, sending its icy fingers toward the sea. Ohnalee shivered, then turned to Mokeema.

"I will go there one day and convince her to leave," she promised, a silvery tear escaping from the corner of her eye.

Mokeema held her jacket so Ohnalee could easily put it on, then slipped over the ledge into the water. Ohnalee took one last sad look at the house on the bluff, then dove in, grabbing Mokeema's hand as they swam west.

STEPHANIA & THE SEA DRAGON

Chapter 20

THE FIRST MIGRATION

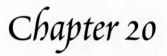*A* *few weeks later, Mokeema attended a gathering of the nobles at the palace to discuss the leaving time to move south. It was October, and soon the wild winds of winter would churn the sea into a maelstrom of storm and fury. It was time to go.*

Mokeema dressed Ohnalee warmly in her leather suit and hood, warning it would be a difficult journey to the land of the warm islands. Knowing this migration would be difficult for his pregnant mate, Mokeema called upon several of the sea people to swim closely by her side, carrying her on their backs when she tired. No other human had yet attempted this journey, but Ohnalee was not afraid.

Seeing that Ohnalee seemed sad to leave their dwelling, Mokeema assured her they would return in the spring, and everything would be waiting, untouched.

"When we reach the enchanted isles of the large lizards," Mokeema said, "you will swim in crystal clear water and recline on sandy beaches with the hot sun on your skin, and when our child is born, you will teach it about the things of the world, including the creatures that fly with wings and those that crawl and walk."

Ohnalee rubbed her belly, feeling the child stirring within, wondering whether her baby would resemble Mokeema's body, or hers. Would the little one have a strong lower body and powerful tail like Mokeema, or weak, inferior legs that would forever mark it as being human? Mokeema gave her a golden crucifix he found in one of the treasure boxes from a ship, hanging it on the pretty chain around her neck with her scallop shell, and Ohnalee rubbed the cross several times every day, praying her baby would be like the sea people. She did not want her children to feel like outcasts in the society or be discriminated against because of their human 'deformities,' but Mokeema assured her the child would be loved and cherished no matter what.

"We are not like the people of the Dragon Mer," Mokeema grumbled, showing his sharp teeth. "No one will hurt our child."

On the way south, Mokeema entertained Ohnalee with more tales of the wondrous sights she would see when they arrived in the offshore islands.

"Your eyes will see creatures that exist nowhere else in the world. There are giant lizards, tortoises and sharks as big as a whale," he promised, "and I will make a pair of leather flippers for your feet, so you can swim more easily, and dive to the bottom to play and search for shells." Ohnalee thought it would be nice to have a pair of sandals as well so she could venture farther away from the water. I'll ask him to do that, *she mused.*

Sometimes they stopped to rest at small islands and groups of rocks along the route where Ohnalee begged Mokeema to sleep in the open air under the stars rather than below in the underwater caverns and ledges the Mer people preferred. Mokeema laid down a blanket of sealskin to cushion Ohnalee's tender white skin, and they curled together in the darkness, looking up at a starry sky. Mokeema was tender and loving, rubbing Ohnalee's back as they rested, seeming to know exactly how to use his fingertips to ease her discomfort and weariness. His strong, cool fingers searched out the painful spots on Ohnalee's back, massaging deep to quiet the snakes coiled tightly within, making them relax so Ohnalee could rest.

Ohnalee filled her lungs with the cool salty air, thinking how much better her body felt at sea level. Even though she had adjusted well to life in the deep, it was still a joy to be human with her mate by her side. Ohnalee frowned for a moment, knowing the migration to southern waters and back to the Pacific Northwest would tax her body and spirit twice every year. She remembered how she used to dread the bumpy journey to Florence, and smiled, thinking how ridiculously easy that now seemed.

"No matter, dearest one," Ohnalee whispered lovingly, "wherever you travel, I will go with you; wherever you stay, I will be by your side. Your people are now my people, my love, as it was foretold in the holy book." Ohnalee kissed her man tenderly, her heart so full of love and emotion she could not resist the temptation to sing.

> *I will follow you,*
> *Follow you where ever you may go,*
> *I'll swim any ocean to stay by your side,*
> *The path may be stormy,*
> *But I will stay with you.*

Ohnalee did not regret her decision to leave her home in Oregon, feeling it was her destiny to be one of the "wanderers" who are happiest moving from one place to another. Not for her, life in a small cabin, going to church on Sundays, living as others thought she should. She wanted and needed the excitement of change, and life with the Merfolk was a constant challenge for survival. She chose to leave with Mokeema of her own free will and never looked back.

We are two parts of the same individual, she thought, one incomplete without the other.

It was almost four weeks later when the tribe arrived at the archipelago where they wintered every year. Mokeema was jubilant as he raced toward the steep, mountainous island with the moon-shaped harbor he preferred. Other tribes wintered on some of the other cays, but Mokeema said his people had been coming here for untold centuries. It was their special place, he said, where they felt safe as the animals here had no predatory nature and were unafraid of the Mer. Only the great white shark, their mortal enemy, presented a danger, but they seldom appeared in the area.

Ohnalee was exhausted by the long voyage, and her birthing time was near, so Mokeema set the people to work to prepare a comfortable place where she could rest after the delivery. On the western side of the harbor, close to the water's edge yet protected from the wind by craggy formations of rock streaked with reddish brown colorations, was a snug cave. Approaching from the open sea, a swimmer could easily enter the cave, gliding close over the top of a colorful shallow coral reef, teeming with schools of elegant blue tang, black angelfish, and red snapper.

The people understood that breaking off pieces of the coral was like destroying a living organism, so they avoided flipping their powerful tails as they passed over, also being careful not to touch the stands of red coral that would burn the skin. The people knew it was important to guard and protect the environment. Once inside the cavern, Ohnalee saw a flat rocky shelf where she could be snug and dry.

The interior walls of the cavern and the ceiling were illuminated by beams of sunlight flooding through a square opening in the rock at the side, painting the surface in shades of purple, pink, and green. This window, facing west, opened to a rocky beach on the outside, and as Ohnalee peered out, she could see the crimson face of the sun as it approached the horizon, flashing green as it dipped beneath the sea.

Just off the rocky beach, brown pelicans floated in schools of tiny flashing fish so dense it was impossible to see the sea bottom beneath. Other pelicans soaring overhead, took aim on their prey, then dove down kamikaze style, hitting the water with such force that the tiny fish were stunned, a sort of mercy killing since they were immediately scooped up and swallowed whole. Fat white seagulls landed on the backs of the pelicans, screeching "share, share", as others crowded next to the pelicans, gorging themselves with the kill.

Dense green vines, intertwined with wild orchids, hung in colorful tangles from the high cliffs overhanging the beach, and from the top, calls of tropical birds were caught on the breeze, their voices reaching the interior of the cavern.

Ohnalee beamed with approval, wrapping her arms around Mokeema's broad shoulders, kissing his lips and rubbing her nose against his. Then Mokeema took a short step back from this affectionate moment to instruct his people in the preparation of the nest for the baby after the birthing.

The people searched along the rocky ledges along the water, collecting hundreds of soft feathers from numerous species of birds, some of which were as soft as goose down, piling them carefully on the rocky platform inside the cave. Over this fluffy cushion, soft and supple sealskins were stretched, providing comfort for the human and the baby soon to come.

Mokeema and Ohnalee reclined on the flat rocky ledge when the nest was finished. They curled their bodies, fitting together like two spoons, with only a blanket of stars to illuminate their love and contentment, and in the morning, on the day before the full moon, Ohnalee felt rhythmic sharp pangs in her belly, a sure sign her time was near. Mokeema called several of the women to instruct in the giving of birth, according to their traditions. They suggested that Mokeema leave, joining the males, as was the custom, but he refused to go, saying he would stay close and observe all.

BLACK ANGEL FISH

Chapter 21

PRINCESS AQUENAE MAGENA

O *hnalee's natural inclination was to remember how women gave birth in Oregon rather than learn new ways, but the women convinced her their way would be less painful, quicker, and better for the baby. Ohnalee had often seen birthing, human style, with the woman on her back in bed, with only women in attendance while the men stayed out of the way. Sometimes they were told to boil water, and this task seemed to make them feel needed. Ohnalee remembered her aunt holding on to a piece of rope tied to the headboard of the bed, screaming in pain as the baby came.*

Women of the sea tribe gave birth underwater as they knew the warm salty water felt soothing to the birthing mother. The feeling of weightlessness calmed and tranquilized the mother, diminishing her pain as the contractions tightened. They said they had a ritual that would divert Ohnalee's attention so she could relax and go with the pangs, allowing the baby to move smoothly from the birthing canal. Ohnalee learned that once the baby was gulping air, it would immediately be taken down under the water for a few minutes until it was breathing easily underwater as well.

Ohnalee knew the importance of this birth as Mokeema would succeed his mother as ruler, and after his reign, his child would take the power. If the child had dominant human characteristics, it would be more difficult to adjust and integrate, particularly to the long journey back to the winter hunting grounds.

Mokeema and several women of the tribe gathered in the warm clear water of the sea cave, taking Ohnalee's hands and leading her outside into the sunlight.

"Swim, swim," the women counseled as they joined hands, making a long line, with Ohnalee in the middle. Mokeema held her right hand as they swam along the bottom of the seafloor, about thirty-five feet below the surface, passing over small brown starfish and larger knobby yellow ones resting in the sea grass by rose-coral flowers exquisite as fine porcelain. Moray eels and puffer fish peeked curiously from dark holes in the reef while schools of blue and black tang performed their graceful underwater ballet, sometimes barely moving as if suspended from invisible strings, then suddenly sprinting off together to a new location. Green sea turtles joined the people in this birthing dance, and a few of the children hitched a ride on these friendly creatures, holding tightly to their shells as they surfaced to get a breath of air.

Fat yellowtail snappers cruised the area, sometimes accompanied by green and purple parrot fish whose faces seemed to be frozen in a permanent smile, but Ohnalee loved the elegant black angelfish best of all.

Two immense rays glided gracefully along just above the swimmers, and Ohnalee thought she had never seen anything so beautiful. Their upper bodies were inky black with white spots, and Ohnalee could see the white underbodies as they soared smoothly and fluidly, almost without effort, through the clear sky of the ocean.

"We call these magnificent animals the eagles of the sea," Mokeema said, "but treat them with respect, always keeping a safe distance, as contact with the sharp barb at the end of their tails could result in death."

Despite the pangs in her belly, Ohnalee found herself grinning with amusement as the line of swimmers led her through dense schools of tiny minnows, past the seagulls and pelicans who seemed oblivious to their presence.

"Swimming will make the child come faster," the women advised Ohnalee, "and soon you will spin as the whale people do when giving birth."

Ohnalee paused from time to time, squeezing Mokeema's hand firmly, gritting her teeth and grimacing as the contractions came ever closer and more intense. Finally, when she felt as if she could swim no longer, the line of sea people began swimming round and round in a large circle, holding Ohnalee's arms outstretched, whirling and twirling her body faster and faster, as if she were a top.

They spun her all the way from the bottom, and when her face broke the surface of the water, Ohnalee's child was born. Mokeema caught the child in his arms but held her face out of the water until she took her first lusty breath of air.

The infant squealed loudly, and a triumphant grin danced upon Mokeema's handsome face. Ohnalee watched anxiously as her infant disappeared beneath the water in the arms of her father. Several minutes passed before he surfaced with a loud whoop, holding the baby high for all to see.

"See here, the Princess," he shouted to all, gently placing the baby back in the water, "behold this child of two worlds, my daughter, and my heir."

Ohnalee watched with amazement as her tiny baby bobbed comfortably at her father's side, first floating lazily, then with a flip of her tiny tail, diving deep.

"She is beautiful, my baby," Ohnalee exalted, "a true child of the people." A look of sadness shadowed her lovely face for an instant as she wondered if she would ever see her mother again and wished her Mom could see this grandchild and share her happiness.

Mokeema led Ohnalee back to the sea cave, positioning her lovingly on the soft cushioned ledge, then gave his daughter to her mother's warm arms so Ohnalee could investigate every part of her new baby's anatomy. All mothers think their babies are beautiful, but everyone agreed this was the most flawless infant anyone had ever seen. Several of the women in the tribe had given birth since their arrival in the enchanted islands, but these children all had the olive skin, high cheekbones, thin pointed noses, soulful dark eyes, and black hair of the people.

The child of Ohnalee and Mokeema had skin the color of snow and a full head of curly black hair streaked with strands of green and silver. Her large round lavender eyes, rimmed with long thick ebony lashes, glowed in the dim light of the cave's interior. The high cheekbones and facial structure resembled the face of her father, but below her waist, this child radiated color. The tiny scales of her lower body were incandescent with luminous flashes of pale green and darker shades of purple. All agreed this child was indeed a gift from the gods, a being to be treasured and honored.

That night, Ohnalee and Mokeema swam with their child as the bright white light of the moon shone down on the quiet waters of the bay. Although she had been birthed but a few hours ago, this tiny person already displayed a mischievous spirit and independent mind. At first she stayed close beneath Mokeema's body, but soon she was swimming free, flipping her wee tail from side to side, igniting bioluminescent flashes that twinkled in the darkness.

"She will be a force to deal with," her proud father pronounced as he watched the child dive deep, playfully winding her way along the top of the reef, then putting her baby finger to the top of a sea anemone which quickly withdrew from her touch.

Ohnalee did not realize the full importance of her standing as the mother of this wondrous child until she received a visit from the priestess of the tribe, accompanied by her faithful companion and secretary, Eagalia.

Eagalia followed Magdalena Meda everywhere, ready to assist with any job, no matter how small. The two were inseparable as Magdalena Meda trusted her friend to help organize the many details of her busy life. Eagalia had a brilliant mind and considered Meda to be her teacher and guide to the workings of the spiritual world in and beyond the kingdom of the sea. Eagalia believed, without a doubt, that her mentor was a gifted prophet and healer, worthy of her total love and devotion. She had no life of her own to speak of, no other friends or family, but seemed content to dedicate herself heart and soul to Meda.

She is my soul mate, *Eagalia thought,* and I will serve her until the spirits call her to be with them in the afterworld.

"Don't be foolish," Meda huffed, clearly hearing her friends words, "when I pass over to the land of our fathers, I will send another who will steal your heart and take my place."

Eagalia knew better to argue with Meda, and despite the knowledge that her prophesies were usually correct, found that difficult to believe.

Ohnalee knew it was customary for Magdalena Meda to bless a new child before choosing the name by which it would be known, as her dreams *and visions were believed to be messages from the Great Spirit. The powerful voice of this seer was heard and respected by the old queen, who listened intently to her advice in all things.*

When the seer saw Ohnalee's baby, she knelt, touching her brow to the seafloor.

"I give thanks to the Great Mystery," Magdalena Meda prayed, "for this messenger from the ancestors. This child will be a link between two worlds and a blessing to our people.

Give thanks," she chanted, her voice loud in Ohnalee's mind, "this is a child of the ancient ones, a creature of the gods. Her name will be Aquenae, meaning 'peace,' and Magena, 'daughter of the moon'."

Ohnalee smiled, putting the child to her breast, suckling her as human mothers have always done as other members of the tribe came to pay homage. In the days following the birth she welcomed the peace and tranquility of the islands, often taking the child with her when she left the water to wander on the white sands, whispering soft words of love and assurance to the infant. She discovered the child could communicate with the voice of a human child as well as telepathically, so Ohnalee sang the same lullabies her mother crooned to her, so long ago. She was happy her child would speak both the human tongue and the mind-centered language of the Mer. Being bilingual was a good thing.

Two frisky chipmunks scampered up and down a tree near Margaret Rose, but she was not aware of their chattering antics, as memories unfolded, one page following another, one experience after another, flashing bright with visions of life with Mokeema and his tribe. *I remember Magena,* she murmured, then laughing out loud at the joy of it.

GATHERING CONCH

Chapter 22

MAGENA'S SURPRISE

*T*he newborn infants of the tribe grew strong and flourished and soon a giggling troop of children swam happily in the clear waters, led by the Princess Aquenae Magena, who was called simply Magena. Mer children grew quickly, becoming about the size of an eight-year-old human child within months. Ohnalee learned it had always been this way since ancient times since this immediate growth provided some measure of protection from their enemies. The new batch of children would be able to swim safely next to their parents by the time of the migration north, although they still had much to learn from the adults in the tribe. Ohnalee noticed the children of the Mer were adored by their mothers and spoiled by their grandparents, in much the same way as human children.

During one of her first explorations ashore, Ohnalee was excited to see dense stands of bananas and mangos growing in lush groves close to the beach. Here in this oasis of plenty, she discovered citrus fruits of many kinds, including sweet miniature pineapples, which were a delicious addition to her diet.

Just beyond the vegetation of the shoreline, Ohnalee found several clear springs where the water was effervescent with crystal-clear bubbles. Following *the rivers leading from these springs, she discovered one waterfall that tumbled down from high cliffs into the sea and another which thundered into a clear pool of dark blue water. She threw herself headlong into the water, splashing happily, then made her way beneath the falling water on a narrow ledge where she could peek out at the world, unseen by anyone who appeared. The sparkling water was cool and delicious to the taste, and Ohnalee still enjoyed this human necessity even though she could go months without it while under the sea. These islands were truly enchanted in more ways than one.*

The Merfolk had never eaten fruit while they were in the winter islands as they had not ventured from the sea into the area where these were found. Mokeema said they had seen coconuts floating in the water and often threw them at each other, in a playful game, but did not know they could be eaten. Ohnalee gathered the nuts from the ground under the tall palms, then showed the people how to open the shells by forcefully dashing them down on a sharp rock.

She demonstrated how to peel away the tough outer fibers, then used a sharp piece of coral to puncture the eye, so they could taste the sweet milk inside. After the first tasting of the milk, the people craved it, constantly begging Ohnalee to go ashore to get the nuts. Ohnalee used a sharp rock to dig and gouge at the firm white flesh, shredding it into succulent piles, then showed the Mer how to break the meat into pieces for a crunchy and delicious snack.

Baby Magena was especially fond of bananas, impatiently biting through the skin with her sharp baby teeth, not bothering to peel away the wrapper as Ohnalee had taught her.

"More, more," Magena demanded, pointing her finger at the hill where the stands of bananas grew in abundance.

"Not now, Magena," Ohnalee scolded, "Mama has to go with Poppi to find some conch for the evening meal. Stay here and play in the shallows with the other children until I return."

"No, no," she protested, "Magena go with you."

"Don't be so disobedient," Ohnalee begged. "Tell you what—you can recline on the rocky ledge and comb your hair in the warm sunshine while I am gone. Later you can help tenderize the conch by pounding it on the rocks."

"Don't want to comb hair," Magena pouted, sticking out her plump lower lip. Ohnalee watched with amusement as her head strong child clenched her

157

chubby fists, smacking her tail on the surface of the water, sending sparkling plumes of spray in all directions.

"That won't work with me, girl," Ohnalee laughed, taking Magena by the hand, gently but firmly placing her on a flat rock in the sun.

"Your father and I will return shortly; don't cry now, Miss Wild Child," scolded Ohnalee as she glided out into the deeper water where Mokeema and some of the others were already gathering conch off the bottom.

What a temper that one has, *Ohnalee mused, a grin on her beautiful face as she spotted a large conch lying in the sea grass about thirty feet down. Ohnalee was wearing a sling which hung from her shoulders. It was made of sealskin and could be used to carry a child as well as any other food or items that the people salvaged. She glided along the bottom, picking up large queen conch as she swam, and when her sling was filled to capacity, she and Mokeema headed for the shore to harvest the shellfish for dinner.*

The people loved the delicious white body of the conch, especially since Ohnalee had invented a new method of tenderizing the meat. Normally they pounded the conch against the rocks until it broke apart, then pulled out the snail-like creature from its pink-lined shell, which they later used for making jewelry. They sliced the meat using a sharp shell, then pounded it with a rock until it was tender. The men believed that eating the "pistola" of the slimy slug would make them virile and bring many children. Ohnalee scoffed at this idea, watching with disgust as they swallowed the clear pencil-like protrusion, thinking, Men will be men, in any culture.

Ohnalee discovered that squeezing the juice from the small round yellow limes which grew on the island would make the conch tender, almost as if it had been cooked. This technique brought a whole new dimension to the menu, and Ohnalee wished she could bring a supply of the fruit to Oregon when she returned. At first Mokeema and the people thought it was silly to go to all this trouble just to change the taste of a perfectly delicious piece of seafood, but after several meals developed a liking for this strange new concoction.

When Ohnalee and Mokeema surfaced close to the beach, they were astounded to see their daughter standing by the water's edge with a stalk of small fig bananas in her hand and a mischievous smile on her elfish face.

"Got my own bananas, Poppi," she announced, racing toward her parents with a triumphant grin on her face. Then, with one graceful leap, Magena dove into the water.

Ohnalee and Mokeema gasped at this demonstration. They had just seen their daughter run toward them on two beautiful human legs, then transform in seconds back to her Mer form. Her shimmering purple and green tail flashed in the water as she dove deep, taking the bananas below.

"By the gods," Mokeema exalted, "this girl is indeed a miracle as the shaman has foretold. She will be the bridge between two people, truly walking in both worlds, bringing peace as is her name."

"We know," Mokeema said, "that some special children can be either human or Mer. This ability appears suddenly, sometimes years after birth; it is one of the great mysteries of our people. Magena has only to sit in the sun until dry for her human characteristics to overpower the Mer. Then she may walk on the land as a human, but when she wishes can return to the sea, being as one of the people again."

The implications of this staggering discovery made Ohnalee dizzy with excitement. Magena could walk with her mother on the land as well as swim with her under the sea. Now, Ohnalee saw a new world of limitless opportunities for her child, and she wondered where Magena would choose to live her life.

"Do any other members of the tribe have this gift?" Ohnalee asked Mokeema, wondering why her child was so unique.

"The Queen, my mother, can walk among humans in this way, and so can Magdalena Meda," Mokeema said.

"Mother has lived on the land at different times during her life but always returned to the sea. At this stage of her life, she has no desire to leave her people."

"And Magdalena Meda has done the same?" Ohnalee inquired, wondering if she would be able to talk with the shaman about her experiences.

"Yes, at many times," Mokeema said, "often with my mother."

"Are there others in the tribe who can do this?" Ohnalee persisted, even though Mokeema looked impatient with the conversation.

"None that we know," Mokeema declared with a sad look on his face, "and it is mostly for the females, this gift, usually not for the males."

Ohnalee realized Mokeema understood this was a part of his daughter's life he might never share, and the knowledge was hurtful.

"I will be with you always, my love," Ohnalee reassured her mate, "and we will worry together if Magena decides to spend time on the land when she reaches full maturity."

Soon it was spring, and time to return to their northern hunting grounds, but the journey north was easier this time for Ohnalee, and she was anxious to return to her home in the deep waters off the Oregon Coast. Mokeema and Ohnalee taught Magena to be proud of her biracial heritage so she would respect both cultures, so she could fulfill her destiny to become a connection between the two races in the future.

My daughter, my baby, Margaret Rose cried, remembering her child, and longing for her touch.

SEA TURTLE

Chapter 23

QILLAC

*T*he following fall, Ohnalee was pregnant for the second time, but the journey south felt familiar now, and she was happy her second child would be birthed in the sea outside the beautiful cave. This time, a boy was born to Ohnalee and Mokeema after a fast and easy delivery. He was strong and beautiful, with the same black hair as his father, and instantly adapted to underwater breathing.

The shaman named him Qillac, placing him under the protection of the sea lion clan as she dreamed of a sea lion the night before his birth. Qillac's large round black eyes did indeed look like those of the sea lions, but when he was agitated or wanted food, the eyes came alive with deep purple or green flashes, like his father and sister. His skin was darker than his sister's, more like the olive skin of Mokeema. Aquenae Magena was proud of her new brother and immediately took over, bossing him about ruthlessly, leading him to her favorite reefs and sea caves where she and her friends loved to play. Qillac did not often communicate verbally as did his mother and sister, but Ohnalee heard her child's voice clearly in her mind, as she did his father's.

Mokeema, his Mother, and all the other members of the tribe habitually raised their voices in song when happy, afraid, or melancholy. Their songs expressed every possible aspect of their feelings, but the high-pitched tones were more like those of the violin, the harp, or the flute. When the people sang while relaxing and reclining on rocky perches above the water, seabirds responded, screeching in harmony.

Aquenae Magena's lyrical soprano voice, which combined human sounds with the tones of her father's people, blended beautifully with this chorus, bringing tears to Ohnalee's eyes. No legend could have imagined the beauty of such a voice, and Ohnalee had no doubt this glorious sound could indeed entrance and entice any human to follow. Perhaps the stories of sailors being lured to their deaths by sea sirens were true, *she mused.*

Margaret Rose remembered that she often thought about her life on the Oregon Coast, especially when she was teaching the children. During her first winter in the enchanted islands, she discovered the children were very curious about her presence, wanting to know where she came from, what it was like living there, and what games she played.

At first, only a few children came to talk and listen as she told them about her dog, her brother and sisters, and her parents, but they seemed fascinated with her stories, and before long brought their siblings and friends to the "learning time." Ohnalee had enjoyed teaching the children at the schoolhouse at Heceta Head, and Mokeema agreed it would be a good thing for the Mer children to learn more about the world above the sea.

At first the sessions were loosely organized, but then Ohnalee began to take her job much more seriously. Two-hour classes were held at a certain time every day, but the children came early so they wouldn't miss anything. Ohnalee taught them about the history of the world, adding in some simple mathematical ideas and a little science. She found the children to be headstrong but artistic, and before long they were making simple jewelry and drawing pictures on the walls of some of the caverns in the area. The adults were all in favor of the school as it gave them a few hours of freedom from the mischievous imps who were their children.

Ohnalee's children joined the classes after their birth, and Magena soaked up knowledge like a giant sea sponge. Qillac was slower, often finding it hard to compete with other children his age, particularly if the task involved speaking out in class in front of his other classmates. Qillac was a boy of few words but had a loving heart. Older sister Magena helped with his studies and proudly cheered him on as he excelled at sports and martial games. All males trained in military tactics as they knew they could be called on to defend their people against more warlike tribes.

One day Ohnalee led the younger children on an excursion to explore some shallow rocky ledges close to the shore. Although she did not know the proper names of the various kinds of corals, she enjoyed pointing out all the different varieties, showing the children how to glide carefully over the tops, avoiding any contact which could cut or burn them. As the exuberant troop swished and frolicked over the sandy bottom close to the reef, Ohnalee spotted a narrow opening in the rocks. Outside the hole was a pile of small shells, emptied of their previous occupants. Carefully she peered inside, slightly nervous at the possibility of disturbing a green or brown moray eel, but instead, she discovered the dwelling was inhabited by a small octopus. The creature was a light brown color, with a body about the size of a large melon, and as Ohnalee and the children watched, one of his tentacles protruded from the cave, displaying his round suction cups. The children were very excited, pushing and shoving to be the next to peer into the cavern until the animal took fearful flight, disappearing into the dark depths of his rocky home.

Ohnalee found a small fighting conch shell nestled in the sand and positioned the shell just outside the hole. She told the children they would return the next day to see if the octopus had accepted their gift as this kind of animal loved to dine on the delicious juicy contents of shells like the conch. When they arrived in the afternoon, they found the conch empty.

"He likes the tasty meat from the shells," Ohnalee smiled, "so we will bring him another treat on our next visit." As the weeks went by, the children continued to bring shells for their new friend, hoping that one day they would see him emerge from the hole to take the shells for his dinner. The visit to the Octopus Cavern became a highlight of every day, and finally, they saw the creature reach out from its' hiding place. The powerful suction cups on his arms seized the shell firmly, then pulled it quickly inside, out of sight. The children danced and sang in an abundance of enthusiasm, hoping that one day the octopus would come all the way out of the hole.

One of the older boys of the tribe heard about the octopus feeding and followed the children on their daily visit. He watched as the little ones placed another conch near the entrance and grinned as the creature slowly emerged to take the gift. This time, the octopus glided slowly out of the cavern, thrilling the children as they took their first good look at their new friend. The octopus seemed to look at the children, and they gasped as he took the shell. Then disaster struck.

The older boy was carrying a spear fashioned from a long straight stick with a sharp tip carved from a piece of dead coral. The tip was attached with thin strips of dried sealskin, making an instrument perfect for self-defense or food gathering. The boy came in fast and hard, plunging the tip of the spear directly into the center of the octopus's fat round body. It died instantly, its tentacles quivering before it was finished.

The wicked boy pulled the animal from the seafloor, drawing back the spear, then hurling the dead octopus up onto the sandy shore. The children cried and moaned, striking at the boy with their fists, but he pushed them away easily, laughing as he swam away.

Ohnalee was sad and shocked when the children told her about the murder of the octopus. This was a tragic lesson that showed them how little respect some people had for life.

"Never kill for fun," Ohnalee begged the children. "Life is precious, and the gods love all their creatures." She put her arms around the devastated children, hugging and kissing them with great affection. Mokeema just laughed when she told him about the incident. "Don't worry about that boy, my love, he'll make a great warrior."

Ohnalee thought a lot about her parents, especially when she was telling the children about how human families lived. She especially remembered the mundane events of her childhood, like snuggling on her mother's lap as they rocked back and forth on the wooden chair on the porch. The memory was so sharp she could almost smell the flowers in the gardens around the lighthouse, and she wondered if her parents were well and if they ever thought of her.

Mother knew that one day I would go, *she reasoned, suspecting she knew about her daughter's true heritage. She remembered her mom's warning not to spend so much time at the beach and her relief when she agreed to be married.* She didn't have to watch me so closely, *Ohnalee thought,* when I became the responsibility of Minister Coombs.

Chapter 24

A QUEEN'S SACRIFICE

*A*gain *the winter months passed quickly, but at the end of February, a terrible event occurred that would change life forever. The people had chosen this island as their annual winter residence as it was far from any human contamination, but this year, the solitude was destroyed by the arrival of a large sailing vessel that appeared at the mouth of their favorite harbor. The ship was flying a large black flag with a white skull and crossbones, and the people worried as they watched it approach, drawing closer and closer to the shore, finally dropping an enormous anchor from the bow. From their vantage point beneath the waves, the merfolk saw the anchor crash onto a beautiful stand of staghorn coral, breaking and pulverizing the branches, destroying everything it touched before settling to the bottom. Lengths of heavy chain then followed the anchor, the iron links dragging ruthlessly across the coral as the ship was caught broadside by a strong gust. After plowing a path of destruction across the reef, the anchor finally held fast as the vessel came up into the wind, pointing her nose to the beach.*

When the vessel was safely settled, the crew dropped heavy rope ladders down her side, then lowered a small wooden boat into the water, tying it alongside the dark hull of the boat.

Several of the bearded brawny pirates threw themselves over the side into the harbor, bellowing and splashing while others seemed content to stay aboard, lifting brown bottles of rum and grog to their lips and singing loudly. After baiting large hooks with dangling strips of salt pork, several crew members tossed hand lines into the water, hoping to catch a few large red snappers for dinner. Most of the crew were so occupied they did not notice the three men who grunted and groaned as they manhandled several heavy iron chests into the tender. The boat rode low in the water as the men rowed slowly toward the entrance of the sea cave.

Ohnalee and the children fled from the cave to the far side of the harbor, and as they watched fearfully, the men entered the cave, pushing off the sides of the entrance with the oars as they disappeared from view. Ohnalee was relieved; it was late morning so the interior of the cave would not be well illuminated as she worried the men might see evidence of their presence. When the dinghy reappeared, only two men were visible, and the boat showed some of her bottom as if some heavy object had been left behind in the cave.

The people hid quietly in the deepest part of the harbor in small caves, and on rocky ledges, waiting until night to feed, terrified they might be seen by the scurvy-looking lot of pirates who crewed the ship. The youngest members of the tribe chafed at this sudden restriction of their freedom, longing to get loose from their parents to take a closer look at the mysterious intruder. None of them had ever seen such a ship before, and as most children are, were fearless, unbelieving that anything could actually hurt them.

Late in the afternoon, several of the older children found an opportunity to escape when their parents were momentarily distracted by a large killer whale that entered the harbor. Most killer whales were the enemies of the people, but this one seemed uninterested in their presence. It passed silently overhead, casting a dark shadow, then moved away from the area.

The Queen Mother was swimming toward the area where she had last seen Mokeema and Ohnalee, having slipped away from the four Guardians who were responsible for her safety. Sometimes Maru grew weary of the constant surveillance her position required, and it became a game to see if she could escape the Guardian's watchful eyes, if only for a few moments. She would say she planned to nap for a while in her chambers, leaving her watchers stationed at the door, then slipping out by a narrow passageway. Often she donned a brown sealskin cape, pulling the hood down over her eyes so she could pass unnoticed among her people. Freedom was exciting and stimulating.

After all, I'm a queen, *she thought,* and I can do what I like.

As she neared her son's location, Queen Maru was the only person who saw the children swim toward the ship, their small bodies undulating as their tiny tails swished from side to side. By instinct, she quickly followed, with no fear for her own safety.

The children came up under the bottom of the pirate ship, gliding along the keel, their faces curious as their fingers traced along the bottom of this mysterious hard object. The Queen swam up beneath them, grabbing two of the urchins by their tails, motioning sternly for them to go below, but two others, surprised and confused, splashed to the surface, alongside the boat, thus announcing their existence to the ship's crew.

"By god, me hearties," one of the pirates growled, pointing to the water, "what the hell kind of sea monsters are those I'm seeing with me own good eyes?"

In seconds, other men ran to the rail, pointing at the two sea children who were plainly visible.

"Kill 'em, kill 'em," they howled, scrambling to grab the two heavy harpoons that always stood ready for use.

The men drew back their arms, then hurled, aiming for the children. One of the harpoons hit the water, narrowly missing its target as the Queen threw herself in front of the children's retreating forms.

"Go, go," she screeched in terror as the second harpoon landed hard in the center of her back, inflicting a mortal wound.

"I hit one, hit one," gleefully screamed one of the shooters, frantically hauling in the heavy length of line attached to the harpoon, dragging the Queen closer to the boat.

"My god," he muttered, making the sign of the cross on his brow, "what abomination is this?"

Several of the men then hastily scrambled down into the dinghy, pulling the body alongside.

"A female," they grunted, "but not human, this thing with the breasts of a woman and the tail of a fish."

Hearing the commotion, the captain stomped from his cabin, barefoot and furious at this interruption of his enjoyment of the female prisoner who was confined to his cabin. The pirate was a fearsome and disgusting sight as he pulled up his britches and fastened the front of the loose trousers that reached just below his knee. It was not an easy job as the man's bulging belly protruded over his belt, making the bronze buckle almost invisible to the eye. A frizzy black beard hung in tangles over his hairy chest despite an obvious attempt to control the growth by twisting it into ringlets tied with bits of hemp. The black kerchief tied round his head protected the captain's bald dome from the sun and helped to control the greasy locks which hung down his back, coiling like tiny snakes around massively muscled shoulders and arms which were covered with colorful tattoos of naked women and grinning skulls.

"What the hell," the captain roared as he clapped his leather tricornered hat on top of his head, getting his first glance at the sad dead creature whose blood now flowed in torrents from her wound, staining the clear waters of the harbor.

"You've killed a mermaid, you sniveling lot of half-wits," bellowed the captain, "and now bad luck will follow us forever.

You frigging idiots," he screamed, "I'll have your mangy hides.

Give me the miserable bilge rat who did this," he demanded, "and I'll flay his back to ribbons before he walks the plank as a peace offering to the gods of the sea.

This thing's fiendish friends will slaughter us in our beds as we sleep, then sink this ship to the bottom of the sea," he ranted as beads of sweat ran down his brow, and frothy bubbles of drool foamed from the side of his mouth.

"Give me that dam fool, I tell ya," he screeched frantically, grabbing the cat-o'-nine-tails from a large hook by the helm.

The poor unfortunate soul who harpooned the Queen was dragged across the deck by two of his mates, who slammed him hard against the mainmast, his back facing the captain. The first mate tied him tightly, then ripped the shirt from his body, waiting for the captain to give the order.

"Twenty strong lashes, then into the sea he goes," the captain ordered as the sailor screamed for mercy. His body shook convulsively as the cruel lash fell over and over, cutting his flesh, sending blood splattering in every direction.

"No mercy for you, moron," he shouted, "you've brought down the wrath of the sea gods upon all of us. Over you go, and good riddance. The captain laughed like a maniac as the crew dragged the helpless man to the rail and threw him into the sea.

"Get down on your scurvy knees and beg, you imbeciles," the captain raged, "pray we can escape from this anchorage with our lives."

The doomed sailor splashed frantically in the water, begging and crying as the blood from his tattered back mixed with the blood of the murdered sea queen, turning the water a dark sapphire red. "No, no," he pleaded, seeing large fins cutting through the water in his direction. As the sharks attacked ferociously, the water around the sailor exploded as arms and legs were torn from his body. Other body parts appeared, then disappeared, leaving small white patches of skin and bone floating in the horrid frothy pink layer of foam and bubbles on the top of the water. The large fish fought each other for the big meaty parts, tearing, and gobbling, then swallowing them whole. In seconds, the corpse disappeared completely, leaving only a few bits and pieces for the smaller fish to enjoy.

"Haul the anchor," the captain roared, taking the helm. "Make preparations to sail. We must leave these waters now, or we will be here forever."

"And the creature, what shall we do with the creature?" the sailors begged, quavering at the sight of her body, fearful the captain might decide a few more should die to compensate for this one miserable abomination.

"Leave her," he screamed, "let the sharks have the bitch, and ye better hope nothing remains. We must be gone from this place quickly before the fiends find she is gone."

The crew hoisted the mainsail as the captain tacked up over the anchor so the men could winch the heavy chain back up on deck. They sweated and strained, cursing and moaning with the effort, and when the anchor was in sight, they found its flukes were fouled with mud, large pieces of broken coral, and purple sea fans. It had to be cleaned before hauling it the rest of the way to the deck, so two crew scrambled out on the bowsprit carrying wooden buckets tied with strong lengths of rope. They threw the buckets down, filling them with briny water, then pulled them back up to splash on the anchor. When the mud was gone, one man scrambled down, agile as a monkey, and pulled the coral off the anchor, throwing it in the sea.

Even before the anchor was safely back on deck, the captain brought his ship about, turning stern to the beach as he fled the harbor, running before the wind toward the setting sun.

Meanwhile, down deep below the surface of the harbor, the children waited quietly, afraid to tell their parents they had disobeyed. They had no idea the

Queen had been killed and fearfully awaited her arrival. What punishment was in store, they wondered, staying very obedient and quiet but expecting a lashing from the Queen's sharp tongue, at the very least.

After a short while, the Queen's Guardians approached Mokeema.

"The Queen has disappeared," they cried, "we can't find her anywhere."

"You are supposed to keep her safe, and she has made fools of you once again," Mokeema grumbled, his voice strained with worry.

"She's probably fine," Ohnalee said, "just taking a little private time for herself; you know how she likes to do her own thing once in a while."

"Follow me," Mokeema growled to the Guardians as he headed to the surface, leaving Ohnalee below. The men quickly scanned the area, surprised the ship was gone, but then they saw a ghastly thing floating on the surface of the water.

What Mokeema saw appeared to be a piece of an arm with a hand attached, and on that hand was a finger with a long curved nail and a ring with a blood red ruby. And there, in the shallow water near to the shore, left as if the sharks had eaten their fill and were saving a snack for later, was the mutilated head of the Queen Mother and her upper torso.

Ohnalee and the people, resting far below, then heard a sound so mournful it pierced the sea from top to bottom, and from one end of the earth to the other. Even the angels in heaven must have heard that awful cry of pain, that howling and wailing, that sorrowful sound that came from Mokeema's lips when he found his mother's corpse.

"Vengeance, vengeance," he moaned, pounding his chest and shaking his fist at the sky.

Ohnalee and the rest of the tribe rushed to the surface, knowing something terrible must have happened. They cried and moaned, paralyzed with terror, sickened and nauseated at the sight of the good Queen's remains. At first they thought the Queen had been killed by sharks, but then on closer investigation, they saw she had been speared from front to back.

Mokeema was almost insane with grief. Tears gushed from his expressive eyes as he swam round and round in circles in the deep water near his mother's pitiful remains, gathering speed until his body was almost invisible to the eye. Suddenly, with one powerful thrashing thrust of his mighty tail he came out of the water, almost twenty feet up in the air. "I invoke you, oh powerful god of wind and sea, find the beasts and send their ship to the bottom," Mokeema screamed, his clenched fists reaching toward the heavens. "Show them no mercy."

Hearing the voice of Mokeema, the god gave his answer, sending howling winds that created gigantic swells to overtake the fleeing ship. Great green waves almost as high as the mainmast, curling at the tops with foamy white crowns, engulfed the vessel, smashing and hammering the hull, which groaned and creaked from the stress. As the mighty storm raged, water flooded into the bilge from cracks in the seams, sending the ship's rats scrambling over the sailors in their bunks. The men rushed out onto the deck, slashing each other with their swords and knives as they fought to get to the lifeboats. In their haste, they tripped on the rats, who paused from their crazed frenzy to feast on the blood and flesh of the injured pirates. One extremely large gray rat actually ripped off the right ear of a pirate who was lying unconscious on the deck. The disgusting trophy still protruded from the rodent's bloody mouth as he slid out through a scupper hole into the sea.

The captain watched fearfully as his men fell on their knees, praying and begging for mercy, but it was to no avail. With a thunderous roar, one of the largest waves anyone had ever seen broke over the aft deck, washing the men from side to side in waist-deep water, smashing them against the masts and rails, then hurling their battered bodies over the side. The captain tied himself to the wheel, his face frozen in terror, and there he stayed as the boat broke into pieces, its remains falling deep to a cold watery grave. No lifeboat was launched, and no member of this crew would ever return to the enchanted islands or the treasure left there.

"It is done," Mokeema shouted, knowing his prayer had been answered.

With tears flowing from his dark eyes, Mokeema ordered his people to take the Queen to the sea cave where she could be laid to rest on the soft bed used after the birthing of his children.

"No one will ever see the inside of that cave again," he vowed. "We will seal it off with large boulders and logs. The Queen will rest, forevermore, in the darkness of the morning with the rays of the setting sun shining through the window of stone."

As the people entered the cave, bearing the remains of the Queen, they were surprised to see several large chests sitting in the darkness, far back

172

on the ledge in the interior of the cavern. Ohnalee swallowed her fear and being careful not to lose her balance on the slippery dark rocks, made her way to the trunks. She found them not to be locked and, opening the lids, stepped back in amazement as she saw the treasure inside. Two of the treasure boxes were so full of priceless jewelry and ornaments that their contents spilled over the top and onto the ground in glittering mounds. Ohnalee saw diamond necklaces and earrings, bracelets with rubies and emeralds, ropes of pearls, and heavy crosses of hammered gold with insets of precious stones. The other box contained a king's ransom of coins and large gold bars. A large silver chalice, inlaid with gems, was another of the many artifacts the pirates had hidden until a future time when they could return. Slumped by the side of the chests as if guarding the body was the gruesome corpse of a dead sailor. His head had been caved in by the bloody axe which lay by his side.

"Get him out of here. He is food for the sharks," ordered Mokeema. Two of the strongest males grabbed the sailor's feet, roughly dragging him out of the cave, towing his carcass far away from the island to the edge where the water changed from pale green to deep indigo blue.

After the ledge was cleaned and purified, Mokeema placed the pitiful remnants of his beloved mother carefully on the soft couch, remembering how happy he and Ohnalee had been in the cave after the birth of their children. The people covered Queen Maru with seaweed, then with a layer of clay from the shore outside. Ohnalee climbed through the window of the cave, onto the adjoining rocky beach, so she could pick the wild orchids that hung from the cliffs to decorate Big Maru's tomb.

After the grave was finished, Mokeema's warriors removed the coins from the chest, covering the body with their splendor, and then, over the gold, they heaped up all the remaining treasure. On top of these jewels, Ohnalee laid her blanket of wild orchids. It was indeed a mausoleum fit for a queen.

It took several weeks of hard work to move large boulders into place which would block off the entrance to the cave forever, and these boulders were then reinforced with heavy logs pulled from the beaches. When they were sure the Queen's remains were safe from intruders, Mokeema and his tribe sang the songs of leaving that would be heard in the heavenly houses of their ancestors. They sang of the Queen's accomplishments and virtues, sang of her good deeds and generous nature, and sang of their grief and sorrow.

For seven days and seven nights, Queen Maru's people sang and cried, refusing to eat or play, and when the time of remembrance was passed, the people accepted Mokeema as their king, guardian of his people, and Ohnalee as their queen. The two children watched sadly, but proudly, as their father accepted his mother's crown, but they did not understand what this really meant. Ohnalee was the first human ever to share the throne of the Pacific Mer with one of the Kings of the Sea.

MOKEEMA'S REVENGE

Chapter 25

MOKEEMA, RULER OF THE MER

He is so strong, Margaret thought, thinking how Mokeema took charge after the murder of his mother.

One of Mokeema's first priorities was to deal with the Guardians who had failed to provide the protection his mother deserved as he knew he would never again trust them to provide safety for any member of the royal family.

Rather than subject his traumatized people to the stress of a trial, Mokeema decided that banishment was a punishment his mother would have approved, so he sent the cringing Guardians from his sight, saying they were no longer welcome.

"Go, and do not return," he said sternly, "you have failed to do your duty, and this has resulted in the death of your queen. Do not show your faces in our lands again."

Mokeema and his family now had the constant protection of new Guardians, who vowed to give their lives rather than let harm come to the royal family. The disgraced Guardians eventually made their way to the land of the Dragon Mer where they begged the protection of Dragone.

"Why should I take you in?" he sneered. "How do I know you are not spies sent by Queen Maru?"

"We have information of interest, Sir Dragone," they said as they cowered in his presence.

"Tell me what news you bring. If I like it, you will live; if not, you will die."

"Queen Maru is dead," they whined, "and Mokeema has taken the throne with his mate."

"Good riddance," Dragone growled. "Is that all?"

"More, more, we have more," the Guardians stuttered, almost unable to speak.

"Out with it then. You are wasting my time and testing my patience," said Dragone as he drew his sword, brandishing it over their heads.

"Mokeema's mate may be of interest to you Sir. She is human and was taken near the lighthouse that stands on the cliff near the large sea cave."

Dragone's eyes flashed as he waved his hand in dismissal.

"That is all. You can stay, but I want to be kept informed of Mokeema and this woman."

Chapter 26

CAUGHT IN THE NET

*A*s the Mer returned to northern waters, word of the old queen's death reached ahead of the travelers, passed along by the sea lions, their good friends. Traveling through the different kingdoms of these animals, Mokeema and his tribe were welcomed with noisy cries and moans of grief. Mokeema accepted this tribute as a token of their respect.

When the travelers passed from the California coast to the Oregon Coast, they rested on a large offshore group of rocky cays just offshore of Coos Bay. Here, they spent several days socializing with another tribe of sea people, sharing food and listening to each other's songs. Ohnalee was pleased when her rival Stephania became enthralled with a male from the other tribe as it was difficult to deal with the woman's continuing fixation on Mokeema. Ohnalee felt she was always in the background, watching for any opportunity to step in when and if Mokeema found fault with his human mate. When she requested permission to leave, Mokeema happily gave his approval to the match, inviting the couple to visit whenever they came past their tribal area.

Mokeema, Ohnalee, and the two children were swimming with their Guardians and a sea lion escort as they passed the entry to the Siuslaw River *off the town of Florence. They noticed a fishing vessel in the area laying nets, but Mokeema's plan was to stay well away from the boat, passing to the west as they neared their summer home, only a few miles to the north.*

The family was wearing their hooded leather jackets, so the casual observer probably would not have distinguished them from the sea lions who were accompanying the group. Mokeema and the children moved quickly and easily in the water, but Ohnalee was cold and tired, resting from time to time as the rest of the travelers left her a short distance behind. She called for help, but the Guardians were concentrating more on the children than the adults, and her voice sounded like that of a seabird. Again, the Guardians failed to do their duty.

Ohnalee struggled to swim against the strong current that appeared to be setting toward shore when suddenly, she found herself surrounded by a barrier under the water.

With a terrified cry of recognition, Ohnalee realized she was entrapped in a large net, which trailed a long distance away from the fishing boat. She struggled to escape, screaming for Mokeema, but the net was moving swiftly, dragging her closer and closer to the vessel. Dive, dive, *she thought, going deep to see if she could swim under the net, but it was closed beneath her. Closer and closer the boat came, and she could see three men on the deck, hauling in the net.*

"Mokeema, help," she sobbed, being helpless to move as hundreds of large fish surrounded her body, almost crushing her with their weight.

Mokeema looked back, perplexed by the distant cry. It took only an instant to realize that Ohnalee was not close behind with her guardians, and he understood the danger immediately. Ohnalee had been caught up in the net and, unless he acted quickly, would be captured. Several of the Guardians and twenty sea lions followed Mokeema as he sped back to the south while others stayed with the children.

By the time the agitated group arrived on the scene, they could see Ohnalee caught up in the heavy knotted strands, struggling to get free. Mokeema and the others threw themselves at the net, hoping to break the fibers, but it was too strong.

"Go, go," shrieked Ohnalee as she saw the captain raise the shotgun to his shoulder, "go to the children, it is too late for me.

Flee quickly, they will kill you," she begged, "go, Mokeema."

The sea lions and Mokeema dove deep, just barely escaping the blast from the gun, but just before the net came up on deck over the wide rollers, a large wave struck the ship broadside, throwing the net against the side of the hull. Ohnalee's head was bashed so hard against the wooden planks that she lost consciousness.

Chapter 27

FINDING MOKEEMA

Margaret Rose sat on the porch of her cabin on the Oregon Coast, staring out at the sea as if waiting for an answer on what to do next. Now that the memory of the events of the last four years had returned in vivid detail, she knew for certain that the life of Ohnalee, Queen of the Mer, was not merely a dream or a figment of her imagination. Tears welled up, spilling from the corners of her sad blue eyes as she thought of the beautiful children who waited just beyond the horizon.

Ohnalee remembered the calls she had heard so many times since her return, those mysterious wailing sounds carried on the back of the wind, from the sea and up the cliffs, making her feel uneasy and depressed. "Motherrr, Motherrr," came the cries, catching at her heart, provoking an aching pain in her body that would not cease.

They have been calling to me, trying to get my attention, Ohnalee now realized, her body shaking uncontrollably. *My God, did they think I heard, but would not come? Perhaps that is why the sounds came so often when I first returned home but now are heard only now and then. They cannot know I was injured when captured,* she worried, *or that I lost all memory of them until now.* The thought that she would abandon her children willingly was almost more than she could bear as Margaret now sobbed loudly.

Magena came to find me, Ohnalee wept, remembering that day when she saw the strange girl peering through the window of the church. *And I did not recognize my own child.*

The flood of memories was almost overpowering as Ohnalee remembered the man who had been her best friend since childhood. *Mokeema, Mokeema,* she begged, *please speak to me, and let me know you are all right. Let me know you still love me.*

Now, coming up the path, Ohnalee saw the reverend, who was returning from a visit to the sickbed of one of his parishioners in Yachats. She struggled to calm her nerves, knowing she could not share this shocking revelation with her husband. He must never know, she decided as she waved and wiped her eyes, realizing she had made no preparations for supper.

"How is Mrs. Connett?" Ohnalee inquired, trying to show interest.

"Not well," he replied, "she would very much like to see you soon. Perhaps you could bake one of your delicious apple pies for her and go with me next week when I visit again."

"A good idea, dear," Ohnalee agreed, trying her best to concentrate as she followed the minister into the kitchen, gratefully accepting a fat red slab of salmon he received from one of the town's fishermen.

"I'll just put the kettle on and get some dinner ready for you quickly," Ohnalee said as she laid out the china cups and saucers. "It will take less than half an hour to make some salmon chowder," she promised, cutting out the eyes of four white potatoes, then slicing an onion and two carrots.

Those morels I picked earlier will go nicely with this dish, Ohnalee thought, dropping the potatoes into the boiling water, followed by the vegetables. In about fifteen minutes, the potatoes were slightly soft, so she laid the piece of salmon on top, then put the lid back on for a few more minutes. The mushrooms were quickly wiped with a kitchen towel before adding them to the pot for the last few minutes of cooking where they soaked up some of the stock, becoming plump and delicious. Just before serving, Margaret poured in a cup of heavy cream whisked with a touch of cornstarch to thicken the broth.

"Excellent, my dear," the minister raved, soaking a piece of bread in the stew, energetically licking his fingers.

"Why don't you eat something, Margaret?" her husband begged. "You are thin as a rail."

Ohnalee picked at the stew in her bowl, finally snagging a small piece of the fish with the spoon. As she raised the morsel to her lips, a flash of memory hit her so forcefully that she dropped the spoon, spilling the creamy white liquid onto the white tablecloth.

We don't eat the salmon. she remembered, almost gagging in disgust, *they are sacred to the people.*

Ohnalee scrambled to her feet, hastily dabbing at the spilled food with a corner of the kitchen towel.

"Sorry, husband," Ohnalee apologized, "my stomach is feeling queasy today, so I'll just have a cup of tea."

"Perhaps you could be pregnant, my dear," the minister suggested, not noticing the look of dismay that swept over his wife's face.

Ohnalee placed her hand on her belly, thinking, *It is a bit round these days, but surely one hasty act could not result in a pregnancy.* The idea was unthinkable, so she shoved the thought to the back of her mind where it could not interfere with her plan to get away as quickly as possible.

After the meal was cleared away, Ohnalee sat on the porch by herself while her husband read by lantern light. *Why doesn't he go to bed?* she thought, feeling itchy and impatient. After the minister was in bed, Ohnalee planned to go down the steep path to the sand and call for Mokeema.

He must hear me, he must, she agonized, her mind tormented with a vision of Mokeema riding on the foamy white top of a breaking green swell.

"You should turn in soon, dear," the minister suggested as he turned out the light before going to bed.

"I will, and thank you, sir, for being such a good and understanding man," Ohnalee replied in a soft quivering voice, not sure he had heard. *I may not be here in the morning*, she hoped, her heart pounding at the thought.

The moon was high in the sky, lighting the way down the sandy path to the beach as Ohnalee ran wildly toward her destiny. She seemed mindless of the stones and rocks along the way, feeling no pain as her bare feet were cut by the sharp points and edges.

"You must come, you must come," she chanted out loud, hoping Mokeema and the children would hear.

"I am here, and you must come," Ohnalee shouted to the sea, now sobbing as she reached the bottom of the path. Across the soft sand dunes she ran, stumbling several times until at last she reached the water's edge. Moonbeams danced on top of the gentle waves, illuminating the rocky ledges and caves along the shore, but there was no sign of either sea lions or Mokeema.

"I am Ohnalee," she screamed, "I am Queen Ohnalee, and I command you to come for me, Mokeema. Come, I beg you, my king. Come and take me home to our children, my love."

High on the cliff to the north of the beach where Ohnalee now stood, the beam from the lighthouse at Heceta Head swept the sea from side to side, warning of dangerous shoals, keeping mariners far offshore in the deep water. Margaret and her friends had played at the foot of this lighthouse since she was a child, often hiding in the darkness, sometimes imagining they saw the resident ghost pacing back and forth in the Light Tower. Now Ohnalee dropped to her knees in the surf, eyes searching the sea as the light illuminated the entire offshore area.

Hours passed and Ohnalee became more and more exhausted, finally retreating to higher ground as the tide came in full. Her frock was wet, and she shivered in the damp night air. Her teeth chattered loudly as she curled her body in the damp grass, knees to chest. After a few moments, fatigue and stress ruled as Ohnalee fell into a deep slumber, not seeing the thick marine layer of fog that moved over the land, enveloping her body like a fluffy gray blanket.

Gentle briny swells crept slowly toward Ohnalee, kissing the bottoms of her feet with soft salty tongues, yet still she slept, dreaming of soulful black eyes with flashing green jets of light and silvery voices calling her name.

Then the beam from the lighthouse spotlighted some activity in the water far out on the horizon. It seemed to be a school of large fish feeding or perhaps whales breeching and spouting or possibly sea lions playing in the moonlight. An observer might have thought that three sea lions were approaching the beach, swimming hard, flipping their tails against the lazy swells, but these were not sea lions.

"Motherrr, Motherrr," called one of the animals as it neared the shore, followed closely by the other two.

"Motherrr, Motherrr," the creature screamed, throwing back its hood to reveal a white face and head of wild dark tangled hair as it rode a friendly wave up onto the shore, beaching just inches from Ohnalee.

"Wake," the female demanded as she curled her body alongside Ohnalee, intertwining her fingers in Ohnalee's hair.

Blue eyes red from weeping opened wide and Ohnalee screamed with joy as two deep lavender eyes stared back at her. "Aquenae, my baby," she yelped, throwing her arms around her child.

"Also me, Mother," came the deep calm voice of her son, Qillac, lying now by her side on the sand.

"And me, my love," called Mokeema, drawing close, his handsome face filled with emotion.

Ohnalee sprung to her feet, stumbling over her children, falling into Mokeema's waiting arms. She was so overcome with love and emotion that speech would not come, but Mokeema knew well the feelings of her heart.

"We called to you many times, dear one," Mokeema said, his large eyes a pool of liquid onyx, "but you did not hear, and we worried, knowing you would come if you could."

"I searched for you, Motherrr," Magena said, pushing out her lower lip as she always did when displeased or sulky.

"Father said I must be brave and go far from the sea to find you, so I covered my body with my cloak and climbed the steep path to the church," complained Magena. "The sharp stones on the trail cut my feet."

"I didn't know, I didn't know, my darling," Ohnalee wept, "please forgive me."

Ohnalee held Magena close as she listened to her elder daughter's story.

"I saw you in the church through the window, Motherrr," Magena whimpered, "but you did not recognize me, and I was afraid to come inside."

Ohnalee told her family about the events of the last months, reassuring them of her love and devotion, promising never to leave them again.

Mokeema confessed his failure to rescue Ohnalee on the day of her capture. "The wicked man threw a heavy club with a sharp hook, making a deep hole in my shoulder," Mokeema said. "I tried to follow, but the wound was deep, and I was weak."

Ohnalee wept, knowing that only an extreme injury would stop Mokeema from coming to her rescue. "The Guardians arrived to help," Mokeema admitted wryly, "better late than never, but shortly afterwards a Great White Shark was seen in the area, attracted by my blood. My brothers of the Sea Lion Clan surrounded us, three deep, ready to fight if the shark attacked, but we returned home safely."

Later, as dawn came creeping over the mountain tops to the east, Mokeema said they must go, and Ohnalee agreed, knowing the minister would wake and find her gone.

"The suit, Ohnalee," Mokeema asked, "where is the suit that keeps you warm in the sea?"

Ohnalee gasped, remembering the day when Mokeema told her she must never lose the suit of sealskin.

"I don't know where it is," Ohnalee cried, remembering the day of her capture.

"I was wearing the garment when I was taken," she said. "Can't you make me another?"

Mokeema's face looked both stern and sad at the same time, and his dark eyes flashed.

"Do you recall when I told you how it took many years to make the suit?" Mokeema reminded. "I always believed one day you would come to be with me, so I knew it must be ready for the Day of Choosing. The shaman blessed the garment with magical powers, chanting your special name as it was constructed.

Without the suit of sealskin, you would freeze in these cold waters, especially now that you are not accustomed to the sea, and your body must adapt again," Mokeema said.

"I'll be OK, I'll be OK," Ohnalee begged, "I must come with you."

"Find the garment," Mokeema commanded, his face contorted with grief and sadness. "I cannot take you without it."

Ohnalee wrapped her arms around his neck and twined her legs around his waist, holding on with all her strength. "You cannot leave me," she pleaded. "I would rather die than stay here without you and the children."

"If a person with a bad heart finds that suit, great harm could come to our people," Mokeema said.

"With that suit a human could find the places where we rest deep below the surface. We must keep our existence a secret, or we will be hunted as the seal and the whales.

Go back, Ohnalee, go back to the humans who found you, and get the suit," Mokeema directed. "Retrieve it quickly so you can return to me and the children."

Aquenae Magena and Qillac howled as Mokeema gently pulled Ohnalee off his body, brushing the tears from her cheeks. "Be strong, my love," he whispered, "you will find the suit, and I will be waiting for your call."

"Motherrr, Motherrr, we love you, we love you," Magena whimpered, brilliant silver and green flashes of light shooting from her glorious violet eyes. At that moment Ohnalee recognized even more clearly the truth of her daughter's noble heritage and aristocratic bloodline. *"Purple is the color of the great dragon, wise Mother of all*," she heard Mokeema whisper ever so softly as if he was reading her mind.

"I love you, Mother," Qillac said quietly, touching her face gently with great reverence. Ohnalee smiled, taking his hand in hers, understanding the depth of his feelings despite his stoic and cool-headed exterior.

"We must go now," warned Mokeema. "Come, children, kiss your mother goodbye. We must leave quickly as the tide is going out. We must not be stranded."

Ohnalee watched her family move slowly away from the shore, waving as they reached the deep water, then diving deep and disappearing beneath the waves.

"Love you, love you," she heard them say distinctly, deep in her head, as her eyes filled with tears.

I will be strong, she promised, turning her back to the sea, feet retracing her steps, following the path back to the cabin. *I can do this, and I will be with them soon.*

By the time Ohnalee returned, her husband was awake, fully dressed, and pacing back and forth on the porch.

"Where have you been all night?" he demanded testily, scowling at her wet and sandy clothing and disheveled hair.

"I couldn't sleep," Ohnalee shrugged, "so I went down to cool my feet in the surf. You know how that always calms my nerves.

Then I lost my balance and stumbled on some rocks," she lied, "and a big wave broke on top of me, almost washing me out to sea."

"My God, Margaret," said the minister, "how many times do I have to tell you to be more careful?

"I know, I know, dear. I'll be more careful, I promise, but rest yourself while I put the kettle on for tea. Let me get these wet things off, and I'll make you a nice breakfast."

A few minutes later Ohnalee emerged from the bedroom dressed in a clean housedress, her hair now neatly tied back with a ribbon. Tying an apron round her waist, she heated an iron skillet for the ham, then warmed some white gravy for the biscuits. When the ham was browned, Ohnalee cracked three large eggs into the hot grease, frying them until the white part was lacy brown and crunchy on the bottom but the yolks were still runny as the minister preferred them. Ohnalee flipped the ham out onto a plate, then covered it with the fried eggs, setting the meal before her husband. The smell of the food cooking made her feel slightly nauseous, but she blamed this queasiness on her new remembrance of the fresh diet she had learned to enjoy in the land of the sea people.

Reverend Coombs soaked up the last bit of runny egg yolk with his biscuit, smacking his lips in appreciation. "That was lovely, dear," he praised, "I must run now. I am expected in town for a meeting and will be gone most of the day. I see neighbor Bill coming along the road now with his buggy as he has kindly offered me a ride."

Ohnalee could hardly wait as he buttoned his waistcoat and straightened his tie. She was anxious to proceed with her plan to find the sealskin garment as soon as possible.

"Perhaps you can lay up some preserves today," the reverend suggested, "rather than frittering away your time lying in the sun and daydreaming."

"Perhaps," said Ohnalee agreeably, accepting a peck on her cheek, thinking it would be the last he would ever place upon her person.

"Goodbye, sir," said Ohnalee with a curious note of formality in her voice, "I thank you for all your kindnesses."

Ohnalee watched as the buggy headed north along the road in the direction of Yachats. When her husband finally disappeared around the bend, she dashed inside to collect the things she most treasured. Ohnalee grabbed the handsome wooden box her father had made for her sixteenth birthday, lifting the lid to make sure it contained her journal. Then she opened the bottom drawer of her dresser, removing the pink dress the captain's wife had given her a few months before. She placed the dress in the box with the journal, then reached in the next drawer, pulling out the Trumpet Triton shell Mokeema had given to her so many years ago.

Ohnalee placed the shell inside the box, closed the catch, then hurried out the door to the barn where she threw a saddle on the old spotted mare. For a moment, she considered hitching up the buggy to make it easier to carry the box but decided to tie it securely to the back of the saddle instead. Putting one foot into the stirrups, Ohnalee took one last look at the cabin, then turned her back, heading south to Florence. She hoped she would never return, but for a moment regretted she had not washed the dishes from the morning meal. *He will be so aggravated,* she thought, a hint of a smile on her face.

OHNALEE, DAUGHTER OF THE DRAGON MER

Chapter 28

QUEST FOR THE MAGIC SUIT

Ohnalee had not been back to Florence since she was rescued by the captain of the *Daniel T.* several months before. She tied her horse up near the captain's dwelling on Lincoln Street and pulled down the wooden box.

When she got to the front stoop the door opened, and she was greeted by the captain's lady.

"Goodness gracious, what are you doing here, Margaret?" the woman inquired, giving her a warm hug as she took the box and followed her visitor up the steep stairs.

"I must talk to you," Ohnalee said, her face flushed and her heart beating fast.

"I am so glad to see you," Laydie assured her, "but where is your husband?"

"I came by myself," Ohnalee said, "I need your help, dear Laydie."

Ohnalee's friend bade her sit down and have a cup of tea before they talked, saying the captain had taken the children to Eugene for a few days.

"We can have a nice chat," the hostess assured her guest, "without fear of interruption from the little ones."

On the way to Florence, Ohnalee racked her brain to decide the best way to convince the captain's lady to help recover the suit, knowing her story sounded unbelievable. *If I tell the truth, Laydie will think I am out of my mind, a complete lunatic. Nobody could believe I can breathe under the sea and swim like a fish.*

"My memory has returned at last," Ohnalee blurted out. "I remember everything that happened during the four years I was gone."

"Oh, my dear," Laydie murmured, rising from her chair at the kitchen table to stand by her friend's side. Patting her on the shoulders, she took a white napkin from the table, dabbing at Ohnalee's eyes.

"There, there, dear, don't cry. Tell me everything. It will make you feel ever so much better."

Captain Dan and his wife had discussed several possible explanations for Margaret's disappearance, including the idea that she might have been washed out to sea by a rip tide, then rescued by a passing schooner. Perhaps she was walking the beach when a large wave hurled a piece of driftwood through the air, knocking her unconscious. This could explain the amnesia, but what happened after that was anyone's guess.

Ohnalee decided to lie to her friend rather than blurt out the incredible truth.

"I was visiting the sea caves one day when the tide came in high, trapping me inside," she explained. "I tried to escape by slipping through a narrow crevice which seemed to lead to higher ground, but I must have knocked my head against the side of the rocky opening.

The next thing I remember is lying on the grassy slope high above the caves, but when I tried to sit up, I was dizzy. I looked around but couldn't see anything that looked familiar, so I just sat there, totally confused, not knowing what to do."

Ohnalee described how a group of Indians gathering clams on the beach saw she was injured and came to help.

"One man tore strips from the shirt he was wearing and wrapped it around my head. They were very kind. They cleaned the blood from my face, and asked where I lived so they could escort me home. My mind was a complete blank," Ohnalee continued, "and I had absolutely no idea where I lived. I must have blacked out again as the next thing I knew, I was lying on the ground on a pile of furs in a small native-style house. It was very smoky in the place, and I found it hard to breathe. There was a small hole in the roof of the house to let the smoke out, but it didn't work very well.

I was so scared." Ohnalee continued, seeing she had the full attention of her hostess. Laydie was swallowing the story, hook, line, and sinker.

Then Ohnalee described in detail how a woman was cooking some food on a woodstove in the house, and when she saw her guest was awake, helped her sit up.

"You sick, you must eat then sleep again," the woman grunted, offering her a bowl of delicious hot, steaming broth.

"I ate the soup and then slept for a whole day," Ohnalee fibbed, finding it hard to keep a straight face. "And when I woke, I still could not remember anything—not my name or where I came from."

"Oh, my dear, this is terrible," Laydie sympathized, fanning her face as the room was very warm.

"I wanted to leave," Ohnalee said, "but I had no idea where to go."

Ohnalee embellished the story as she spoke, trying to make it sound plausible. It was certainly more believable than the truth, she thought.

"I felt welcome and they seemed happy to have me there," Ohnalee said, "I helped the woman and her husband with the children, and one day they introduced me to their elder son, who had just returned from another part of the state."

"Oh my word," Laydie interrupted, "and what happened then, my dear?"

"I have children," Ohnalee cried, burying her face in her hands with a heartrending sob that was not fabricated.

"I have remembered my two children, and I must return to them."

"These are Indians, Margaret?" Laydie questioned. "You have been living with Indians in one of their settlements?"

"Yes," Ohnalee whimpered, "I have been living with a man of a different culture, and in my eyes, and his, we were truly man and wife."

The captain's lady seemed overwhelmed with this account, but Ohnalee felt she believed it.

"Please, you can't tell anyone," Ohnalee begged. "My husband would not be able to hold his head up high if people knew the truth. Please, I beg you, you must help me. I must return to my children. I will die if I cannot."

"Of course, dear, I understand completely," Laydie assured her distressed friend, putting her arm around the girl in a sincere gesture of love and friendship.

"What can I do?" she asked. "But tell me why you were found in the ocean, wearing that strange leather garment. A person can become unconscious in just a few minutes in that freezing water."

"I don't clearly remember all the details as yet," Ohnalee responded, "but I believe my man and I were fishing in the ocean for salmon in a small skiff, and I was wearing the warm suit. My man cut and stitched that garment himself to keep me warm, and I think he made me wear it every time we went fishing," Ohnalee lied, feeling guilty and upset at her deception.

"I remember how the wind started blowing hard from the north, making the sea very rough, so we decided to come back in. My man sailed back into the mouth of the inlet, tacking back and forth across the river, but it was difficult making headway against the outgoing tide. Suddenly a fierce gust of wind laid our small craft over on its side, putting the rail clear under the water. I held on for dear life, thinking the boat would never come upright, but when it did, another gust laid us down again, breaking off the mast just above the deck."

Ohnalee's narrative was flowing easily now, and she was satisfied Laydie was believing the explanation without any problem whatsoever. Since she often accompanied her husband on his fishing expeditions, the captain's lady was well aware of the dangers encountered by men fishing the offshore waters in that area.

"Oh, my dear, please continue," begged the captain's lady, her eyes wide.

"My man scrambled to pull the broken mast out of the water, hauling the wet sail and broken rigging back on deck, but by the time this was done, we were in terrible danger. We had oars, but it was difficult to row against the current, and within minutes we were swept across the bar at the mouth of the river and out to sea.

Enormous waves were breaking over the boat," Ohnalee explained, her voice quaking, "and we were bailing water with a can and a small bucket as fast as we could. I was tired and cold, and the wind was howling so loud I could barely hear the voice of my man screaming instructions."

"Keep bailing, keep bailing" he shouted, "I'll try to rig a small sail."

"The fog lay heavily as a blanket over the sea," Ohnalee whispered, "so we could not see anything whatsoever of the shore."

"Keep talking, I'm listening," Laydie said as she poured two more cups of tea, then cut two warm wedges of marionberry pie from the round dish on the stove. The flaky crust crumbled as she served the desert, warm juices running from the filling, the slice more like a serving of pudding than a pie.

"Sorry about that, dear," Laydie apologized. "The pie would be better if it cooled awhile, but I think we both need the nourishment at this moment. A nice dollop of cream on top will make it nicer," she said, spooning a large mountain of whipped cream over each serving.

"What happened then, girl?" Laydie asked, licking cream off her fingers.

"I don't remember much after that," Ohnalee said, "but I think a large breaker capsized the craft, pitching us overboard."

Ohnalee sniffed at that remembrance, wiping at her eyes. "My man must have drowned," she moaned, "but luckily for me, your husband, rescued me."

"Praise the Lord, darling girl. What a terrible ordeal you have been through."

"I must go to my children immediately," cried Ohnalee, "but I need your help."

"Anything," Laydie promised fervently. "Do you know where to find them?"

"My horse is waiting outside, and I feel I must head east from Florence, following the river. I believe it is not far, and I can be there in several hours."

"I'll make some sandwiches for you to eat along the way," offered Laydie, clearing away the dishes from the table and bustling into action in the kitchen.

"Thank you so much, my friend, but I need two favors before I go."

Ohnalee then asked her friend to help find the sealskin clothing she was wearing when rescued by the captain.

"I must return those garments to the village. My man worked many months sewing the suit, and I want another woman to have it."

Laydie told Margaret she believed the suit was still aboard the vessel *Daniel T.*, so it should be easy to find. "The mate is aboard the boat," Laydie said, "so let him know I sent you to recover your belongings."

Ohnalee was overjoyed. The mission seemed easy to accomplish, and soon she would be on her way to join Mokeema and the children.

"Thank you, Laydie," Ohnalee said, reaching for the wooden box. "There is one more favor I must ask."

"Anything," her friend agreed.

"Please, dear Laydie, this box contains my most precious possessions. The pink dress inside belongs to you, and I am returning it as I promised. Also in this chest is my personal journal and a beloved memento of my childhood. I beg you to keep these things safe as I hope to return for them one day. If not, perhaps one of my children will come in the future, wanting to learn more of her mother."

"The dress is yours to keep, dear Margaret," Laydie said, "so I will leave it in the trunk with the other things.

Have no worries, my friend. I promise that no one will be allowed to look in the chest or through the pages of your journal. These things will be safe with me, and I will ask the captain to put a strong lock on the box when he returns."

"You are so kind," Ohnalee said, "I can never thank you enough. Now I must go to the *Daniel T.* to find the garment so I can return home quickly."

The two women gazed at each other sadly with misty eyes, and Ohnalee wrapped her arms around Laydie, holding her close. The exotic scent of amber radiated from her friend's long blond hair, and she thought she would never forget that sweet memory.

Under the sea, the people could not experience the joy of delicious aromas and smells. It was only when they came up from the deep into the fresh air of the human world this was possible. Ohnalee hoped her daughter, Magena, would one day experience the special scents of being human, inhaling the sweet floral scent of lavender; the pungent, sweet smell of cinnamon; the clean, fresh aroma of cedar; or the hospitable smell of vanilla. Ohnalee felt there was nothing in the world that smelled so good as a fresh-baked apple pie cooling on the windowsill.

"Is there no possibility you can retrieve your children and then return to Florence?"

"I think not," replied Ohnalee, sadly. "I fear they might suffer discrimination because of their mixed blood. In the village, their grandparents will teach them the ways of the tribe. Perhaps they will choose to leave one day, but for now, I feel they will be safer where they are. I cannot put this burden on Minister Coombs."

"It is getting late, Margaret," Laydie said, "you should stay with me until tomorrow morning and then proceed to your destination."

"No, no," Ohnalee protested, "I must go now. My children have no idea I am alive, and I cannot wait another day.

Don't worry, I'll be fine," she assured her friend, "I learned much in the land of the Siuslaw and Coos people, and I am not afraid."

"Then go with my love, and return one day, dear friend," Laydie begged, "but always remember that your children are welcome to come and stay with me. They will be lovingly treated as members of my family."

"Will you promise to keep my secret from your husband and others?" Ohnalee asked. "I fear if the truth were known, some would feel compelled to pursue me. I don't want to bring trouble down upon my adopted people as they have been very kind to me and my children."

"I cannot promise to keep this information from my husband," Laydie said, "as we share all things, but he would never break a confidence.

You can trust us to keep your secret," she promised, "no matter what."

The two women hugged, and Ohnalee gratefully accepted two ham sandwiches, wrapped in white paper. "I love your ginger cookies," she called up the stairs as she left, biting into one as she closed the door to the residence.

Chapter 29

THE LAST VOYAGE

Ohnalee sped down the street to the river. When she reached the *Daniel T.* it was almost full dark, and she could see a dim light glowing from a porthole in the bow of the boat. She thought this indicated the mate was in his cabin, perhaps reading by lantern light. She planned to ask nicely for her suit, thank the man for his kindness, then run to her horse. Ohnalee knew the trip back up the coast in darkness would be difficult, but she wanted to stop by the sea lion caves, an easy place to call Mokeema in to pick her up. The horse could be let loose there. *He knows the way home,* Ohnalee speculated, *it's not far.*

"Hello, hello," Ohnalee called, knocking gently on the side of the boat. After a few minutes she walked toward the bow of the boat where she had seen the light, knocking even harder on the hull.

"Hello, is anyone there?" she shouted again more loudly, walking back toward the aft deck, trying to peer inside the wheelhouse.

Ohnalee stepped quietly onto the aft deck, intending to knock again. "Ouch," she squealed loudly as she stumbled on a pile of greasy engine parts hiding in the darkness, and fell to her knees.

As she painfully picked herself up, afraid her ankle might be sprained, Ohnalee heard a noise up on the foredeck. Looking toward the bow, she saw a man emerging from a hatch. He was carrying a lantern in one hand while pulling his suspenders up over his shoulders with the other.

"What cha want?" the man shouted gruffly, shuffling along the gunnel to the aft deck, holding the lantern high to better see his visitor.

"I am Margaret Rose Lavell," Ohnalee began timidly, her voice soft and quavering. "Do you remember me, sir?"

"Goll darn sure I do," the man retorted gruffly, setting the lantern down on the deck. The bright silvery light from the kerosene lamp swept upward, illuminating the man's face, giving his features a strange and evil look. He reached down in his pant pocket and pulled out a pipe, sticking it in his mouth as he reached in another pocket for a pack of tobacco. Margaret felt worried and uncomfortable as he tamped the dried leaves down, then struck the match on the bottom on his shoe.

The mate scowled as Ohnalee shifted her weight from one foot to the other, nervously taking the measure of the man. He looked about forty, but life had obviously been difficult as his body was bent and contorted. His hands were gnarled and calloused, probably from years of working with heavy lines and nets, and there was a long scar across one cheek.

"Sure do remember you, ma'am," he repeated with a sinister leer on his pockmarked face, looking her up one side and down the other as if he could see straight through her frock and under her petticoats.

"Helped the captain get you out of that tight leather suit, I did," the mate muttered in a slimy lecherous voice, showing two gaping holes in the front of his mouth. The man's remaining teeth were broken and decayed with disgusting streaks of black and green on their surface.

201

Ohnalee was terrified, knowing she should get ashore as fast as possible, but if she did, she might not be able to retrieve the suit.

"Thank you for your kindness, sir," she smiled, trying to look as weak and feminine as possible.

"You and the captain saved my life, and there is no way I can ever thank you enough."

"Oh, you could thank me, my pretty," the man leered coming closer, "in more ways than one."

Ohnalee winced, stepping back on her injured foot as the mate grabbed her arm.

"Stop, sir, I beg you," Ohnalee pleaded, "I need to find the leather suit I was wearing when you rescued me. If you will get it, I will leave and let you get back to whatever you were doing."

"So what will you give me for that suit, girl?" he demanded sarcastically, grabbing her by the hair, then roughly pulling her into the deckhouse, "cause I know how valuable that thing is and why you want it so bad."

"Stop, please," Ohnalee begged as he dragged her down into the lower depths of the vessel, brutally pulling her along by a strand of curly hair.

"Shut up, bitch," the man growled, roughly throwing her down on the floor. "Been wondering when you wuz gonna show up here for that suit."

"Help, help," she screamed as the mate slapped her hard across the face.

"If you don't shut up, you'll never get that suit," the mate threatened, "but we may just make a deal here if you'll close your yap and listen."

Ohnalee's head was throbbing, and so was her swollen ankle, but she took a deep breath, calmed herself, and thought about Mokeema. *I'll be strong*, she thought, *I'll get that suit, and I'll be home soon.*

"What do you mean, make a deal?" Ohnalee sniffed, drying her tears on a corner of her sleeve.

"I been talking to some people about you," the mate said, "and I know where you wuz for all them years. Thought it was a crazy yarn at first, but then things started meshing together, know what I mean?"

Ohnalee had pulled herself up into a sitting position and was now leaning against the wall in the corner, her knees drawn up to her chest. She tucked the hem of her long skirt firmly around the bottoms of her feet as if to guard against any unwanted approach.

"No, sir. What do you mean?" she said softly. "All I want is my suit, and I will go. My man made it for me, and he was drowned in the sea, so I want to take it to his mama in the Indian village."

"Drown, hell, he ain't drown for sure," the mate whispered, squatting down in front of her then thrusting his hateful face close to hers, "and he sure as shit ain't no Indian."

Ohnalee almost gagged at the smell of the man's sour breath. He reeked of stale beer and whiskey, and she recoiled in terror as he traced his finger down her nose, across her mouth and chin, then down her neck and under the neckline of her dress. The other hand snatched and clawed at the buttons on her shirt as she screamed loudly.

"No, no, please stop," she begged, pushing him away. "I don't know what you mean."

"The hell you don't," he sneered. "Let's quit playing with each other, and I'll tell you what's gonna happen here.

Ged up," he growled, dragging Ohnalee to her feet. "I'm gonna show you something, and then you better goddam listen close to every word I say. Don't you dare give me any more lip, girl."

The man grabbed Ohnalee by the back of her neck, propelling her roughly through a narrow hallway, then past a filthy hanging curtain into the small cabin in the bow. There was barely enough room to stand in the small area where the crew slept, and Ohnalee grimaced as Martin leaned close to lift the lid on the small locker between the berths. Inside was the suit, and at that moment, she wished for a weapon. *If I had a knife*, she thought, *I'd stick it deep in his cold heart, and take my suit*. Ohnalee would hesitate at nothing to achieve her goal.

"Here's whut you want so bad, little lady," the mate whispered in a teasing voice, picking up the bundle of gray leather clothing.

"How 'bout taking off that pretty dress, and we'll see if this outfit still fits," he suggested. "Looks like you're a bit swollen around the middle."

Ohnalee instinctively put her hand on her stomach, wondering if it could be true. Was it possible she was pregnant? The thought was so disturbing she turned white, suddenly feeling faint.

"Please give me the garment, I beg you, sir," Ohnalee pleaded, "you have discovered my secret. I am pregnant and must return to my husband who is waiting for me just up the street."

"Just up the street, my foot," sneered the mate. "More like just out to sea is what you mean. I've got this thing figured out, and you and me better make a deal.

No deal, no leather suit," he growled, grabbing her by the arm, pulling her back toward the aft deck, the suit slung over his shoulder.

"Settle yerself now," he commanded, pushing Ohnalee down on the planked planked deck. "Jist sit tight and pay attention. No running away girlie," he giggled as he tied her hands and feet.

"Please, you've tied my wrists too tightly," she protested, "my hands are going numb."

"Too bad, fish lover," he snarled, curling his lip meanly, then giving Ohnalee a shove with his foot.

"Now I been over at the logger's tavern talking to some folks about strange goings on up the coast. First I thought them guys was too full of rum, seeing and hearing things that did not exist, but then it all made sense. Said their kids saw some strange sea lions that looked almost human, and also found drawings on the walls of one of the big caves up there, probably been there hundreds of years. Maybe Indians put 'em there, or maybe some other people, I don't know, but the pictures show people with fish tails."

Ohnalee remembered seeing these etchings in the back of the big cave, and Mokeema told her they were placed there by ancient Native American peoples who knew of the existence of the sea tribes.

"Dam kids been keeping this a secret all along, so I went up to them caves to have a look see," the mate said, "took a lantern, climbed down that fisherman's net and saw em for myself; it all made sense then."

The mate disappeared down into the galley of the boat, coming back with a bottle of whiskey.

"Have a tot," he urged, sticking the mouth of the bottle under her nose, his chin whiskers inches away from her face.

The smell of the whiskey mixed with his foul body odor was more than Ohnalee could bear, and she gagged, almost vomiting.

"Whoa, lady, hold on there. Don't puke all over my deck," he warned, taking a big swig out of the bottle.

"One night I decided it was time for a real heart to heart with my old squaw woman, know what I mean?

Used to be she was content to stay with me at my shack in town, but lately she been living with her people, and that suits me fine. Bitch, bitch, bitch, all she did was bitch 'bout me having a bottle of booze once in a while, so ya can't blame me for slapping her upside the head now and then.

Anyway," he continued, lifting the bottle to his lips again, "I snuck up by her squat real quiet like so no one knowed I was there and listened a while to make sure she was alone. The bitch was surprised to see me fer sure. Had to give her a slap and pour some whiskey down her yap so she'd keep quiet, sniveling slut. Took a bit more convincing before she'd talk bout them fish people, know what I mean? Can't believe her keeping that stuff from me all those years, and me working hard to keep vittles on the table.

Said several men in the tribe were out fishing one day and saw the fish men, actually had some kind of powwow with 'em but agreed they would never talk about the thing outside the tribe. They had pretty baubles strung round their necks, and one had a gold coin tied up in his long hair.

Tell you what," he announced, "I'm gonna fire up the old diesel, so we can get on with the plan. We've wasted enough time. You want the suit, and I'll tell you what I want when we get out the channel and over the bar."

Ohnalee was terrified and confused. What was he thinking?

Within minutes, the mate had cast off the dock lines and was heading west toward the inlet. Ohnalee was still sitting on the deck, leaning against a tall pile of net, and for just a few minutes, her mind wandered. She had a vision of herself sitting at the piano, dressed in a beautiful frock, admired by friends who were enjoying her music. What in the world was she doing here, sitting on the deck of a smelly fishing boat, in the control of this horrible man? *Stop feeling sorry for yourself,* Ohnalee's strong voice sternly instructed the weak Margaret Rose. *You'll never get out of here in one piece with that attitude.*

I am Ohnalee, loved by my people, and I will not be stopped, Ohnalee decided. *It's a pretty pickle I'm in, but I intend to get out of it alive. I must not get excited. I must stay calm and make this man think I will go along with whatever he has in mind. Then, when the time is right, I'll act and get what I came for.*

The mate steered the boat toward the sea, and since the wind was light, easily ran across the bar on a tranquil sea.

"What are we doing out here, sir?" Ohnalee inquired politely, ignoring the throbbing in her hands from the tight bindings.

"Well there is jist one more thing I didn't tell ya before, and it took some hard work on my part to get it out of my squaw woman. Knuckles are still sore, but I got the real story."

At that point, Ohnalee had an idea what he was talking about but tried hard to keep a confused look on her face.

"The old bag confessed that some of the old folks in the tribe told stories about strange yellow people with slanted eyes who came across the ocean on sailing ships in ancient times. Seems they was caught up in somethin' the natives call the 'black current,' a river in the sea so swift they couldn't sail out of it, getting swept clear across the Pacific to the shores of these parts.

My old woman said several junks wrecked along the coast in the old days, but their bones were covered by the constantly shifting sand on the beaches. Rumor has it that several of these sailors survived and were taken in by the tribes living in the area. I always wondered why some of those Indians have funny eyes, look like goddam Chinamen or somethin', so it makes sense.

She showed me a coin her uncle found on the beach, and it had some crazy-looking language written on it. Lots more where those came from," she taunted, "but she said no way was she about to tell me where it was.

Knocked out a couple of teeth and split her upper lip," he bragged, "ugly bitch won't get another man now for sure, but she wouldn't say more. Dam squaw ain't got much sense anyway.

The thing is," he went on, "some of those ships went to the bottom before they hung up on the rocks, and the legends say they were carrying the riches of the orient.

Thought I was on to something when I returned to town, and then knew I wuz right when I picked up this leather suit of yourn." The mate picked up the suit from the chart deck where it had been tossed.

Martin put down the bottle and drew close to Ohnalee, pointing his gnarled finger at her nose, poking it back and forth in front of her face. He held the suit up high, pointing gleefully to the row of buttons sewn on the front.

"See here, girl, gold coins they are, and covered with funny Oriental writing. Took one of these to a Chink I know, and he got all excited. Yellow devil was mumbling something 'bout fung su, or fu swang, or some devilish name like that, crazy story about a ancient Japanese civilization somewhere on the Pacific coast, and ships laden with treasure bound for these shores.

Had to kill 'em, poor devil," the mate confessed, making the sign of the cross on his forehead. "Not human anyway, and couldn't stop him from running his mouth.

So here's the deal, girl. You are gonna call up them fish people, and tell em to go to the closest shipwreck and bring me back as many gold coins and precious jewels as they can carry.

They better load up real good, or I'll just keep sending them back down for more until I say stop. Always wanted to go to San Francisco and live high on the hog, so I figure this is the way to do it. Get me enough money to buy me one of them Nob Hill places, get some fancy-dancy furniture, dress like a gentleman, and never have to work a single day ever again."

Ohnalee was incredulous. "You think I can 'call up fish people'? Are you simple-minded, sir?"

"Crazy as a goddam fox," he boasted, "and you know I can fix it so you'll never get that suit. I'll throw it in the stove, turn it into charcoal, you don't agree. So shut up, and don't open your trap until we are near where they are. You'll call 'em, or I'll fix you so you can't call anybody, ever again."

The mate reached up on the chart deck, grabbing an evil-looking fillet knife. "You won't look so purty once I'm done with ya," he threatened, brandishing the knife in her direction.

"You tell me when to slow down and what direction to go to find 'em," he directed, "and we'll get this over with fast. Then you'll get the suit, and I'll get this boat back to the wharf so Captain Dan don't know I took it."

"Captain Dan's wife said you were a kind man," Ohnalee said boldly. "How could she have been so wrong?"

"Thinks I'm his right-hand man, he does for sure," Martin grinned. "What he don't know won't hurt him none."

Ohnalee's pretty face no longer looked scared, and if the mate had looked closely, he would have seen a fierce new determination. She concentrated hard, calling to Mokeema, knowing he would know what to do, and soon, she heard his voice.

I am here, Ohnalee, do not be afraid.
Tell the man to slow the boat, and we will bring what he wants.

"You must slow the vessel," Ohnalee directed, "and your demands will be met."

"How do you know that?" the mate demanded. "I don't see any fish people around here."

"Your request will be granted," said Ohnalee, "and you will give me the suit. Then you will take the boat back to the dock and never tell anyone what you have seen, or you will suffer the consequences. That is what the people say."

The mate pulled back the engine speed to idle, then pointed the *Daniel T.'s* bow into the swells. The boat rode gently up and down as the waves slid beneath the keel. The night was very dark, with just a sliver of moon, but the sky was full of stars.

"Don't see a dam thing out there," the mate grumbled as he searched the horizon with the ship's binoculars. "You sure this is the right place?

Holy Jesus God," the mate bellowed, seeing the sea erupt all around the boat. "What the hell is that?"

Ohnalee's heart pounded as she saw hundreds of sea lions emerge simultaneously from beneath the sea, and intermingled with the animals were at least fifty of the strongest warriors of their tribe. Mokeema surfaced at the starboard side of the vessel with one of the Guardians close by. Even with the hood covering most of his face, she would recognize those flashing dark eyes anywhere, but she had never seen him look as fierce and dangerous as he did now.

Mokeema and the other warriors had decorated their cheeks and foreheads with black zigzag symbols, and as they came close to the boat, the mate seemed to quake and shiver fearfully.

"Free my hands," Ohnalee begged, "please."

"No way," he argued, grabbing the shotgun from its rack on the overhead. "Tell them to get my treasure."

"They have it now," said Ohnalee, seeing several of the sea people raise their hands, showing large pouches.

"Those bags are filled with gold and precious gems," Ohnalee assured the mate, "they will throw them on the deck once you have freed me and given me the suit."

"Treasure first, then the suit," growled the mate, "or else the deal is off.

Tell em to throw them pouches over here, then go down again for more," he demanded.

Hearing that, Mokeema motioned for the sea people to throw their sacks up on the deck of the boat. The heavy leather pouches landed hard, hammering the decks with their weight, and several split open, scattering their precious contents near the piles of net.

"Now you will be the richest man in California", Ohnalee pleaded. "Give me the leather suit and I will go."

The mate looked nervously over his shoulder at the hundreds of sea lions and warriors now surrounding the ship, as if he suddenly realized his vulnerability. Ohnalee sensed that the patience of the sea people was close to the breaking point as she could hear the deafening clamor of their voices in her head. The sea lions were partners of the sea people in battle against their enemies, and their barks and roars seemed to be increasing in intensity as well.

"OK, girl, this will be enough for now," Martin agreed, grabbing the shotgun. "We're going back. You tell those devils to git back down to their lairs, and we'll be back another day for more. No sense in being greedy, I guess."

Ohnalee was defiant as she faced her captor, eyes flashing, and jaw set.

"You promised to let me go. Now free my hands and let me go."

"Changed my mind, I did," the mate chuckled, "terrible liar I am, ha ha. You and me is gonna get to know each other a whole lot better, and if ya know what's good for ya, you'll shut your trap and do what I say. A real man will be a whole lot better for a pretty thing like you anyway than one of those inhuman animals. I'll just shoot a bunch of them evil-looking beasts if ya don't," he threatened.

"You'll be sorry," Ohnalee murmured under her breath as the mate turned the vessel back to port, holding the shotgun with his right hand, steering with his left.

Then Ohnalee saw Mokeema swim close to the port side of the vessel, coming so near she could almost reach out and touch his hand.

The mate panicked seeing this approach. He grabbed the shotgun with both hands and fired in Mokeema's direction. Mokeema dove deep, and Ohnalee knew he was unhurt, but she had no idea what would happen next.

Suddenly there was a tremendous crashing noise from under the hull of the *Daniel T.* It was so loud that Ohnalee thought of dynamite, but she knew that was impossible.

"We're going down," the mate screamed as he peered below. "Them bastards are sinking the *Daniel T.*"

With that, he got off a few more shotgun rounds into the darkness, and Ohnalee heard a bellow of pain as the blast hit one of the sea lions.

A tremendous roar then came up from around the boat, a sound so raw and frightful even Ohnalee was afraid. The sea boiled as hundreds of sea people burst from the water, strong muscled tails thrusting their bodies high into the air toward the sinking boat. Like mythical sea monsters, the enraged warriors landed hard on the foredeck, the top of the deckhouse, and on the aft deck, their high-pitched screeches penetrating the darkness. The tremendous weight of this army of attackers pushed the vessel low in the sea as seawater rushed into the boat from the hole in the bottom, filling the engine compartment, releasing thick black oil from the pans beneath the engine. The foul-smelling mess floated on the top, coating the interior with an oily black sheen.

Hundreds of noisy sea lions then climbed on board the vessel, sealing its fate. The *Daniel T.* was minutes from going under when Ohnalee threw herself against the mate who was raising his gun to get off another round, knocking him away from the helm. She grabbed the suit from the chart deck with her bound hands, just as Mokeema hit the deck full force, knocking the mate unconscious with one swipe of his powerful arm.

Mokeema swept Ohnalee and the suit up into his arms, holding her tightly as if he would never let her go again. With a victorious whoop of sheer joy, he leapt high in the air, landing in the water clear of the sinking boat. The Mer King reached for the sharp knife he kept tied on a leather belt around his waist, freeing Ohnalee's hands and feet, and the couple watched as the *Daniel T.* started her downward plummet to the bottom. It was only a few seconds from the time when the bowsprit went under until the stern took its last look at the sky, and Ohnalee knew the mate would never lay a hand on any woman again.

"He was a bad man," Mokeema whispered, "and he will cause no more suffering."

Chapter 30

AN ERRAND FOR MAGENA

Ohnalee slipped into the warm suit, assisted by her man of the sea, and together they descended to the world of her chosen people. Mokeema was proud of the Guardians, and anyone could see by the grins and smiles on their faces that they were very happy to have their queen back again.

Down, down the couple descended, hand in hand, through the lush forests of swaying kelp, to the land where the children waited for their mother. Ohnalee's joy was so great, she feared her poor human heart would burst out of her chest, but Mokeema squeezed her hand hard as if to say, *I am here, I am here, and I will never let you go again.*

Mokeema's face was triumphant as the party of warriors entered the settlement, and in her mind, Ohnalee compared the experience to that of Indian braves returning from battle in the human world. The women gave their men a hero's welcome, dropping necklaces of gems and shells around their necks, singing their praises with melodic high-pitched songs. Many of the women wound themselves round their man's body, some even climbing on their backs, showing plainly the erotic character of their intentions. Within minutes, the warriors scattered, subjugated by the amatory desires of their mates.

Magena and Qillac rushed toward their parents, screaming with excitement. "Mother, Mother," they cried, their sweet voices overflowing with love. Magena, always intense and hyperactive, clung to Ohnalee's body, stroking her face and back, demanding her mother's full attention, while Qillac, always controlled and unemotional, stood back, allowing his dramatic sister to take center stage.

"I missed you, Mother," Qillac finally interrupted, displaying a wee bit of jealously.

"Oh, my dear boy, I missed you too," wept Ohnalee, now showing the full extent of her emotions. *He is so tall and strong,* she thought, as she ran her hands over the sculptured muscles of his upper arms and back. Although he was now only a child in human years, this boy looked like a full-grown man of the Mer.

"You make me very proud, my son," Ohnalee said as a vision of her parents crossed her mind, casting a shadow on this happy moment.

"I wish your grandparents could see you, my beauties," Ohnalee said sadly. "They will be so hurt when they hear that I have gone again without saying goodbye."

"Your mother will know you have returned to your people," Mokeema speculated, "and she would not want you to worry."

Ohnalee smiled, not wanting this happy moment to be spoiled, but she vowed that one day her mother would know the full extent of her happiness.

Later, Mokeema and his lady queen rested together, their hearts and bodies melding together in spasms of total enchantment and contentment. The fire ignited at their very first touch had not cooled in the least, and if anything, the heat was more intense. Ohnalee felt the strong attraction they shared would last forever, and past forever, and believed it possible they had been together in previous lifetimes. *Perhaps Mokeema and I lived together in the ancient Motherland before it was destroyed,* she theorized.

The next day, Ohnalee talked with Mokeema about the *Daniel T.*. She was very sad because she understood how hard the captain and his wife worked to support their family. The loss of the *Daniel T.* would be catastrophic as without the boat, there would be no income from fishing or crabbing.

"Please, Mokeema," Ohnalee begged, "I must do something to help Laydie and Dan. They were so kind when I was captured."

Before long, the two lovers decided on a plan but they needed Aquenae Magena to make it work.

"Magena, my darling, I have a task for you," her father said. "It is dangerous, and you must be careful, but we trust that you can do this good deed."

Magena was enthusiastic as usual, thinking there was no task too difficult for her to accomplish.

"I can do it, Poppi, whatever it is," Magena promised, anxious to get started immediately.

Ohnalee was worried since this was Magina's first visit to a populated area, but she knew that every mother must recognize the time to give freedom, hand in hand with responsibility.

"The gods have given you the ability to go ashore as a human woman, but you must be careful to follow our instructions exactly," Mokeema warned.

"Take this pouch of coins and precious stones to the home of your mother's friend," Mokeema instructed, placing the heavy bag in her hand. "Listen carefully so you will know exactly what to do.

We will accompany you to the mouth of the harbor," Mokeema directed, "where you will climb up on the rocks and dry your body in the sun. When you are completely dry, quickly put on the pants and blouse your mother has sewn from the sealskins, then wrap your upper body in the hooded cloak."

"Keep the cloak wrapped around your body," Ohnalee cautioned, "as it is not seemly for a young woman to walk into town, unescorted, and you must be careful not to draw attention to yourself in any way.

When you reach the dirt street that runs along the river, you will look for a street running to the north. On the east side of that street, you will see a white building that says 'Bank,' and next to that is a narrow two story building with a green roof. Laydie and Dan live upstairs."

Magena was itchy to leave, rolling her eyes, impatient at her parent's detailed explanation.

"I know, I know," she interrupted, "knock on the door, give the people the bag of pretty rocks and shiny metal, then leave quickly. I can do it, no problem."

Teenagers! Think they know everything!, Ohnalee thought. *Wish Qillac could walk on land. He would do this job properly, without all the drama.* She grinned at that thought, thinking Drama Queen was a better title for her daughter, Princess Aquenae Magena.

"I will tell you exactly what to say to my friend," Ohnalee said. "She is very dear to me."

"Fine, fine," Magena said dismissively, waving her hand in the air as if she were already on the throne.

Mokeema, Ohnalee, and a contingent of sea lions set forth on the mission, leaving Qillac in charge at the settlement. He said goodbye to Magena with his usual inscrutable stare, not being a good communicator of his emotions, but Ohnalee knew he was worried about his older sister.

"She'll be fine, son," assured Ohnalee, "we must trust her with this important chore. There is no alternative."

When the small band reached the entrance of the Siuslaw, Magena pulled herself up on the rocks on the north side of the river, stretching lazily in the sun as if she had nothing better to do than get a suntan. Mokeema and Ohnalee watched from a short distance offshore, frustrated as they realized the girl had fallen asleep on her warm perch.

"What is that girl doing?" Mokeema complained. "Can't she ever be on time for anything?"

"Wake up, lazybones, wake up," Ohnalee cried as the girl rolled over on her side. Her gorgeous purple tail had disappeared and two shapely legs had taken its place.

"I am, I am," Magena protested.

"Magena, hurry up, get dressed, for heaven's sake," bellowed her father. "Don't want someone to come by and catch you like that."

Finally, Magena yawned, then slowly sat up, rubbing her eyes and scratching idly at one of her toes. She pulled her knees close to her chest, so she could study those strange objects more closely. *Like fingers on your feet*, she decided.

Mokeema had given her a pair of soft sealskin slippers before giving her a boost up onto the rocks, saying she must wear them on the walk into the town. "Humans do not go about in their bare feet," he warned.

It seemed like an eternity to Mokeema and Ohnalee as they waited for Magena to dress herself and get ready to leave. Mokeema was frustrated at the delay, watching her fiddle with her long dark hair, combing it straight with the golden comb she carried everywhere, then twisting it into ringlets with her fingers. *Good thing she didn't bring her mirror*, he thought, *we'd never get her moving.*

Teenagers are so aggravating, Ohnalee agreed. *Hope it doesn't take this long getting her back in the water after the job is done.*

Magena scrambled down off the rocks, gave her parents a jaunty wave, then skipped away along the sandy path toward town. Ohnalee and Mokeema watched anxiously, knowing they should not worry, but it was difficult not to. Their daughter was going into town on her own for the first time. She was a stranger in a strange new land, and they would not be there to protect her.

Glancing over her shoulders toward the breakwater where she had last seen her parents, Magena grinned as she tossed back the long cloak over her shoulders. The garment billowed out behind her body as she literally danced along, stopping here and there to pick a blackberry from the numerous wild bushes along the path. By the time she reached the outskirts of the village, her mouth, tongue, and fingers were stained purple from the delicious wild fruits. *I love the sweet treats of the land*, she thought, *so much better than the salty tidbits from the sea.*

Magena's arrival in town was not noticed as it was early, and the shopkeepers were just arriving at their stores. Remembering her parents' warning to keep a low profile, Magena drew her cloak closely around her body, covering her hair with the hood. Despite this attempt to appear plain and nondescript, a closer look would immediately confirm that Magena was something very special indeed.

The ever-present fresh, salty breeze from the sea caught hold of the girl's long damp black hair, twisting and tangling the tendrils into even tighter curls, creating a fanciful and unique coiffure that refused to stay within the confines of the hood. The serpentine coils squirmed and writhed, escaping over her shoulders to cascade lavishly across her bosom, glinting with splendorous streaks of purple and silver, much like the different species of sea snakes in the land of the people.

Magena paused in front of a whitewashed wooden shop building, her magnificent orchid colored eyes wide with astonishment. The display in Florence Mercantile's window featured the very latest in ladies' bonnets and elegant frocks from San Francisco and Portland, but Magena was particularly drawn to a fanciful creation decorated with plump silk cabbage roses in shades of pale lilac and plum. A perky veil crowned this opulent chapeau, which was obviously designed for a lady with discriminating taste and wealth.

Inside the shop, Mr. Marcus Graves energetically bustled around, filling the till in preparation for a busy day. He had already swept the hardwood floor and rearranged a display of Sunday dress shirts for gentlemen, then quickly ran a comb through his slicked-back hair before opening. As he approached the front door to pull open the latch, his eyes darted to the window.

The young man stopped dead in his tracks, actually gasping out loud as he spotted Magena looking in the window. She had removed her hood, and the cape was again carelessly thrown back over her shoulders, revealing a slim but voluptuous figure clad in strange gray leather pants and top. The outfit looked almost tribal, he thought, but her features did not resemble those of any Native American he had ever seen.

Marcus opened the door and stepped just outside to take a closer look at the woman peering in his window. "Come in, miss," he invited, his voice cracking with emotion. For some unexplainable reason, he felt that getting her inside the store was the most important thing that would ever happen in his life.

Magena turned her face toward the shopkeeper, a look of hesitation evident. She knew dillydallying was not the proper thing to do as her parents were waiting for her return, but it would be only for a few minutes, and no one would know.

"Perhaps you would like to try on one of the beautiful bonnets," Marcus suggested, extending his hand in her direction. Magena paused for only a moment, then offered her hand to be led inside. The man's heart actually skipped a beat as he escorted Magena into the interior of the store. He shivered with delicious excitement as a tingling feeling emanated from her fingertips, a sort of electric energy that made him almost light-headed.

Magena wandered around the store, curiously touching the neatly arranged piles of ladies' fine accouterments, wondering if she could ever become accustomed to wearing so many layers of clothing. Then Marcus approached, bearing two bonnets from the store window, one of which was the hat covered with roses. Magena's eyes fluttered as she pointed at the veiled beauty.

"May I approach, miss," Marcus inquired, "to position the hat correctly on your head?"

Magena nodded her agreement then took a seat on a comfortable chair in front of an ornate mirror with roses carved into the heavy wooden frame. *Motherrr would love this glass,* she thought, smiling at her reflection. "With your permission, Miss," the clerk said, as he carefully placed the bonnet on Magena's head, then pulled the veil down just to her eyebrows.

"Beautiful, beautiful," he gushed, almost at a loss for words as he stared at her reflection in the glass. She seemed totally out of place in the little store, and he knew that none of the expensive items displayed were really good enough for this regal person.

"You really should have it, miss," Marcus suggested, feeling as if he were in the presence of royalty.

"OK," Magena said, rising from the chair, "I take it."

Then she headed for the door still wearing the bonnet, much to the clerk's dismay. *Oh my gosh,* he thought, *the girl is leaving without paying.*

"Stop, miss," he begged, "that hat is four dollars—a little spendy perhaps, but a very reasonable price for such an elegant and unique chapeau."

Magena hesitated at the door, wondering what the man meant. He just said she should take the hat, now he was changing his mind. "I *will* take it," Magena said, a haughty look on her face.

"My employer will be unhappy if you go without paying," Marcus pleaded, visualizing the elderly lady who owned the store. "You must pay, miss."

Magena turned toward Marcus, coming so close he could smell the sweet scent of her body. His feet felt as if they were nailed to the floor as she placed the open palm of her right hand gently against his cheek. Marcus's body seemed to quiver, and his eyes stared blankly as Magena murmured quietly into his ear.

"You will not remember that you have seen me, human, but I will leave a pretty thing that will make you happy."

Magena reached into the leather bag, pulling out a large black pearl, then slipped her hand deep into the side pocket of his trousers. Despite his state of trance, the man's body shook and his eyes blinked as Magena removed her hand.

"You will find the pretty stone and tell people you found it in a large oyster," she directed, "but you will not remember Magena."

With a toss of her head, Magena turned on her heel and sped out the door. *Motherrr, will not know I gave the nice man a stone,* she reasoned, *and I can give the pretty head covering thing to her friend.*

After a few minutes, Marcus shook his head, straightened his tie, and opened the door. *Beautiful day,* he thought, totally without any memory of what had just transpired. Later, when he returned home, he reached into his pant pocket to retrieve his keys and found the pearl. *What luck,* he thought, *finding an oyster with a pearl like this is a rare occurrence, but I don't remember eating oysters lately.*

The more he thought about it, however, the more he remembered finding the pearl in the oyster until finally the story was embedded firmly in his brain, and anyone who asked would be convinced by the tale. A few years later, Marcus used the pearl to purchase the building on Front Street from his elderly employer, becoming a powerful and successful businessman in the local community.

A BONNET FOR MAGENA

Chapter 31

TRUTH VERSUS LIES

An elderly man walking his dog along the river stared at the vivacious girl hurrying along the wooden sidewalk. The fancy chapeau on her head was a strange contrast to the leather britches and shirt that fit her lithe body like a second skin. Stopping dead in his tracks, the man seemed entranced. He watched Magena until she disappeared from sight.

What a handsome young woman, he thought, wishing he was young again.

"I'd follow that one to the ends of the earth," he muttered under his breath.

Magena turned on the street her mother described and within minutes located the building where the captain and his wife lived. Her nose twitched at the odor of baking bread emanating from the upstairs window as she approached the stoop and knocked loudly on the door. Magena was not one to address a task timidly, and she was excited about meeting her mother's friend.

The door opened wide, and Magena saw a petite woman dressed in a blue cotton frock, standing in the entry. Her fair hair was plaited in two thick braids which were pinned up by each ear, and she had a white apron tied round her waist.

"My Motherrr sends me to talk to you, Laydie," Magena announced, holding out the hat to the woman in the doorway.

"You like the pretty head covering?" she asked. "It is gift for you from me."

The captain's lady looked confused as Magena pushed the hat toward her. It was the most beautiful creation she had ever seen, but more incredible than the hat, she thought, was the exotic creature standing on her stoop.

"My Motherrr, the woman you know as Margaret Rose, sent me to you, Laydie," Magena repeated. "She is sorry about the boat falling to the bottom of the sea."

The captain's lady was never at a loss for words, but at this moment felt as if she could not speak at all. Who was this girl, and what did she mean about Margaret Rose?

Magena frowned. "We go to your living place, Laydie," she demanded, "not talk on the street."

"Of course. How rude of me," Laydie apologized. "Come along, and I will make us a hot cup of chamomile tea so we can relax and chat."

Magena followed Laydie to the upstairs apartment. It was the first time she had ever climbed stairs; just one more 'first' in the day's adventures.

"Sit, my dear, and make yourself comfortable," Laydie invited as Magena removed her cloak, throwing it over the banister. The girl was close on her heels as her hostess turned into the tiny kitchen to make the tea. Meanwhile, Magena took the opportunity to investigate everything that was happening in the steamy room. She pulled open the oven door, peering inside at two loaves of baking bread, then stuck her finger into the large puffy batch of dough rising on the counter. The curious finger poked into the pot of jam, then trailed in the butter as Magena licked and tasted every edible

223

item visible. She smacked her lips, drinking milk from a bottle on the counter, all the while making a strange musical trilling sound.

Laydie watched as her visitor opened drawers and cupboards as if she owned the place. Magena appeared to be particularly interested in the floral designs on the English china plates, tracing the patterns with her finger. *Who is this bold girl?* Laydie thought, astonished by Magena's regal bearing and self-assurance.

"Come, my dear," she directed, taking off her apron, "the tea is ready, and we can drink it in the parlor while we talk."

The captain's lady sat on one of the comfortable chairs by the window after placing two cups of steaming tea on a small table. She motioned for Magena to sit on the davenport, but Magena ignored the suggestion, instead sitting on the floor by Laydie's chair. When Magena placed her hand familiarly on Laydie's arm, the confused woman flinched as she felt an electric tingling in her fingertips.

"You are the most beautiful child," Laydie whispered, leaning forward to stroke Magena's hair, feeling as if she was looking at an angel. Then Magena raised her face towards the captain's lady, opening her exotic violet eyes wide as she stared into the face of her hostess. Laydie stared back, transfixed, almost as if she was bewitched.

"I will tell you about Motherrr now," Magena purred, laying her head on Laydie's knee.

The two women sat absolutely still for almost fifteen minutes as Laydie learned everything about the incredible journey of Margaret Rose. Not a word was spoken, but words were not necessary as Magena told the story of Ohnalee to her mother's friend. Magena knew some humans had the ability to understand the silent language of the sea people, and the captain's lady was one of these. When Magena was finished, her new friend took a sip of her tea, feeling strangely calm and at peace. "This revelation brings me great joy child," Laydie said quietly, "but the mystery is why I feel like I knew it already." Magena grinned, a saucy look on her animated face and her pert little nose twitched as if catching a whiff of some scent or aroma.

Then she jumped up like a mischievous child, hitting the small table with her elbow, knocking her cup of tea onto the floor.

"Oh, so sorry, Laydie," she giggled as she loosened the drawstring on the leather pouch she carried, spilling its precious contents into the lap of her hostess.

"Motherrr wants the Captain to have a new boat," Magena said, a triumphant look on her face, "because she feels very bad the bad man took it."

The captain's lady sat silently, her lap spilling over with heavy gold coins and precious stones, but instead of picking them up or running her fingers through the pile, she seemed unable to take her eyes off Magena. The treasure Ohnalee had given her friend was more than enough to purchase the finest boat and engine on the market, but she felt the greater treasure was the presence of this fascinating magical child.

"I must go now," Magena said, "Mommy and Poppi will worry. They think I am still a baby, even though I am almost five in human years."

The captain's lady now fully understood everything about the people of Ohnalee's new world, so this was not surprising.

"Please tell your Mother that I love and miss her," Laydie requested, "and I thank her for her generous gift. When the captain returns home today, I will explain everything, but he is a good man, and I can promise he will never reveal the existence of your people to anyone."

Magena put her arms around Laydie, hugging her tightly. "Can I come back and stay with you, if Motherrr says it is permitted."

"Of course, of course," Laydie agreed warmly, "you are always welcome for as long as you want. If you would like to attend school in Florence, we can say that you are my niece, come to visit for a while.

The school is just up the street, in the next block, actually," Laydie explained, seeming excited at the idea, "so it would be very convenient for you to live with me during the school year. You could help out by babysitting with the children while I am baking."

Laydie's eyes danced with delight as she thought of a particularly delicious idea. "Perhaps you could be Queen of the Rhododendron Festival one year. I know that would make your mother very proud."

"Thank you, Laydie," Magena said politely, remembering how her mother taught her to respond to kindness. *It might be neat to be queen of the humans,* she thought, *bet no other Mer princess has done that.*

"I must go quickly now, back to the place where Motherrr waits, but I can wear the hat when I return, yes?"

"Of course you can," Laydie promised as she took off her apron and grabbed a warm sweater from the hook by the stairway, "but now I'll walk with you."

"One more thing I must give to you," Magena purred as she donned her cloak. From a deep pocket inside the garment, Magena removed a large scallop shell, placing it by the doorway inside the hall. "It is the mark of our people," Magena said, "blessed by Magdalena Meda to bring you good fortune and happiness."

"There it will stay," promised Laydie as she locked the door, "if I can keep the children from taking it to their room."

The two women held hands as they walked along the street toward the river, chattering happily as if they had known each other for years and years. There was an immediate connection between the two, and Magena felt she now had a beloved auntie who would help her to navigate easily back and forth across the bridge between two worlds.

When they reached the mouth of the river, Magena let loose a series of loud whoops as she shucked off her leather suit. Completely natural and without any shame at all, she stood naked on a large gray rock, her arms outstretched. The lady watched, enthralled, as Magena dove gracefully into the water, carrying her leather clothing in her arms. As her body disappeared beneath the sea, the captain's lady got a quick glimpse of a shimmering purple tail that smacked the surface, then was gone.

The captain's lady waited for a while until daylight was waning, hoping to catch a look at her friend, but all she saw was a few sea lions swimming just offshore. Just in case her friend was watching, she gave one last sad wave of her hand before heading back toward town. *What a tale I have to tell the captain,* she mused, thinking how his eyes would sparkle at the thought of a new boat.

Ohnalee, Mokeema, and Magena watched and waited until Laydie disappeared behind the sand dunes. It was time to swim toward the setting sun, then down deep to the land of the Mer. Magena was absolutely hyperactive, swimming back and forth from one parent to the other, babbling nonstop about her visit to town and the captain's lady, telling and retelling each and every moment of her adventure until her parents finally begged for quiet. Ohnalee smiled as Magena told about the beautiful hat she had given to Laydie, and for just a moment, she felt a certain sadness for the things she would never enjoy in her chosen life, such as beautiful feminine dresses, and a hat with a veil.

"Can I go live with Laydie sometime, Mommy, please, please," Magena begged. "She says I can come for as long as I want, even go to school."

"We'll see, darling," Ohnalee promised. "Your father and I will discuss it when we get home."

Mokeema grinned, thinking maybe a "babysitter" on shore might be a very good idea.

Chapter 32

OPALINA

When Reverend Coombs returned home and found his wife gone again, it was almost more than he could bear. This time, however, he found a note sitting on the table in the kitchen. It said simply,

I will never return.
Please forgive me,
Margaret Rose.

The Reverend sat down on one of the wooden chairs by the table, crumpling the paper in his hand. *What have I done to deserve this*, he thought, his gray eyes spilling over with tears. *Haven't I been a faithful servant of the good Lord? Haven't I treated Margaret kindly and done everything possible to make a good home for her?* His thin body slumped as he rested his elbows on the table, cradling his head in his arms. The cabin grew dark as night fell over the Oregon Coast, but the somber wail carried on the breeze was not the sound of the wind, but the despair of a wounded soul.

When the reverend woke the next morning, he was still sitting at the table. His clothes were rumpled and his body stiff.

"Dear God," he moaned as he pulled himself up painfully, stretching his arms and scratching his head, "help me accept this burden."

My wife is dead, he decided as he placed a few bits of kindling in the stove to take the chill off the room. *She is dead to me, just as dead as if she fell off a cliff into the sea. I must be calm and rational, and with the help of my Lord and Savior, Jesus Christ, I will survive this misery.*

When Margaret Rose disappeared the first time, the reverend seemed unable to resign himself to her loss, letting the pain affect every part of his life, making him a bitter and judgmental person. But now, a kind of peaceful understanding came upon his heart as he placed his anger and frustration in the hands of his Lord. *It is a part of the plan for my life,* he realized, *and I must accept this trial with patient submission.*

The reverend suspected Margaret Rose had left him for another man, but in the weeks to come, he found the strength to forgive her.

Every night he knelt by his bed, praying silently, *Surround your servant, Margaret Rose, with the pure white light of your protection, and give me the wisdom to accept and forgive.*

Laura Leigh often came to visit, and he found they had many things in common. *Perhaps I married the wrong sister,* he reflected. *But I can never marry again, knowing my wife still lives, somewhere.*

Several months after Ohnalee sent Magena to the captain's lady with the pouch of precious stones and coins, Laydie stirred in her bed, hearing a soft knock on her front door. It was almost midnight and the moon was full, hanging low over the river, its metallic silvery glow illuminating the dark streets of the town. The captain was away on an overnight trip with his new vessel, and Laydie and the children were sleeping soundly.

The knock came again, louder this time, rousing Laydie from dreamland. She sat upright in the bed, rubbing her eyes as the vision faded. Something about catching a really big tuna, she thought regretfully as she heard the knock again.

Who the heck can that be at this hour, she wondered as she crawled out of bed, then grabbed the warm robe from the hook by the door. Thrusting her feet into slippers, Laydie padded down the stairs, placing her ear on the door.

"Who's there?" she whispered, hoping bad news had not arrived at her stoop. A captain's wife always worries when her husband is at sea, and Laydie was no exception. "It's me, Margaret Rose," Ohnalee called, her voice just above a whisper. "I need your help, please."

The captain's lady opened the door, astonished to see her friend and Magena huddled together outside. Magena's arm was wrapped around her mother, who was doubled over as if in pain.

"Help Laydie," Magena pleaded, "Mommy is having a baby."

Ohnalee whimpered as the captain's lady put her arms around her friend, pulling her inside. "Oh, my dear," Laydie exclaimed, supporting her friend from behind as they climbed the narrow stairway.

"I am so sorry to trouble you," Ohnalee moaned, "but this baby is coming fast, and it must be born on land or it will die, I fear."

"I don't understand," the captain's lady said in a quiet voice, "but we must get you into bed immediately."

"No, no," protested Ohnalee, "I have learned a better way to tolerate the pain of birthing a child. In the world of the sea people, the females birth their young easily and without pain. Will you help me have this baby in the way I have been taught by the Mer?"

"Of course, my dear," the captain's lady agreed. "Tell me what you need Margaret, and I will help."

"I can help, Mommy. I can help too," Magena interrupted. "I'm a big girl now."

The captain's lady was bursting with curiosity, but put all her questions aside to concentrate on the task ahead.

"Will you kindly call me by the name my mate has given?" Ohnalee asked?

"I am so sorry, my dear Ohnalee," her friend agreed, "I have said your new name often since sweet Magena came to see me."

Ohnalee grimaced as a strong contraction wracked her body. She realized it would not be long before her baby arrived as it had been only a few minutes since the last pain.

"Can you please fill your bathing tub with warm water?" Ohnalee requested as she removed her cloak, exposing her round tummy. Magena helped her into the bedroom where she removed Ohnalee's damp sealskin shift with plenty of room for her swollen belly, then propped her mother up against the pillows on the lady's bed.

"I can wear your warm garment, lady?" Magena inquired as Laydie removed her robe, slipping into a clean housedress.

"Of course," Laydie agreed with an amused smile, noticing that Magena had already donned the housecoat and was grooming her hair with the silver-plated brush that belonged to Dan's grandmother.

The captain's lady bustled around the kitchen, filling several pans with water, then bringing them to the boil. Back and forth she trudged, from the kitchen to the bathroom, dumping the boiling water into the tub.

"How much water do you want in the bath, dear?" Laydie asked as she added cool water to the hot water, producing a perfect temperature.

"To the top," Ohnalee requested.

"Magena, put that brush down and come away from the mirror," Ohnalee commanded sternly. "You're frittering away your time as usual." She grinned for a minute as she recognized she was saying the same words to her daughter as the Reverend used on her during their marriage.

"Sorry dear," Ohnalee apologized, "but you need to act like a big girl, I need your help."

Magena frowned but obediently put the brush down, following Laydie into the kitchen to get more water.

Laydie wondered what Ohnalee was going to do with all the water she was pouring into the claw-footed iron tub, but she was content to be patient to see what her friend needed.

When the tub was almost full, Ohnalee got up from the bed and moved into the small bathroom. She was panting hard now as the contractions came one after the other. Ohnalee put her elbow into the water to test the temperature, then gingerly put one foot after another into the tub, finally settling down into the tepid water. The captain's lady watched in amazement as her friend pulled her knees up almost to her armpits, spreading her feet wide apart. Magena crouched close to the tub, holding her mother's hand. With each contraction, Ohnalee cried out in a high shrill voice. Magena seemed attuned to her mother's discomfort as she joined in with her own melodious voice, the two producing a rhythmic pulsating symphony of orgasmic sound.

Suddenly Ohnalee cried out one last time, and Magena plunged her hands deep into the water between her mother's legs. With a triumphant yell, she brought forth a tiny infant, holding it just out of the water. Almost instantly, the baby started to squall, and Laydie reached for a spool of heavy white twine to tie the umbilical cord, neatly cutting it with her sharp sewing scissors. Ohnalee lay back against the tub, exhausted but exhilarated at the same time, watching as her friend placed the newborn on a white towel. The lady sponged the tiny body clean, then wrapped the infant in a soft blanket, handing the child to Magena.

The girl danced around the room singing. She cuddled her baby sister in her arms as Ohnalee smiled with obvious pride. Laydie was enchanted by the high, trilling sound coming from Magena's lips. The song dipped and soared like a tropic bird, filling the room with its bewitching melody. The girl swayed back and forth as she moved, and Laydie thought she heard a giggle from the newborn as Magena placed her finger in the cherub's pink mouth. *Impossible. I must be hearing things*, she decided.

Laydie wondered why a baby born like this would not immediately breathe water into the lungs, but Magena seemed to be reading her thoughts, as usual, saying, "Babies have a special gift which prevents them from taking immediate breath underwater when born. Children of the Mer must first breathe air before they adapt to breathing underwater, but this baby is more human than Mer and cannot survive beneath the sea while she is so small."

Laydie thought that explanation left word for interpretation, wondering if the child would be able to live with the Merfolk when she was an adult, but Magena answered the question without hesitation.

"With the magic of the gods, and her full consent, it may be possible," she said, "but I will keep my baby sister close to my heart, even when we are apart."

Laydie was amazed by this easy birth. She saw how the warm water relaxed the mother, enabling her to better control the pushing reflex. She had delivered many babies but never had she seen such a fast and painless delivery.

Ohnalee stood up in the tub, then carefully stepped out, requesting a pan to birth the placenta. Laydie wrapped a warm shawl around her friend's shoulders as she squatted near the tub, and after the placenta was delivered, made her comfortable on her own soft bed. She covered Ohnalee warmly with a feather comforter, then placed the new infant in her arms. Magena curled her body next to her mother, watching as Ohnalee placed the child to her breast for her first feeding.

Laydie stood at her bedroom window, watching the sun rise over the Siuslaw River, its shimmering light casting a myriad of orange reflections on the placid surface of the water. Her guests said they were starving after the birth, and devoured several flaky hot biscuits slathered with butter and jam. After they finished their tea, Ohnalee and Magena fell into a sound and comfortable sleep.

Hope my little ones sleep awhile, Laydie thought, *I could use a nap.*

I will feel absolutely great when I wake, Laydie commanded her brain, *not tired in any way, with every part of my body feeling strong and healthy.* Anytime Laydie was weary, getting late to bed with only a few hours of sleep, with much work to do the next day, she used this mental exercise to awake feeling rested and mentally alert. When she fished with the captain, often alone on the helm during the night watch, she used the same kind of mental affirmation to stay awake, ready for whatever was required.

Laydie settled down on the sofa, thinking about her friend, pondering about the newborn child and its future. Obviously the infant was more human than Mer, and the lady wondered what plans Ohnalee had for the little girl.

About eight in the morning, the children of the household awoke, rousing their snoozing mother by climbing onto her lap. The girls had already peeked into the bedroom where the new baby slept, and only a glass of milk and a muffin would convince them to be quiet until the visitors were awake. When Ohnalee was wakened by her baby's cry, she saw two sets of curious eyes watching from the doorway, and the minute she smiled at the children, they climbed up on the bottom of her bed.

"Shoo, shoo, you two," Laydie said, waving the rascals down and out of the room. "Play quietly with your dolls, girls, and we will take a walk later on," she promised.

After bringing a breakfast tray to her hungry guests, Laydie pulled a chair alongside the bed so they could chat while devouring the last tidbit of coffee cake. She was full of questions, and Ohnalee was ready to tell her friend everything.

Ohnalee grasped her friend's hand tightly as she confessed this baby was indeed the child of Minister Coombs, the unexpected fruit of the one night when the minister lost control of his sexual desires. Ohnalee told Laydie she had not realized she was pregnant and ignored the obvious signs like feeling nauseous in the morning, particularly when cooking the greasy sausages her husband preferred for breakfast.

A few months after her return to the sea people, Ohnalee said she felt a stirring in her tummy and went to the tribe's shaman for advice. Magdalena Meda placed her hand on Ohnalee's stomach to determine if the child was human or a child of the Mer. She warned the child was human and could not survive in the cold water of the Pacific or be able to make the long migration to the enchanted islands for the winter.

"The child must be called 'Opalina,'" the shaman pronounced, "as she will be a happy child, with a glowing inner flame that will burn brightly when she reaches her full maturity. She will need protection and peace in her early years, but perhaps in the future, she will choose to reconnect with our people."

Ohnalee wondered how that could happen, but she knew better than to question the vision of Magdalena Meda. She had faith that Meda was divinely inspired and used her gift to guide the Mer along the correct path.

Mokeema understood Ohnalee's account of the encounter with Reverend Coombs and was her loving support during the last months of her pregnancy, but they understood the child must be born on land.

Ohnalee told Laydie a little about the history of the Mer people, saying that often children were left onshore to be raised by humans. "Families all over the world are descended from our people," Ohnalee said, "as our women must sometimes choose what life and what world will be the best for their children."

"I must give this child to its father," Ohnalee told the captain's lady, "even though it will break my heart." Tears welled in her eyes as the baby suckled at her breast, and within minutes, all three women were sobbing.

"I would raise this baby willingly, Ohnalee, as if it were my own," Laydie suggested, but Ohnalee had already decided what course must be taken. "The minister must have his child," Ohnalee said, "and I would like Laura Leigh to be involved in her life. Her grandparents will be ecstatic when they see this beautiful child, and perhaps it will make up in some small way for my decision to leave them behind."

Ohnalee wiped her eyes, then blew her nose on a handkerchief provided by her hostess as she gazed lovingly at the tiny creature enfolded in her arms.

"Will you take this baby to Reverend Coombs, Laydie? Beg him to love her, even though I am her Mother. I know he must hate me because of the hurt and embarrassment I have caused, but I want my baby to be with her father."

Laydie assured her friend she would take the child to the minister and make sure he would accept the baby before leaving.

"If he does not," she promised with determination, "I will go to your parents, and they will not refuse me."

Ohnalee and Magena rested during the day, and when darkness fell, they made ready to leave.

"Must you go so soon, my friend?" Laydie said. "You are not yet recovered from the birth."

"Dear Laydie, we cannot stay," Ohnalee said. "It is almost time for the people to migrate south for the winter, and my place is with them."

Ohnalee wept as she relinquished her child to the arms of her friend and leaned forward to kiss the tiny rosebud mouth one last time. Magena grinned, placing her finger in the little hand of her sister.

"I'll be back soon," she promised, "so me and Laydie can come and play with you and your daddy."

Laydie bade farewell to her visitors, and within minutes they had sped away into the darkness. In many ways, the swift departure was a blessing as Laydie knew any delay would be even more painful for her friend. The tiny baby in her arms was a treasure, and Ohnalee's heart would never fully heal from the loss of her child.

When the captain returned from his fishing trip, he was shocked to hear a baby's cry as he climbed the stairs. He found his wife gently rocking in her favorite chair in the living room, a Madonna-like smile on her face. Laydie put a finger to her lips. "Shush," she murmured, anticipating a stream of loud questions.

"We have an angel visiting for a few days, luv," she whispered, handing the child up to his kind calloused hands.

The captain held the baby close as his wife recounted the story of Ohnalee's visit.

"Taking her to the father is the right thing to do," Captain Dan agreed, "but we'll bring her home with us if he hesitates for a second."

Ohnalee's gift had made it possible for the captain's family to have a prosperous and comfortable life with a new vessel equipped with the very latest equipment for fishing or crabbing. The debt was impossible to repay, but both the captain and his lady knew their family would be forever connected to Ohnalee and her family.

The next morning, Captain Dan borrowed a horse and buggy and the couple headed north along the coast. When they finally reached the cabin, they could see the minister and a lady sitting on the porch. The two waved when the captain and his wife approached, then hurried to the gate as the visitors tied the horse to a tree near the picket fence.

Ohnalee's sister greeted the visitors with obvious enthusiasm, saying how happy she was to see them. Captain Dan helped his wife down from the buggy seat, and for the first time, the minister noticed she was holding a small bundle in her arms. He and Laura Leigh exchanged puzzled glances, and the captain's lady imagined she saw a spark of familiarity on their faces that was more than friendship.

Laydie heard a tiny squeal coming from her bundle, then pulled the blanket back so the minister and Laura Leigh could see the baby's face. Opalina blinked her bright blue eyes as the sunlight fell upon her translucent white skin and red gold curls.

The minister gasped, stumbling a few steps backward, as he gaped at the tiny cherub in the lady's arms. Even though this child was only a few days old, she was the spitting image of Margaret Rose. There was no mistaking who this child's mother was, and tears started flowing from Laura Leigh's dark eyes.

"Where is she? Where is my sister?" she demanded. "I know this is her child."

"I don't know where Margaret Rose has gone," said Laydie softly, "but she is safe and well. This is your child, Minister Coombs, and Margaret begs that you and Laura Leigh will raise her with love and affection."

The captain's lady stretched out her arms, offering the child to her father. The man held back, looking fearful and distressed, but Laura Leigh took the baby and smothered it with kisses. The infant gurgled and cooed, making a chirping noise that sounded like *la la la la la la la,* then she giggled with sheer delight as Laura Leigh placed a finger in the center of her tiny palm. Little Opalina clutched the finger with surprising strength, holding tightly, then pulled it toward her pink mouth.

"She's hungry," Laura Leigh whispered as the baby sucked. "I must warm some milk immediately."

"Take her," she demanded, thrusting the baby in the minister's arms as she turned toward the cabin, racing at high speed through the grass.

"Margaret Rose has named the child Opalina," Laydie said, "but she will be content for you to give the child an additional name of your choosing. She suggests the name 'Marie,' the name of your mother, as a good possibility."

"Where is Margaret? Where is she?" the minister begged to know. "Will she ever return?"

"I am sorry for you, dear man," the captain's lady replied, "but Margaret Rose must travel far away with her new family and cannot take this dear babe on the difficult journey. She said to tell you she is sorry for the distress she has caused but hopes you will treasure this child and understand her decision. Margaret Rose feels she cannot be a proper mother for this child at the moment and knows she will have a better life with you.

The minister struggled to contain his emotions, but several deep sobs escaped his lips as he held his daughter tightly. Baby Opalina Marie smiled again, then giggled again, the tinkling sound sounding almost melodic like a song. "Da da da da da da da," she trilled to everyone's amazement.

"She said 'da da,'" the minister almost shouted, his gray eyes wide with astonishment. "How can a baby only a few days old say da da?"

"She is a treasure, indeed, dear man," Laydie agreed. "Margaret Rose trusts you will keep her daughter safe and give her lots of love, with ample amounts of freedom. She will bring you joy if you do that, and Margaret Rose says she will sense her daughter's happiness from wherever her path leads."

The minister and his guests walked slowly along the path toward the cabin as Laura Leigh emerged with a nursing bottle in her hand. She sat down on one of the rocking chairs on the porch, reaching for the little one held gingerly in the minister's arms. The bottle had been used to feed two baby goats whose mother had died after their birth, but now, baby Opalina curled her pink lips around the nipple, sucking greedily and purring with contentment, like a fat happy cat.

Captain Dan smiled at the scene, knowing Opalina Marie would be well loved with her father and her aunt.

"Time to go, babe," he suggested, knowing how attached his lady had become to this tiny angel.

"The tide is low so we will make good time going back along the beach," the captain said, putting his arm around his lady's small waist. He could see that her blue eyes were misty even though her mouth was smiling.

"She'll be fine, Babe," Dan said as he wiped a tear from her cheek. "You can't keep her; Ohnalee is right, Opalina needs her father."

"I know you're right", Laydie sniffed, but I feel such a strong connection that it really hurts."

After warm goodbyes were said, Laydie turned her face to the sea, retracing her steps to the waiting horse. Dan was ready to assist her up onto the buggy when they saw Laura Leigh running down the path toward them. The couple could see baby Opalina snuggled in her father's arms as Margaret's sister reached the white picket fence. Throwing her arms around Laydie, she murmured something into her ear.

Laydie looked confused for a moment, stammering, "Uh, uh, well, I don't really know what you mean, my dear."

"You do, you do," Laura Leigh insisted, her slim body shaking as she fell back, staring intently as if her pain could convince Laydie to do her bidding.

"Tell me what I need to know, and I'll not trouble you for the details, I promise," she pleaded.

The lady looked to her husband as if for guidance, upset by the tortured look on Laura's face.

"I know about him—that man, that creature," Laura Leigh sobbed, pointing a quivering finger toward the ocean. "How could she? How could she leave us, leave me, leave our mother, to go with that animal, that beast from another world?

I told her not to meet him, not to talk to him, to stay away from the shore, but she wouldn't listen," Laura Leigh raged hysterically, "and she made me promise not to tell Mother, not to tell anyone.

God forgive me for keeping that hideous secret," Laura Leigh wept, "I should have known better, him teasing her, saying she was meant to be his, spinning wild stories about wealth and treasure, making her think there was something better just over the horizon."

The captain's lady stepped forward toward Laura Leigh and put her arms around the shaking woman, stroking her hair and brushing the tears from her eyes.

"It's not your fault, my dear," the lady said softly, trying her best to calm her.

"It was meant to be, and nothing you could have done or said would have changed the outcome.

Be still now, and listen," the lady demanded in a firm voice. "You have a job to do, something more important than anything you have ever done. You have a child to raise, a child with special needs, a child whose mother trusts you to keep her safe. This precious little girl now has two families, one here, and another that travels in a realm where we cannot go, but perhaps one day she will want to know her birth mother and siblings."

"She has a sister?" Laura Leigh asked in a quiet voice.

"Yes, and a brother also," said Laydie, "and one day, if I can, I will bring the sister to meet you as she already has that in her plan. That one has a mind of her own and will not be dissuaded when she sets forth on a course. Magena loves her little sister, and even though she is still a young child herself, helped her mother at the birthing as well as any adult.

She is loved, your sister—loved as you cannot imagine, not only by her mate, who treats her as a queen, but by her people as she really is their queen."

Laura Leigh's mouth fell open in amazement as she struggled to regain her composure.

"You say Margaret Rose is a queen?" she said, trying hard to envision her very own sister sitting on a throne under the sea.

"It is true, but it will be better if the minister does not know of these things," Laydie suggested. "I hope you will not speak of thrones and creatures from the sea in helping him to accept your sister's gift."

Captain Dan nodded his head in agreement as the women talked for a few minutes more, then watched as his wife kissed Laura Leigh affectionately on both cheeks before giving her a gentle shove in the direction of the cabin.

"Bye, sweetheart, please come and visit soon. And bring darling Opalina when you come," Laydie shouted as the girl returned to the porch where she took the sleeping baby from the minister before settling back into the rocking chair. Laura Leigh felt a sweet contentment as she cuddled Opalina close, running her finger along the edges of the tiny scallop shell hanging on a cord around her neck, exploring the folds behind her delicate ears. *I'll get you a golden cord for that shell one day,* Laura Leigh thought as the baby opened her eyes wide, a hint of a smile curling the corners of her winsome rosebud mouth. "La la," she trilled, in a singsong voice, "la la la la la la la."

"It's impossible," Laura Lee said out loud, looking up at the minister as he stood close by her side, hand on her shoulder, "I swear she just said 'ma ma.'"

Captain Dan settled his wife comfortably on the seat of the buggy, placing a blanket across her lap, then headed south toward Florence. They had traveled about a mile down the trail when Laydie clutched his leg, throwing the blanket aside.

"Stop the buggy. Look there, Danny," Laydie cried excitedly, pointing in the direction of the sea where several sea lions seemed to be swimming just offshore.

"She's there. Ohnalee is there. I know it," Laydie exclaimed as she stood, trying to get a better look.

"Just some sea lions," the captain said, squinting his eyes in the face of the sun, which dangled like a fat round juicy orange in the western sky.

The captain's lady hopped down from the buggy, hurrying almost to the edge of a steep drop-off overlooking the rocky shore. She shielded her face with her hand, watching as the sea lions bobbed up and down in the gentle waves. Suddenly, one of the animals raised an arm, waving it back and forth.

241

I see you, my friend, Laydie thought, raising her arm to return the gesture.

"Farewell, farewell, dear Ohnalee," the captain's lady screamed at the top of her lungs, frantically waving both arms back and forth.

The captain rushed to his wife's side but saw nothing unusual as the sea lions slipped beneath the sea. Tears ran down Laydie's cheeks, but she felt a strange sense of peace as she turned her back to the sea.

"Let's go home, my love," she said in a quiet voice. "It has been a very long day indeed."

Out beyond the horizon, in the salty cold water of the blue Pacific, Ohnalee swam close to her mate, holding his hand. Every once in a while, she looked back over her shoulder toward the distant shore as it grew farther and farther away, finally disappearing from view.

"She is safe now, my darling," Mokeema's voice whispered, "safe with her father until *the time of choosing*. In the meantime, we go south to swim again in the warm waters of the enchanted islands." Mokeema grinned, showing his large pointed white teeth, a look of anticipation on his handsome face. His dark eyes glowed as he thought of Ohnalee swimming naked and free through schools of flashing minnows and tarpon, radiating jets of shiny silver light from their heavy scales.

"I will carry you today, my Ohnalee," the male commanded as he swooped her up into his strong arms. *Always and forever*, he promised, knowing spoken words were not necessary between them.

Ohnalee wrapped her arms around Mokeema's neck, entwining the fingers of one hand in his long flowing hair.

I should braid that beautiful hair, Ohnalee thought as they descended far below to the world where she was queen of her tribe and the daughter of Dragone of the Dragon Mer.

MAGDALENA MEDA & THE PURPLE DRAGON

Chapter 33

METAMORPHOSIS

Several days after Ohnalee's return, Mokeema sent couriers to all corners of the kingdom, inviting his people to a special gathering of the Tribe. Although the date was only one week from the announcement, everyone made preparations to leave their homes to see what their king had to say. Such an assembly had been called only a few times in the entire lifetime of the late Queen Maru, so everyone knew the subject must be of great importance.

Mokeema busied himself with the preparations, sending dozens of his most trusted staff members to an underwater mountain range several miles away from the city. They had instructions to prepare for a fantastic celebration, the likes of which had never been seen before.

Magdalena Meda rushed in and out of the palace several times for personal audiences with Mokeema. She flung her purple cloak back over her shoulders as she threw open the doors to his chamber without requesting permission from the guard. The shaman's powerful body was extremely large, seeming to increase in size and weight every year, but this element seemed only to add to her power and importance in the tribe.

"Eagalia has a complete list of everything that must be completed for the ceremony," Meda assured Mokeema, "so everything that must be done, will be done.

The ancient ones have communicated through the magic crystal," Meda confided, "confirming their agreement of the woman's worthiness, so it is only for you to bring dear Ohnalee to the sacred Mountain of Destiny on the night of the full moon where she will ascend the great spiral of knowledge."

"It shall be as you say, Magdalena Meda," assured Mokeema, bowing respectfully to the shaman as a sign of his understanding of her link to the spirit world and the great mysteries.

Ohnalee had fallen into a deep depression after her return home, feeling terrible sadness and guilt about the decision to abandon her precious baby girl. She believed the choice was morally correct, but her warm, motherly heart ached to hold her child just one more time.

Hear my voice oh sweetheart mine, your Mommy loves you, and I'll come when it is time, she sang silently as she tossed restlessly in her bed, remembering Opalina's sweet face and the smell of her skin.

Ohnalee knew little about the planned festivities as she languished in the dwelling she and Mokeema shared after their joining ceremony. She felt completely devoid of energy, and the hustle and bustle of the palace of the late Queen Maru seemed more than she could deal with in her present state. Mokeema understood her feelings and returned to her side every day after his daily schedule was completed, holding her close and warming her body with his.

It was their agreement never to be separated, and Mokeema did not even consider staying in the palace overnight without her.

"You have given me more joy than I ever thought possible, my Ohnalee," Mokeema whispered as he stroked her hair. His strong hands moved lovingly, massaging her shoulders and arms, then caressing the curves and contours of her lower back. He could feel tension disappear as she finally relaxed and slept. Mokeema felt that time would close the wound caused by her separation from Opalina, but he hoped the ceremony he was planning would pull his mate out of her melancholy and heal her heart.

Magena and Qillac hovered near, concerned about their mother's condition, but she paid little attention to their presence. Ohnalee had thrown off her warm suit, burying her face in the folds of the white fur quilt Magena brought from one of the ships in the area, and even Qillac's silly juvenile jokes failed to make her laugh.

Jade brought Ohnalee delicious snacks to tempt her appetite, but she ate little, preferring to escape into an inner world of dreams and daydreams.

Ohnalee often stared for hours into the moonstone Queen Maru had given her on the day of her wedding, and in the milky depths of the crystal, she saw her child sitting on Laura Leigh's lap, gurgling with delight at a small puppy playing on the porch. She looked so happy with Laura, and Ohnalee whimpered as she saw Opalina's little hand reaching for her sister's smiling face. *Opalina, Opalina,* Ohnalee cried silently, *I see you, I see you.*

A few days before the ceremony, as the moon swelled to its fullest, Mokeema told Ohnalee she must ready herself for a special state occasion.

"Oh, Mokeema, my darling, I really don't feel like going," she protested. "I'm just not feeling myself these days."

"You must get yourself together, my dear, as I need you to be at my side for this special event," Mokeema said. "Magena and Jade will help you prepare, and I will bring a special gown for you to wear. You will not need the leather suit on this special night as we will travel to the mountain of the moon in the chariot of the Pocampi."

"It will be as you wish," Ohnalee yawned, stretching her body as if to rise, but then she curled herself in the fetal position and fell back asleep.

On the day of the ceremony, Mokeema did not go to the palace as usual, preferring to stay with Ohnalee to assist in her preparations for the event. Despite her reluctance, he got her up and moving about, and by the time the women arrived to help her dress, she appeared resigned to performing any duty required.

Ohnalee gasped as the women opened a heavy silver trunk to display the most magnificent garment she had ever seen or dreamed of. The ruby-red dress was made of a gossamer material so fine that it weighed absolutely nothing. The mysterious fabric seemed to flicker and glow hot as the brightest flame.

Mokeema slipped the shimmering gown over Ohnalee's head, grinning with satisfaction as it molded itself to her body. The dress had a round neckline that dipped low in the back almost to the waist, but in the front settled demurely just above the swell of her breasts. The dress followed the curve of her hip, then flared out at the knee. The hem was circular, a little shorter in the front but longer in the back, almost like a train. The long sleeves also flared at the bottom, covering Ohnalee's hands, and when she raised her arms, the fabric fluttered as if alive, reaching almost to the ground. When she held her arms up over her head, the fabric fluttered behind in the current, producing an enchanting illusion much like fairy wings.

Instantly, Ohnalee's spirits lifted as she examined her image in the long mirror in her dwelling place. *Who was this woman?* she wondered with amazement, seeing the regal beauty reflected in the glass. This was certainly not the despondent soul who had been lying around feeling sorry for herself, but a strong woman able to perform any duty required.

"This dress was made from thousands of precious ruby crystals found hidden in a wizard's cave in a far-off land," explained Mokeema, "and there is no other garment like it in the universe. The stones were pulverized into a dust so fine it would disappear instantly if caught on a gentle breeze in the land above our ocean world. That precious powder was blended with the glutinous sap of a rare and magical tree which only grows in the deepest part of the underwater universe, in a place known only to Magdalena Meda.

Legends carried down from our ancestors who lived in the land once called Lemuria say that the ruby crystal was used in temple ceremonies as a way to connect with the spirits of those who had ascended. Just one ruby crystal holds incredible power, so this dress is already healing your weakened spirit and filling your body with energy."

247

Ohnalee did indeed feel energized and healthy for the first time since the birth of her child, and all those attending her saw a rosy aura radiating from her skin. The dress seemed almost alive as it fluttered and moved in the lazy current with every move of Ohnalee's body.

Ohnalee suddenly realized she felt not only beautiful in this dress, but warm. The dress seemed to radiate heat as it swirled around her feet, bringing back pleasant memories of the sweet warmth of logs burning in a fireplace or the glow from a white-hot bonfire flaming on an Oregon beach. She recalled holidays when the children gathered driftwood, stacking it high on the beach for a blazing fire that would last into the night.

Mokeema gestured to two of his most trusted couriers, who approached respectfully, bowing low. One carried an elegant gold chest, and the other stood ready for Mokeema's signal to open the lid.

Jade hovered just behind her mistress, fussing with the long hair which swirled about her ivory shoulders. The strands gleamed with a golden glow as if they were illuminated by beams of the brightest sunshine cascading down from the heavens. Jade seemed every bit as excited as Ohnalee at the sight of the gilded box.

When the servant opened the box, Mokeema reached into the interior, bringing forth a glorious necklace, which he held up for all to see. The piece was made with rows of small ruby crystals alternated with spirals of twisted black kyanite, and hanging from the center was a ruby crystal the size of an egg. Ohnalee was mesmerized as Mokeema approached. Jade swept Ohnalee's hair out of the way so Mokeema could hang the spectacular creation around her lovely neck, fastening the clasp at the back. Then her lover pulled Ohnalee in front of the long mirror so she could see the full effect. He floated just behind her with a proud smile on his face.

"You are beautiful, my queen," said Mokeema, "and I must tell you more of this magical gift, which is yours to keep forever. My mother found this necklace in the ruins of a temple in the old city, and Magdalena Meda immediately understood its power. She has explained to me that the black spirals have many uses for the adept.

Magdalena says that the stone stimulates psychic awareness and is used in combination with the ruby crystal to travel on journeys to the land of the spirits."

Ohnalee looked confused, but she stood quietly, her fingers touching the large stone in the middle of the necklace, not wanting to interrupt her mate's explanation.

"Our ancestors believed the ruby crystal was a record keeper containing knowledge stored by wise ones from an ancient realm. The information is locked in the stone, just waiting to be discovered."

Ohnalee's fingers tingled as he spoke, and she felt a loving whisper somewhere in the deep regions of her mind. The voice was so clear that she released the crystal from her fingers, breaking the connection.

"Magdalena Meda says to tell you, my Ohnalee, that the ruby crystal dress and the stones in the necklace will protect you on your spiral journey to enlightenment."

"Spiral journey to where?" Ohnalee murmured under her breath. "What is that all about?"

"You must not worry, my Ohnalee. Tonight will be the most special night of your life."

Mokeema raised his hand, and two more couriers appeared in the doorway, bearing an ebony chest with silver markings. He raised the lid, removing the most special gift of all.

The red-feathered cap seemed to glow with a magical beauty all its own, and when Mokeema placed it on her head, Ohnalee closed her eyes. A whirlwind of visions rushed behind her lids as she saw emerald green mountains and tawny sand beaches.

"This cap belonged to Kerry, the Muiroigh mother of my mother, Maru," Mokeema said.

"The shaman has kept it safe for this day as Maru knew you were destined to wear the cap and be granted its power. I place it on your head, my queen, as a symbol of my mother's love and confidence."

Mokeema gave his men a sign, and Ohnalee heard a commotion at the door of the dwelling. She took Mokeema's hand as he swept her out the door to the waiting carriage. The team of Pocampi pawed the ground, their eyes glowing as they waited the signal to run. Ohnalee had never been carried in the Queen's coach before, so she was thrilled as Mokeema covered her lap with a warm leather coverlet. "I'm fine, darling," Ohnalee assured her mate, "I am toasty warm and very happy."

Mokeema snuggled down next to her, giving the driver permission to go. "We go, we go," Mokeema called. "We have a date with destiny tonight."

Ohnalee held tightly to Mokeema's hand as the sea horses sped through the water, their eyes shooting out jets of light that penetrated the darkness. The carriage flew through forests of kelp, then headed up toward the surface. Hundreds of sea people followed the carriage, and some swam alongside, but it was hard to keep up with the powerful Pocampi as they raced toward the tallest peak of the undersea mountain range.

Ohnalee could see the reflection of the moon on the water now, and as the carriage slowed, she saw they were passing through a wide undersea valley surrounded by taller hills and peaks. The carriage flew just over the tops of massive stands of elkhorn coral, and in the distance, Ohnalee could see mysterious glowing orbs of light that illuminated the water as well as a thousand oil lamps or candles.

Mokeema grinned, and his dark eyes sparkled with delight as he leaned over and kissed Ohnalee on her cheek. "All for you, my Ohnalee," he chuckled as the carriage came to a halt.

"Will you carry me tonight?" Ohnalee asked.

"No need for that," Mokeema said, as several of the men approached carrying a shining golden chair. The sides and back were carved with intricate designs showing Mer people in various activities, but Ohnalee had only a moment to study the meaning.

"Fit for a queen," Mokeema said, lifting Ohnalee in his arms then placing her in the chair.

The throne had two rails extending from the sides, and before she realized what was happening, two strong Mer swimmers were speeding her along toward the flickering lights in the water.

Ohnalee could see they were getting closer and closer to the surface, and the water got warmer, the higher they went. Mokeema had apparently gone on ahead, as Ohnalee could not see him anywhere. She was slightly annoyed he had left her alone, but decided nothing could spoil the joy she felt wearing the special ruby-red dress and matching necklace.

Ohnalee looked about, amazed to see she was surrounded by hundreds of sea people. Males and females floated lazily in the clear water, and others rested on the rocky ledges that surrounded her chair. Sea babies and older children skipped around playfully, hyperactive with the excitement of seeing so many of their cousins and friends in one place. They capered and chased friendly sea otters through crevices and canyons created by the rocky cliffs, darting behind stands of purple sea fans in vigorous games of hide and seek. Looking overhead, Ohnalee saw that the Mer had been joined by their friends, the Sea Lion Clan, as hundreds of the heavy brown warriors floated on the surface, their noisy barks resonating down to the people below.

Chattering flocks of gulls and other seabirds filled the air, sometimes dipping low, then settling for a moment among the sea lions. Frigate birds soared above the gulls, and if one looked closer, several majestic eagles could be seen.

Enormous gray whales cruised around the area, providing a ring of security. Their intelligent dark eyes took note of every suspicious movement or activity as if they were responsible for keeping the peace. Schools of tuna and salmon floated languidly just beneath the surface, basking in the moonlight, which danced off their silver scales.

Ohnalee discovered that the flickering lights emanated from thousands of jellyfish whose translucent bodies not only glowed in the dark, but sent out bright flashing beams that illuminated the noisy throng as they waited for the festivities to begin.

Herds of small sea horses galloped around the sea bottom, looking like miniature brown dragons, then stopped to rest in gardens of purple sea fans where thousands of large red and gold starfish raised their pointed fingers as Ohnalee passed by.

The swimmers carried Ohnalee around every part of the area, making sure that everyone got a close look at their queen. Ohnalee smiled and waved to acknowledge the salutes of her people. This was the first time she actually felt like a queen, and she realized that Mokeema had purposefully left her side, so she could experience the acclaim and homage due a queen.

Among the crowd of admirers, dressed in the traditional sealskin garb of the Mer, were four males who lurked behind some rocky columns as Ohnalee passed. The exiled Guardians had slipped through the safety zone created by Mokeema's guards and teams of cruising whales, to spy for their master, Dragone.

When the swimmers came to a halt, they placed Ohnalee's throne on a flat spot almost at the top of a high peak. With no more than fifty feet of water between her and the surface, the moon was fully visible in the sky, its fullness glowing white hot, casting its beams down upon the mountain below.

Ohnalee giggled with complete enchantment as she saw something she had never seen before. Running up and down the mountain, leaping from one rocky ledge to another, following each other up narrow pathways that looked almost like mountain trails in the human world, were hundreds of small goats. These goats were about two feet high, with sharp horns and pointed beards. They were perfectly formed specimens, except for one unique difference. The front legs of the animals were tipped with sharp hoofs, but instead of hind legs, they had the tails of fish. Suddenly the goats came thundering toward Ohnalee, coming to a screeching halt in front of her chair. Their red eyes gleamed with mischief as each one bent its right front leg in homage.

Ohnalee was breathless with excitement as Mokeema approached with Magdalena Meda at his side. The shaman was resplendent in a billowing purple cape, covered with sparkling stones, and Ohnalee could see her eyelids were painted purple to match the garment.

"Why have I never seen these sweet little sea goats?" Ohnalee asked. "They are the cutest things in all the world."

"They live only in these mountains," Mokeema said, "but usually they keep themselves hidden well. They have come to pay homage on this night of wonderworking."

Out of the darkness, new visitors arrived in a swirl of bubbles and foam. Ohnalee was thrilled when she saw the large pod of friendly porpoises who now surrounded her chair. They nuzzled close, chattering incessantly as she stroked their sleek bodies and accepted their kisses. Two of the largest animals hovered by Mokeema's side, passively allowing him to rest his hands on their backs.

"It is time for your new life to begin," said Mokeema. Then he raised his hands overhead, and the motion brought forth a mighty roar from the assembly. The sound swelled as every species raised their voices in songs of exaltation. The Mer trilled their song of triumph while the sea lions barked, the gulls shrieked, and the dolphins chattered, filling the darkness with their clicking sounds.

Magdalena Meda smiled, reassuring Ohnalee of her kind intentions, then motioned for two large dolphins to come to Ohnalee's side. "Hold tight to these friends, dear Ohnalee, as they will take you to the top of the mountain where you will embark on the most important journey of your life."

Ohnalee held tightly to the fins of the dolphins as they slowly transported her to the highest peak on the mountain. The red dress swirled behind and around her as they swam, creating a fantasy of rainbow reflections.

Then Aquenae Magena and Qillac appeared, swimming close behind their father and Magdalena Meda. Magena was gorgeous in a green cape with a border of white fur while Qillac was elegant in a white jacket and hood. The style matched his father's, and the cut emphasized the men's powerful chests and muscular arms. Qillac's hair was tied in a neat braid which fell down his back, almost to the waist, but Mokeema's hair was loose like Ohnalee's.

Ohnalee still had no idea what would happen next, but with her family close, she was not afraid. Her life had been filled with challenge and adventure since the decision to follow Mokeema into his world, and she had never regretted her choice. Now, she placed herself in his hands, ready for whatever would come next.

Jade followed close behind the family, then came to Ohnalee's side. "I can feel the spiritual energy tonight, my Lady," she whispered in her ear. "Reach to the stars and collect the magic of the full moon. Trust in yourself and those who love you. You are strong, radiant and wise. You are my daughter, my sister and my friend, all in one soul. This is your night, this is your destiny." Then Jade kissed Ohnalee softly on her lips; and Ohnalee tasted a drop of sweet nectar that flowed from the chalice of her friend. "Thank you dear Jade," Ohnalee said, as the woman backed away.

Mokeema extended his right hand to Magena, and his left to Jade. Then Magena held her brother's hand, and the family watched as Magdalena Meda took control.

Ohnalee stood alone, facing Mokeema and her family as the shaman approached. Meda bowed respectfully saying, "You have no idea how powerful you are, but today, you will learn the truth."

Magdalena stepped back, looking intently into Ohnalee's eyes. "You have come to our people twice of your own free will. This freedom of choice is required when a human comes to live beneath the sea. We have known of you since you were saved from the Dragon Mer when your mother died, and the spirits of our ancestors told me you would be the perfect mate for Mokeema. He loved you at first sight, watching as you played on the beach as a child, but waited patiently until you were an adult, hoping you would choose to leave the world of humans and follow him."

Ohnalee nodded her head in agreement, glancing in Mokeema's direction as the shaman continued.

"We honored your first decision to join our people, then were overcome with joy and happiness when you returned a second time. Now, you have made the ultimate sacrifice, leaving your land baby behind to be raised by a human family. I know this pain all too well as I have also left children behind on distant shores. Even though I knew it was the best thing to do, my heart ached for many years each time I made that choice.

The women of the Mer are lusty and sensual, free to choose a mate from the Mer, but they often entertain themselves with human men who are entranced by their beauty. Sometimes they stay awhile, raising their children as human, but in the end, they always return to the sea, leaving these beloveds behind."

Ohnalee thought she saw a crystal tear escape from Magdalena's eye as she continued.

"I found the men of the land of green mountains particularly exciting, and I enjoyed many of these delicious creatures when I was younger. I like to believe my children have traveled to lands around the universe as it is in our blood to journey far, always going through doors of new experience and adventure."

The seer opened her glittering purple cloak wide, bringing forth a tall crystal wand about four feet high. The wand had several brilliant stones fixed along the sides, and Ohnalee blinked as a beam of light flickered from the clear quartz sphere crowning the top.

The people bowed their heads reverently as they watched and listened. Mothers and fathers quieted the children, whispering in their ears to shush, shush.

"This wand is a natural quartz crystal that formed around a rocky center," Magdalena continued, her strong voice resonating with power. "The ancients used a rod like this in their sacred rites in Atlantis and Lemuria," she explained, "and only the high priestess was allowed to touch it. This sceptre crystal and its power has been passed down to me as I will pass it to the one I choose as most worthy."

Magdalena Meda stroked the stone on the top of the wand, bringing forth a clear sweet sound that reached to the heavens. "This is a singing quartz crystal, and its voice can communicate with the celestial beings who will assist in your transformation."

The shaman's fingers then caressed the next crystal on the rod, a pale lavender amethyst.

"This stone comes from the land of Oregon and brings spirituality and contentment to the user. The ancients believed that amethyst could provide a connection between earth and other worlds. It is a symbol of the possibility of complete metamorphosis and will eliminate any dysfunctional or negative energy within your body.

The next crystal on the wand is a red carnelian. It will allow the power of love to overcome any hesitation or negativity while you connect to the higher levels. This stone can also be used in combination with the ruby crystal to send earthbound spirits home to their creator."

At this point, Ohnalee was totally confused about the ceremony that featured her as the star player. All this talk of crystals and transmutation sounded foreign and entirely too complicated to understand. The only statement that really impressed her thus far was the possibility the lighthouse could be cleansed of the uneasy spirit who haunted the lighthouse at Heceta Head by using the power of Magdalena's staff. *Perhaps I can ask Meda to bring the sceptre to the lighthouse one day and ask the spirit to leave, she mused.*

Magdalena Meda pointed at the next crystal on her scepter, a purple charoite. "This stone will stimulate the desire to 'let go' as you become a full member of our tribe, forsaking any possibility of return to your prior life. The gift of this stone is that it will assist you, Ohnalee, to understand that this is where you are supposed to be at this moment in time."

When Ohnalee heard those words, she shivered for a moment as the reality of her situation was made clear. Although she did not fully understand what was to come, the continued use of the word "transformation" seemed to give a clue to the end result of the ceremony. Mokeema saw her moment of discomfort and hesitation and fixed his eyes on her face.

Their eyes locked, and she heard his voice clearly although no sound was heard by the quiet assemblage. *"Trust me, Ohnalee, all will be well."*

Next on the wand was a strange crystal whose stout parts formed a shimmering cross.

"This stone signifies both death and rebirth," Magdalena said. "It is a bridge for crossing over and will help you by providing the 'password' for entry to the land of our ancestors."

The next crystal was actually a crystal within a crystal. Magdalena Meda called this stone a "phantom" crystal as all could plainly see a figure within the quartz. Ohnalee found this stone the most interesting as the shape within the quartz looked like that of a woman.

"This crystal has been growing and changing for thousands of years," Magdalena said. "It represents the numerous phases which may be experienced during one's lifetimes. The ancients believed this crystal could assist in meeting a personal spiritual guide. I will ask this crystal to help heal any emotional or physical distress you may feel after your change."

The last crystal on the staff was a rare pink topaz. Magdalena said this beautiful stone signified true love and would act in conjunction with the amethyst to sooth and stabilize Ohnalee's body after transfiguration.

"All these magical stones will work together with the ruby crystal fabric of your dress to accomplish our fervent desire, " she said.

Magdalena held the staff high for all the people to see. Then she turned slowly in a full circle, waving the wand from side to side.

"I ask the blessing of the spirits of our ancestors in this sacred undertaking. Hear our humble prayers and keep Queen Ohnalee safe as she travels the spiral path to your presence," cried the Seer as she whirled to face Ohnalee.

Ohnalee's heart skipped a beat as she stared into the face of the shaman. The face was no longer the face of Magdalena but a different face with both masculine and feminine characters. The left side of Magdalena Meda's face looked male, with fierce chiseled features, and the right looked female, with softer skin and a more delicate aspect.

Then a deep voice reverberated from the shaman's lips. Everyone present realized this was not the voice of Magdalena Meda but that of a powerful spirit who had entered her body for the ceremony of Ohnalee's rebirth.

"Daughter of the Dragon Mer, Daughter of the Moon, Ohnalee," the voice said, "I offer you the gift of transformation this night. If you accept, you will travel far before returning to this land and the people who love you. Your body will never be totally human again, but you will possess the best traits of both human and Mer."

Now another voice was heard, using Magdalena's lips to speak. A gentle feminine voice emanated from the seer's body, and all could hear the silvery tinkle of laughter as she spoke.

"Be not afraid Ohnalee, as with this gift, you will walk on land and swim as the Mer under the sea. You have already adapted well to your new life, and if you accept, you will rule long beside your mate."

"It is time to decide," the male voice boomed, "as it must be done while the moon is high in the sky. You must give your consent freely as no one can coerce you to make this choice."

Ohnalee took one final look at the faces of her family, before giving her decision to the wise ones in control of Magdalena's body. Her son looked worried, but Magena was positively ecstatic. She grinned from ear to ear, giving a "thumbs up" as she learned to do on her first land visit. "Go for it, Mom," Ohnalee heard her say enthusiastically.

Mokeema spoke silently, not in words, but she could feel the intensity of his emotions. *Forever, forever,* she heard him say, and that was enough.

"I accept the gift of transformation with my own free will," Ohnalee shouted, holding her arms high above her head so all could see. The red dress shimmered, aglow with a rainbow of colors, and the assembly could see spirals of energy shooting from all parts of her body.

Suddenly a purple ray of light streamed from Magdalena Meda's open mouth as she raised her scepter high.

"It shall be done," roared the voice of the Spirit as the purple ray exploded with a blast as loud as a firecracker, becoming a sparkling purple and silver starburst that surrounded the seer's body with jets of shimmering light.

The starburst disintegrated in a few seconds, changing into a transparent fog that formed into the shape of a purple winged dragon, breathing silver fire from its mouth. The apparition flew towards Ohnalee, wrapping itself around her body, it's fierce head coming to rest just above her forehead. Suddenly the phantom disappeared, leaving behind a misty purple fog that seemed to exude from all the pores of Ohnalee's body, bathing her in a luminous aura of silvery violet light. Ohnalee trembled but she did not move, seeming mesmerized by the power of the entity that now possessed her.

The Mer shrieked as they saw the wand fly out of Magdalena's hand, becoming a live and living thing, with an energy of its own. It stopped just in front of Ohnalee, hovering with the top fixed in one spot while the bottom swung back and forth with an even cadence, much like a pendulum suspended from an invisible cord. The rod quivered as it moved faster and faster from side to side as Ohnalee's eyes followed the movement. Suddenly Ohnalee's eyes closed and she swayed back and forth as if in a state of trance. Her slim body imitated the motion of the rod, leaning forward as if to get closer.

Each crystal glowed in the darkness until the colors merged in multicolored bands of luminosity. Bright jets of light from each stone shot toward Ohnalee, sending beams of gold and purple and green and black, which collided on the ruby-red surface of her dress, bursting on impact as if they were meteors crashing down on the red planet.

Ohnalee raised her arms high as if reaching for the sky. She pressed the palms of her hands together, thumbs crossed, with fingers pointed toward the heavens. Suddenly the rod moved from its position in front of Ohnalee to a spot directly over her head. The scepter quivered as it hung slack for a few moments, but then it started to move in a wide slow circle. It moved faster and faster until the scepter itself could not be seen, but the crystals sent the blazing light of their power into a field of light which surrounded Ohnalee on all sides.

Then the large ruby crystal in the center of Ohnalee's necklace began to pulsate, glowing a dark red as if it had caught fire.

Ohnalee's body lifted off the ground, spinning at first slowly in tune to the motion of the rod, then rotating faster and faster until all that could be seen was a blur of hazy purple light and silver sparks.

Suddenly the ground shook violently, the quake scattering small rocks and pebbles in every direction. Mothers and fathers threw their bodies over small children, and most instinctively covered their eyes. Mokeema locked fingers with his children when the tremor struck but did not close his eyes for a second.

The trio watched as the scepter rose, breaking through the surface of the water, spinning fast as it streaked through the dark sky toward the bright full moon, leaving a trail of white light much like a shooting star. Ohnalee's body followed the spiral, but all that could be seen to the naked eye was a blur of silver dust that finally disappeared somewhere near the moon.

Mokeema wept, wrapping one arm around each of his children, not caring that his subjects could see the depths of his terror and distress. "What have I done, what have we done?" he moaned, seeing that even the normally stoic Jade looked dazed and terrified. "Perhaps we have gone too far, asked too much of the gods."

"They are gone, my lord, gone with Ohnalee. Now we must wait and hope for her safe return," the seer mumbled gruffly as if she were coming out of a deep sleep. The purple fog had disappeared, leaving no indication it ever existed.

Qillac was calm, as usual. He never outwardly showed his feelings and could be depended on to be the one to pull things together in times of crises. When he saw Magdalena Meda stagger, attempting to regain control of her body, Qillac rushed to her side, taking her hand as she rubbed her eyes.

"Thank you, boy," she said in a weak and strained voice as she pulled her purple robe close around her plump shoulders, "I am quite myself again."

Magena was her usual high-spirited self, exuberant and hyperactive, bursting with enthusiasm and full of questions.

"Who were those spirits who inhabited your body, Meda?" she probed. "Did you know they were there? Could you feel them? Was it painful?"

"You always need to know all the answers, Magena, but sometimes we don't know what the correct answer really is," said Magdalena Meda wearily.

"I believe the spirits of our ancestors watch over us from another realm. Sometimes you can feel their presence, and sometimes you can't. Shivers and goosebumps can indicate they are near; it's like small sparks of energy dancing on the skin."

"But they possessed your body, Magdalena," Magena said, "speaking from your mouth, and looking through your eyes."

"Things like that have often happened throughout the history of our race," Magdalena said, "and this knowledge and ability has been passed down through the ages to those who could accept the message."

"Will I be able to learn what you know, Magdalena Meda, will I?" Magena asked as she lifted the hem of Magdalena's cape and slipped beneath, then clinging close to her warm plump body.

The seer fondly put her arm around the princess, saying, "We'll see, we'll see, child, but the way to knowledge is long and hard, and you must prove your worthiness."

"Will you teach me, Magdalena Meda?" Magena requested. "I'll be good, I promise."

Eagalia was protective and worried about her friend as usual. She fluttered around Meda, straightening her garments and running her fingers through the shaman's long tangled locks. "Leave her be, girl," she scolded. "Can't you see the shaman is exhausted and weak?"

"So where is Mother, and when is she coming back?" Magena pestered.

"Leave me be, child, there's nothing anyone can do right now."

I can do it, Aquenae Magena decided. *I know I can do it.*

"I'll bring Mother back, I will, I will," Magena told the seer. "Let me try, please."

"Quiet, girl," Magdalena cried, now totally exasperated.

"I called her before, and she heard, even though she was far away. Why can't I call her now and make her come back?"

"All in good time," the seer warned. "We must not risk the wrath of the gods. Transformation is in their hands now, so we must be patient."

Magena was never patient. It was not in her genetic construction to be patient, and there was not a patient bone in her body. She wanted things when she wanted them. Now, not later.

Magena clenched her fists and ground her teeth. *This is making me really mad,* she thought. *What is taking so long?*

I can do it, she decided, *and I will do it now.*

"Motherrr, Motherrr," Magena roared, casting aside her cloak as she gave a swish of her powerful tail, rising to the top of the mountain where the moon still shone bright. Schools of small fish followed, swirling around her body as she soared high out of the water. "Motherrr, Motherrr, Motherrr," she shouted at the moon, "I need you. I need you now."

261

Mokeema and Magdalena Meda watched from below, horrified at the girl's behavior, fearful her actions would endanger Ohnalee, perhaps preventing her return.

Magena splashed down hard into the water, foam and bubbles flying everywhere.

"Do you hear me, Motherrrr?" she wailed, shaking her fist at the heavens. "Do you hear your daughter crying for you?

I will stay right here until you return. Do you hear me, Motherrrr?"

Suddenly a small shadow appeared upon the surface of the moon as if a tiny cloud had passed.

"Motherrr, Motherrr," Magena roared again to the sky, her voice tremendous with emotion and love.

"Mokeema waits, Qillac and I wait," the girl chanted, "Motherrr, Motherrr, Motherrr, come down, come down, come down, come back down to your people."

Mokeema and Qillac then appeared at Magena's side, hoping to put a stop to her hysterical performance by enticing her to come below. Magdalena Meda frowned as she surfaced beside the others, ready to give the girl a good slap, but as she looked to the sky, she saw a shooting star appear in the heavens.

"Motherrr, Motherrr," Magena wailed again as the star sped downward through the dark night sky in their direction, trailing a long tail of silvery sparks as it fell.

The bright orb landed with tremendous force, exploding as it hit, spraying brilliant multicolored sparks in every direction, illuminating the waters below with its brilliance. Every eye in the assembly below saw the impact, and as the foam and bubbles cleared, Ohnalee's smiling face appeared, her glowing hair flowing from underneath the magic red-feather cap.

With a tremendous thrust of her gorgeous scarlet tail, holding the scepter of power in her outstretched hand, Ohnalee dove from the surface to where her people waited.

Magena grinned smugly, a look of triumph on her face as she headed below following her father and brother.

Magdalena Meda, the great shaman of the Mer, smiled with satisfaction as she took a moment to reflect. *The girl is strong,* she thought, *much stronger than the mother. But she will be difficult to train.*

Then Magdalena Meda drew back her arm, flinging a handful of purple dust toward the sky. The dust shimmered in the moonlight for just a moment, but in that instant, Magdalena saw the particles turn into tiny purple winged dragons. They hovered for a second, then shot straight up into the starry sky.

MOTHERRR COME DOWN

Author's Note

In the spring of 2006 I found a book by Matthew Arnold, a Victorian poet and social critic who died in 1888. The faded blue hardcover published in 1927 was in very bad condition with the spine partially ripped away, and the hinges cracked, but I was excited to see the title, *Matthew Arnold, Prose and Poetry*.

I love to open a book that attracts me, picking a spot at random, much like cutting a pack of cards. Then I search the pages for some word or phrase that seems meant for me that day, often finding inspiration, or at the very least learning something new.

Go with the flow, I thought as I shut my eyes, selecting a spot about three quarters of the way through the book, opening it to page 441. On that page, I saw a poem written in 1849, entitled *The Forsaken Merman*. The title jumped off the page, and I saw that the poem was quite long, covering the next four pages.

I have never been interested in mermaids, never collected mermaid art or mermaid statues, didn't read stories about them and wondered why other people did. I never even saw *The Little Mermaid* movie, but when I read Arnold's poem, *goose bumps* raised on my arms. I found it very dark and sad, but it moved me as I understood the merman's grief at the loss of his lover and the sorrow of the poor, sad children left behind. The poem touched my heart and inspired this story.

Ohnalee—Mermaid of Heceta Head, is the first of three books planned in this series. I hope you enjoyed meeting Ohnalee and will look forward to the next part of her journey of love and adventure.

Here for your pleasure is Matthew Arnold's wonderful poem.

THE FORSAKEN MERMAN

Matthew Arnold, 1849

Come dear children, let us away;
Down and a way below!
Now my brothers call from the bay,
Now the great winds shoreward blow,
Now the salt tides seaward flow;
Now the wild white horses play,
Champ and chafe and toss in the spray.
Children dear, let us away!
This way, this way!

Call her once before you go—
Call once yet!
In a voice that she will know:
"Margaret! Margaret!
Children's voices should be dear
(call once more) to a mother's ear;
Children's voices, wild with pain—
Surely she will come again!
Call her once and come away;
This way, this way!
"Mother dear, we cannot stay!
The wild white horses foam and fret."
Margaret! Margaret!

Come dear children, come away down:
Call no more!
One last look at the white walled town,
And the little gray church on the windy shore;
Then come down!
She will not come though you call all day;
Come away, come away!

Children dear, was it yesterday
We heard the sweet bells over the bay?
In the caverns where we lay,
Through the surf and through the swell,
The far-off sound of a silver bell?
Sand-strewn caverns, cool and deep,
Where the winds are all asleep;
Where the spent lights quiver and gleam
Where the salt weed sways in the stream,
Where the sea-beasts ranged all round,
Feed in the ooze of their pasture-ground;
Where the sea-snakes coil and twine,
Dry their mail and bask in the brine;
Where great whales come sailing by,
Sail and sail, with unshut eye,
Round the world for ever and aye?
When did music come this way?

Children dear, was it yesterday
(Call yet once) that she went away?
Once she sate with you and me,
On a red gold throne in the heart of the sea,
And the youngest sate on her knee.
She combed its bright hair, and she tended it well,
When down swung the sound of a far-off bell.
She signed, she looked up through the clear green sea;

She said: "I must go, for my kinsfolk pray
In the little gray church on the shore to-day.
"Twill be Easter-time in the world—ah me!
And I lose my poor soul, Merman! Here with thee."
I said: "Go up, dear heart, through the waves;
Say thy prayer, and come back to the kind sea-caves!"
She smiled, she went up through the surf in the bay.
Children dear, was it yesterday?

Children dear, were we long alone?
"The sea grows stormy, the little ones moan;
Long prayers," I said, "in the world they say;
Come!" I said; and we rose through the surf in the bay,
We went up the beach, by the sandy down
Where the sea-stocks bloom, to the white-walled town;
Through the narrow paved streets, where all was still,
To the little gray church on the windy hill.
From the church came a murmur of folk at their prayers,
But we stood without in the cold blowing airs.
We climbed on the graves, on the stones worn with rains,
And we gazed up the aisle through the small leaded panes.
She sate by the pillar; we saw her clear:
"Margaret, hist! come quick, we are here!
Dear heart," I said, "we are long alone;
The sea grows stormy, the little ones moan."
But, ah, she gave me never a look,
For her eyes were sealed to the holy book!
Loud prays the priest; shut stands the door.
Come away, children, call no more!
Come away, come down, call no more!

Down, down, down!
Down to the depths of the sea!
She sits at her wheel in the humming town,
Singing most joyfully.
Hark what she sings "O joy, O joy,

For the humming street, and the child with its toy!
For the priest, and the bell, and the holy well;
For the wheel where I spun,
And the blessed light of the sun!"
And so she sings her fill,
Singing most joyfully,
Till the spindle falls from her hand,
And the whizzing wheel stands still.
She steals to the window, and looks at the sand,
And over the sand at the sea;
And her eyes are set in a stare;
And anon there breaks a sigh,
And anon there drops a tear,
From a sorrow-clouded eye,
And a heart sorrow-laden,
A long, long sigh;
For the cold strange eyes of a little Mermaiden
And the gleam of her golden hair.

Come away, away children;
Come children, come down!
The hoarse wind blows coldly;
Lights shine in the town.
She will start from her slumber
When gusts shake the door;
She will hear the winds howling,
Will hear the waves roar.
We shall see, while above us
The waves roar and whirl,
A ceiling of amber,
A pavement of pearl.
Singing: "Here came a mortal,
But faithless was she!
And alone dwell forever
The Kings of the sea."

But, children, at midnight,
When soft the winds blow,
When clear falls the moonlight,
When spring-tides are low;
When sweet airs come seaward
From heaths starred with broom,
And high rocks throw mildly
On the blanched sands a gloom;
Up the still, glistening beaches,
Up the creeks we will hie,
Over banks of bright seaweed
The ebb-tide leaves dry.
We will gaze, from the sand-hills,
At the white, sleeping town;
At the church on the hill-side—
And then come back down.
Singing: "There dwells a loved one,
But cruel is she!
She left lonely for ever
The Kings of the sea."

The End

Edwards Brothers Malloy
Thorofare, NJ USA
July 25, 2012